DEADLY TANGO!

DEADLY TANGO!

A GLORIA BERK MYSTERY

GISELA HUBERMAN

TransMedia Group.com
Public Relations • Publishing
• Internet Marketing

Boca Raton, FL

Published by TRANSMEDIA GROUP PUBLISHING
240 W. Palmetto Park Road, Suite 300
Boca Raton, Florida 33432

Publisher's Cataloging-in-Publication Data
Huberman, Gisela.
    Deadly tango / Gisela Huberman
    —Boca Raton, Fla.:
    TransMedia Group Publishing, 2001.
        p.   cm.
    "A Gloria Berk mystery"

    ISBN 1-890819-07-7
    1. Mystery fiction. I. Title.
PS3558. U239 D43 2001   2001-87144
823/ .914—dc21   CIP

PROJECT COORDINATION BY Jenkins Group, Inc. ✢ www.bookpublishing.com

05 04 03 02 01 ✢ 5 4 3 2 1

Printed in the United States of America

DEDICATED TO

Jon, Sue and Mara
Marty, Mariana and David

Lights of my life.

THANK YOU

*Avi Gilad, for showing me
that real life heroes do indeed exist.*

*Mario Cader, for sharing with me
your grandmother's secret potions.*

DEADLY TANGO

CHAPTER 1

D ARK DEEDS ARE EASY TO CONCEAL IN THE SHADOWS of a fading sun, amidst a crowd; and this glorious Washington evening will turn brutal for me and my friend Renata. Her beautiful face will forever bear the scars of this day. And me, well, I will carry the wounds of a passion gone astray; of an erotic relationship turned to fury.

It's the presence of that figure all in black that forewarns me of the impending catastrophe. I'm trying to distinguish the face, but the features are hidden under the shroud of the black felt hat. I'm sure we're being followed as we walk along the busy Georgetown streets.

"What's the matter with you, Gloria? Why do you keep looking back?" Renata's dancing blue eyes stare at me with amusement. "Are you looking for someone?"

"No, no. I just have this funny feeling, you know? Like someone has been behind us since we left the sales meeting."

"Nonsense. Who'd be following us?" She smiles at me but picks up her pace a little, nevertheless. "There are so many people here, we're lost in the crowd." She slides a slender arm around me and pulls me gently. "Come on, you're spooked."

1

"I just had that feeling."

"I know. I know. Ever since your incident with that guy stalking you last year you've changed a lot, you know?"

"What do you mean 'changed'?"

"I don't know exactly. You seem quieter, less bubbly, more... hmmm, I don't know how to put it."

"Cynical, Renata. The word is cynical. He's out, you know. His lawyer got him out only a week ago."

"My God. How did you find out? Is he bothering you again?"

"He's not bothering me. Not yet, at least. Freddy, the police officer who's taking a law course with me called me last night. To warn me. Jesus. Here we go again."

"Who was he anyway?"

"Oh, just a nut who listened to my show and thought I was broadcasting just for him. He thought that every time I signed off with '*love you, guys,*' I was talking just to him."

"What a nut. Are you afraid?"

"Not exactly afraid. Jumpier, more jaded. Problem is, I never thought anyone would dare attack me."

"Why not?" She stops in the middle of the crowded sidewalk and looks at me. "Because you're a radio personality? Because you're well known? You think that makes you invulnerable?" Her vehemence surprises me. "How does your fame protect you at all?"

The delight Renata has shown at the success we just had in our first joint sales promotion campaign for WVVV has vanished. I'm sorry my worries have dampened her joy. A large man in a long grey coat suddenly brushes against me. "Hey, watch out, watch where you're going," I holler at him.

"Take it easy, Gloria, it was an accident."

"Yeah, an accident. Look, he made me drop all the papers and he didn't even look back. Not a word of apology. He probably brushed against me on purpose."

Renata bends down and hands me the station's pamphlets I dropped. Her long blond hair grazes the pavement and she tosses it to one side. She smiles and seems to have forgotten the concern she showed just a few moments ago.

"Thanks," I say as she hands me the papers, and I promptly let them fall to the ground again.

"Are you all right? You're really not yourself at all."

"I think it's because I'm just really tired. And upset that Peter is away and he doesn't seem to miss me at all." Renata smiles and looks away. There isn't much she can give me in the way of comfort. Renata, my girlhood friend. That smiling face always seemed to help a little. She was there for me after my first doomed romantic encounter with my karate instructor. And she consoled me for days after my beloved dog, Oscar, died in my arms. And now, even though we both work at the same radio station we don't seem to have enough time for one another. She's in sales, I'm on the air. There's a chasm between the two departments that has pulled us apart. We in programming think we're true radio, the heart of the station. The rest is just business, even if their sales of on-air advertisements do pay for all our salaries. So we don't mix and match too much across departments. Today I'm just trying to help her out. That's why I went to the sales call with her. She thinks she needs a radio personality to help her in difficult sales.

We quicken our pace. We're getting close to Renata's townhouse only a block from Georgetown University. Nice area. Even though it's impossible to park around here. It's a warm and breezy Friday evening, a beautiful Washington spring. The flowering magnolias perfume the air and the willows have new leaves of the softest, freshest green. I don't feel like going back to my lonely apartment. Not yet. Ever since Peter left for Geneva my weekends have been empty and lonesome. I miss him terribly. *If I just could feel you in my arms, even for just a few minutes. Peter, Peter, why did you have to leave. My whole being needs your presence....*

"Well, we're home," Renata interrupts my daydream. "Thanks for your help today, Gloria. You were great." She opens the door to her townhouse and stands at the threshold. "And thanks so much for helping me carry all these papers home. They weigh a ton." She doesn't ask me in.

"I'm sure somebody was following us, Renata." I linger at the door. She notices and smiles.

"Well, we're here now. Come on in." She opens the door wide for me. I walk into a dimly lit hallway and stumble over a suitcase close to the door. She bites her lower lip and shakes her head slightly. She turns on a light that throws soft shadows all around us, looks at me, smiles a wry smile and says, "I'm leaving." She blushes. "I mean, I'm not really leaving. I'm going on a vacation." She closes the door, takes me by the hand and leads me to the small living room, decorated all in whites. Stylish, exquisite, just like Renata.

"This is beautiful, Renata. I had forgotten what a great place you have. Really great." I walk in and sit on the white leather couch. Soft.

"Thanks," she says as she hands me a glass of sherry. She sits on the stuffed chintz chair across from me, crosses her long legs, tosses her hair to one side, smiles, and in an almost girlish voice says, "Cheers. Let's have a toast to love."

"To love," I say. It's easy to understand why all the men at the station are so crazy about her. She's beautiful in a calm, non-threatening way. Her skin is so pale, it's almost transparent. She looks vulnerable, inviting. Sue Hamilton, our general manager, told me that Renata sells the most contracts of anyone at the station. As usual, nobody can say no to Renata. She has a great future with us, Sue says. And even though she begged me to help her out with this sales meeting today, I'm sure she would've sold the contract without my help at all.

"I love the station, don't you?" she asks me. I think she can read my mind. "And I love your new show, the interviews, the phone-ins. You always have such great guests. It's a lot of fun."

"Thanks. It takes a lot of preparation."

"I can tell. I wish it lasted longer. I never miss it."

"Thank you, Renata." *She's really a wonderful girl. I ought to spend more time with her.*

"Gloria," she says. She's blushing. "I'm very sorry to tell you this. It's really embarrassing, but..."

"What is it?"

"Someone's coming here. To pick me up. I'm leaving with someone." Her eyes are shining. "I've never really told you..."

I bolt up from the couch. "Oh, I'm sorry. I didn't realize I was keeping you." I feel embarrassed.

"No, no. You're not. It's... well, you see, I don't think he would be comfortable if you saw him here. You see..."

"Please, Renata. You don't have to explain. I'm sorry." I quickly put my glass on the cocktail table and reach for my handbag. She rushes to me and envelops me with her arms and her perfume. Her hair brushes my face. It feels silky and smells of shampoo.

"Don't feel sorry. You couldn't know. Oh, Gloria. I'm so excited. So happy. So much in love." She kisses my cheek. Her whole face is shimmering.

"Do I know him?"

"Yes. But... he's married, you know?" She buries her face on my shoulder as we walk together to the door. "That's why I haven't said anything."

I turn around, embrace her and whisper, "Be careful. Have fun, but be careful."

"Oh, I will, I will. I'll call you as soon as I get back."

She gently closes the door behind me and I stand a few seconds outside her townhouse. There's no light on her stoop and I take a moment or two to get used to the sudden evening darkness and to inhale the aroma of the Washington spring. There are couples walking past me, their arms around each other, laughing out loud. I start walking towards Wisconsin Avenue to get to my car and I turn to look at Renata's place one more time. A dark figure is approaching her house. I'm sure it's the same figure that was following us. Strange. I'm sure I've seen that walk before. Those movements. That stance. But where? The figure is standing in front of Renata's house. *It must be her married friend. I left her right on time.* I walk faster. I don't want Renata to see me lingering.

The sounds of the evening seem to be getting louder. The shrill laugh of the girl walking behind me still rings in my ears.

I PARK MY LITTLE BLUE ESCORT BEHIND MY BUILDING IN Adams Morgan. My noisy neighborhood seems louder than usual. Snippets of Spanish and French waft from the coffee shop near me. Francisco, the shop owner, calls after me, "come in, Miss Gloria. A little *café con leche* will perk up that pretty face."

I wave at him. "Not tonight, Francisco. But thanks anyway."

The honeysuckle that covers the building is in full bloom and its aroma sweetens the air. I break a small twig laden with flowers and bring it to my face. Not just to smell it. I want to feel it too. I want to feel its caress, someone's caress, on my cheek. The climb to my third-floor apartment is hard tonight. Too steep.

The flashing light of my answering machine welcomes me. Somehow it makes the apartment seem less empty. I put my honeysuckle twig in a small blue vase my mother gave me. She got it during a trip to Greece and I keep it in the living room always. Just to remind me that one day I too will visit Greece. I pour myself a glass of Chardonnay and turn on the machine.

"Kiddo, I miss you." My hands start trembling the moment I hear Peter's warm voice. My palms are sweaty and I need to put the glass down. *Peter, my darling. I'm so sorry I missed your call.* "It's cold in Geneva. Very cold. In every respect. I hope you're well. I'll call you again during the weekend. Be good, my sweet girl. I kiss your wonderful lips."

Peter was my law professor last semester, and my friend and advisor. He has been gone for barely a month, but my nights have become endlessly empty. I need his presence. I need to know he's close to me, that he would come to me in a minute's notice. I yearn for his mouth, for his warmth. I miss his rugged arms. But he's never asked me to visit him. I want him to miss me, to pine for me. But he's never given any hints I'm important to him. And I feel so alone. So lonely. I think of Renata on her way to a romantic hideaway, simmering, as she was this evening, in the midst of a sizzling love affair. Wouldn't I want to be in her place.

I take a swig of my wine and turn on the CD player. I need some music that will fill me with Peter's being, with his warm laughter and deep voice. I decide on Mozart's 24th Piano Concerto. Caressing. Beautiful. Gentle and understated. Just like Peter. The melodies lift me and I start smiling. Out of my funk.

I need to prepare for my Sunday show, "Let's Chat." My thirty minutes into the worlds of politics and art and music. Thirty minutes of interviewing fascinating people. Sundays at 6 P.M. After begging for this show for months, the general manager let me have it. She said it was my reward for helping solve the murder of the radio station's former owner. For having proved that our night jockey was innocent. I know she gave it to me because I'm a good disc jockey and a hard worker. And the few interviews I had conducted always attracted a lot of listeners. Besides, since people read about my role in solving the murder, my regular daily show is the highest ranking show at the station.

※　※

BETWEEN SIPS OF THE VERY GOOD WINE, A PRESENT FROM Peter before he left—"Don't have this wine with anybody you like too much," is the way he offered it to me—I start writing questions for my Sunday guest. Although I'm afraid that nothing I can do will top last Sunday's program. It was great. My guest was Senator Lowell Beau Clark, senior Senator from Georgia. His last interview before his early retirement. It was the Senator's swan song. Today was his last day in the Senate. The "true gentleman from the South," as he's known by friends and foes alike, has surprised everyone by his sudden and unexpected announcement. In the prime of his life. At the height of his popularity. "Health reasons," was his explanation. He looked just fine to me. His strong stand against abortion and for old-time family values made the show sizzle. The phones didn't stop ringing. The women really let him have it. The Senator handled himself like a real gentleman.

The best part of the show, though, was the presence of his legislative assistant, Alan White. Now that's what I call a legislative assistant. Tall, blond, smart, easy-going. Great smile. Quite agreeable. Quite. When he loosened his tie and opened the top button of his shirt I was so riveted by his movements, I almost hung up on a caller. He noticed. And smiled. I smiled back and wished this show would last a lot longer. I've heard the Senator doesn't go anywhere without Alan White. That he doesn't make a move without Alan by his side, especially when it concerns a public appearance. The show was a great success. I hope this week's show is as good. I spread my papers around me, nibble on my pencil and push away the uneasy, queasy feeling I have about Renata.

I must've dozed off. A loud banging jolts me. "Open the door, Gloria. Open the door right now." It's Sue's voice. "Gloria, are you there?" Piercing, screaming. A staccato of knocks. I run to the door and find a disheveled, pale, almost hysterical Sue. Her usual pageboy hairdo is in disarray, some glossy strands floating over her eyes. Her silk shirt is peeking from under her pale blue jacket.

"Sue, what? What?" I stammer.

"Renata's been attacked."

"My God. Is she wounded?"

"I don't know much. She's calling for you. She was starting a two-week vacation tomorrow. My God. Poor thing. Come on, she's in Georgetown Hospital." We're both running down the stairs. Three floors. Two steps at a time. Her silver BMW is double-parked in front of my building, emergency lights flashing. Doors open. Not a smart thing to do in Adams Morgan. She's lucky the car is still here.

"What happened?" I ask when we're in the car.

"I was at Perry's right around the corner from here, with some friends. We were just finishing dinner. My pager went off. It was the police. They found her unconscious outside her town-house. Someone attacked her."

"Why did they call you?"

"I don't know, Gloria. I don't know. What's happening? In just a few months two tragedies. First our owner is murdered and now my star salesperson is assaulted. I wonder if someone wants us off the air. The competition is so tough."

"That's ridiculous, Sue. You're babbling."

"You really think so? Really? Then tell me why you were stalked and attacked? And he's out now, I heard. Maybe this is the same man who's after Renata now. Who knows?"

"Sue, stop this." I'd rather not talk about the problem I had with the stalker. The feeling of dread is still too overwhelming.

We ride in almost total silence for the next fifteen minutes, each of us wrapped in her own thoughts and fears. The traffic on Wisconsin Avenue on a Friday night is brutal. Even after eleven at night. Sue's weaving in and out, leaning heavily on her horn and making small grunting sounds under her breath, but I can't understand what she's saying.

We drive into the underground lot of the hospital. It's eerily empty. And much too dark. She parks and we jump out of the car. Sue grabs my arm as we walk quickly towards the hospital entrance.

"I'm nervous, Gloria."

"It's O.K., Sue. It's going to be fine." I'm scared to death. We are almost jogging to the entrance.

We slow down in the brightly lit corridor to Renata's room. The room itself is immersed in darkness. Only a small light is on at the bed-stand. I hear muffled sounds. When my eyes get used to the twilight I'm horrified by the sight in front of me. Renata's beautiful face is almost completely swathed in bandages. Two simmering blue eyes rimmed in red are staring at me.

I approach the bed gingerly. Except for those two icy-hot blue pools, everything about her is very still.

"Gloria," the muffled sounds come from under the bandages. I'm petrified. I can hardly breath. "Gloria," it's a plaintive cry. The cry of a child in pain. It pierces my heart.

She manages to extend her arm to me. Slowly, slowly it reaches towards me, but I'm afraid to get close to her, to touch her.

"Renata," I finally say to her, bending down by her bed and taking hold of her hand. "Renata, what happened?"

"It hurts so bad. Burned," she whimpers as a tear forms in her eye and rolls halfway down her bandaged cheek. "They threw something hot and horrible on my face."

"Who, Renata? Who did this?"

"I don't know. I don't know. Please help me, Gloria. I don't have anybody else. Help me. Please. Find Alan White. Please find him." The blistering pools of ice close and her small hand slowly slips away from mine.

CHAPTER 2

"TALK TO ME SOME MORE, PETER. I NEED TO HEAR your voice," I whisper into the phone. The window's open and the May night breezes float into my room, blowing gently over me. I'm barelegged, just wearing a small T-shirt. I'm propped up on one elbow in my unmade bed.

"I miss you, sweets. It would be nice to have you here. What are you doing now?"

"Lying in bed. Thinking of you." *Wanting you desperately. Hungry for you.* "Where are you right now?"

"In my apartment, in the kitchen finishing my morning coffee, getting ready to go to the library. What are you wearing?" he asks suddenly.

"Nothing," I lie.

"Babe..." I hear him exhale.

I need to have Peter want me, to lust after me with his whole being. To desire me as much as I desire him. He didn't want to get intimately involved with me while he was my professor. And then he left for Geneva to teach a course on international law. We never promised each other anything, we didn't commit to one another. He didn't ask and I didn't push. Maybe it was too soon for him, after his wife's death. And yet, I miss him. I miss something. Some excitement. Some involvement. His departure left an enormous void in my life.

"Yes, Peter?" *Please tell me you need me, you can't breathe without my presence.*

"I miss you, you know. I miss your mischief and your delightful laugh."

"What else do you miss?"

"Your legs. Your wonderful, dancer's legs." *Good. He remembers.* "Oh, and that voice of yours."

"Peter, are you coming back soon?"

"Not too soon, I'm afraid."

My heart sinks a little. "Why? Are you enjoying Geneva?" *Say no. No. Say you don't like anything at all if I'm not there.*

"Oh, it's not bad. Great food. Very gentle and civilized people. My students are good. Very different from my American students."

A wave of anger curses through my body. "Different, how different?"

"Older, more mature."

"Better than us?" *Better than me?*

"Well, certainly not better than you, kiddo."

I smile and run my hand up and down my thigh. "Peter," I sigh. "Yes, kiddo?"

"I wish I could be with you right now. It's lonely here, you know."

"You're never far from my thoughts. I've got to run now. I hope your friend Renata recovers soon."

"Call me back soon, Peter. I..."

"Got to run. Do a good job on your show tomorrow. Don't forget to save a tape for me."

"I've saved them all. I'll be thinking of you."

"You do that, kiddo. Be good."

And with that, he's gone. I hang up the phone feeling angry and disappointed. I wish Peter would tell me I'm important to him. That he's passionate about me. I'm reluctant to tell him how deeply lonely I feel without him. But maybe he knows. And maybe he doesn't care.

The Agony and the Ecstasy, the book I was reading when Peter called, slides down the bed to the floor with a loud thump. I don't bother to pick it up. I lie quietly in the dark and run my fingers over my body, over my face. It feels warm. I touch my cheek and lower my hand slowly down my neck and rest it on my breast. I touch my breast lightly. Small. Hard and supple. Ready for Peter's touch. For Peter's mouth.

⚘ ⚘

RAYMOND VELASCO, MY GUEST FOR THE SUNDAY SHOW, IS waiting for me when I walk into our tiny studio at five thirty. He rises slowly and I can't hide my amazement at his girth. He's enormous. He walks slowly towards me and his body seems to overtake the whole studio. As he advances, extending a hand toward me, I start moving back a bit until I feel the cold studio wall pushing against my back.

"Ms. Berk, good to meet you." He takes my hand and surprises me again by the softness of his skin and the gentleness of his voice. He slowly lifts my hand to his lips and kisses it lightly. His short trim beard prickles my skin. I repress the urge to scratch it. "Such a pleasure. Such a great pleasure." He holds my hand between both of his. "Heard a lot about you. You have grit. Was anxious to meet the beautiful and coura-geous Ms. Berk. That's just a sinful combination. Sinful. Come, come." He pulls me gently towards the center of the small studio. "Let's sit. What are we going to be discussing?"

I'm speechless for a few seconds, trying to compose myself after this slow-moving cyclone has taken over the entire studio.

"Nice to meet you, Mr. Velasco," I mumble.

"No, no. There's no such thing as Mr. Velasco. Call me Ray. Everybody does. Except my wife, of course," he winks. "She always calls me Raymundo," he says rolling his R and greatly exaggerating every sound.

"Very well, Ray. Let me explain to you what will happen here."

"You'll ask me questions, the phones will ring, I'll answer them and then you'll go out with me for a nice, quiet dinner. Isn't that what happens?" He sits across from my console in our narrow guest chair and I immediately worry he'll be uncomfortable for the length of the interview. But he unbuttons his blue blazer, places both hands on the console, leans back on the chair, and with a sly smile says, "Let's go."

"Well, Mr. Velasco..."

"Ray, call me Ray."

"Well, Ray, it's not exactly like that."

"What, you're not going to ask me questions?" His smile is truly dazzling and I try to suppress a giggle.

"I don't think the dinner part..."

"We can discuss that part later. Can I smoke?" He takes out a long cigar from his breast pocket.

"Oh, no. I'm afraid not. Smoking isn't allowed anywhere in the building."

"Ridiculous rules. You wouldn't give me away if I took a puff or two, would you?"

I hesitate. I don't know if he's serious.

"No, no. I won't put you on the spot. Don't want to get a beautiful young woman in trouble. Of any kind." He nevertheless continues to play with the cigar, smells it, rolls it over in his fingers, puts it in his mouth.

While I'm adjusting my headphones I glance up and look through the indoor window that looks into the station. My head jerks back involuntarily when I see two very large men, dressed in identical black jackets and black turtlenecks. They're wearing dark glasses. Inside the station. At six in the evening. My hand flies to my mouth and I think I muffle a scream. It sounds as if I'm choking.

Ray quickly leans over to me, pats my hand and says, "It's all right, Sugar. No problem here. They're with me."

"With you? Whatever for?"

"Well... hmmm... Let's just say they're always with me. They're my... hmmm... my friends?"

I look at him and back at them. With a slight flick of his wrist, one that I almost miss, the two men back away and out of my sight.

"Feeling better, Sugar?" He smiles widely.

The interview is fabulous. Ray Velasco is assembling a coalition of Latin American residents of all classes and regions to create a powerful lobby to get more power and representation for the "disenfranchised Latino," as he puts it. He has a plan and is passionate about it. The phones don't stop ringing. I've never seen anything like it. I don't know if the calls have been rigged or if we have a huge Latino audience I know nothing about. Men are calling in. Women are calling in. Even young people are calling in. Ray has an answer for every question, a clever remark, a joke, a quote from a poet or a philosopher. As the show progresses, I become more and more entranced by his rich baritone and the depth of his knowledge. He seems to be enjoying himself tremendously and I myself am having a wonderful time. Thirty minutes have never gone by so quickly before.

"Well, Ray, you were great," I say, smiling at him and pumping his arm. I mean it, he was stunning. "We have to do this again. The phones didn't stop for a second."

His gray eyes are smiling back at me. There are beads of perspiration lining his smooth forehead, just at the hairline. It gives an added sheen to his well-groomed, slicked back hair. He takes out a silk handkerchief that exudes a scent of musk mixed with cigar, wipes his forehead and says, "So, will you honor me with dinner tonight? I'd like to go over the show with you. I promise I'll have you back at your place no later than ten. A solemn promise. Or what, do you have something against eating?" He looks earnestly at me and I burst out laughing.

"Sure," I say. "Let's eat. I'm starving."

The maitre d' at Jean Luc's obviously knows Raymond Velasco very well. He bows, he retreats, he takes me by the arm. "Careful, mademoiselle, please watch your step," he says without taking his eyes off Ray as he leads us to the interior of the softly lit dining room. The aroma in the place is splendid. A medley of spices and chocolate and apples. My stomach growls. I've had almost nothing to eat all day.

"Marcel, this is Ms. Berk," Ray says in a booming voice. "She's not only gorgeous, as you can see, but she's also smart. And just wait until you get an earful of her melodious voice."

"But of course, Monsieur Velasco. All your companions are beautiful." The French accent sounds real enough.

Ray is not happy with Marcel's reply and glares at him without an answer. He walks quickly past him.

I've never been to Jean Luc's, but the chef is famous all over Washington. He has prepared special dinners for the President. I've read he eats here quite often. I look around to see who's here, but at seven-thirty on a Sunday night, candles flicker unnoticed in this almost deserted place.

Ray's two "friends" have followed us in and they quickly position themselves at a corner table, just a few feet away from us. They're facing us, their backs to the wall. They don't seem to attract much attention from anybody even though they're still wearing their dark glasses. I glance at them once or twice. Funny. They don't make me feel any safer.

As soon as we're seated, a busboy rushes over to Ray, *"Don Raymundo, que gran honor!"* He tries to kiss Ray's hand. Both "friends" immediately step towards the small, dark-haired man who appears petrified by their presence.

"Back off," Ray hisses. "It's O.K. *Gracias, amigo.*" He shakes the busboy's hand. "Thank you for your welcome and your friendship. We're going to make it better for you. You'll see."

The busboy bows to Ray and quickly steps back. Marcel has witnessed the whole exchange. He shakes his head and massages his thin, dark moustache with one finger.

"Does this happen often?" I ask.

"Often enough, Sugar. They need somebody to stand up for them."

"You like all this attention, don't you?"

"It's not the attention, Sugar. It's the power." His eyes are glinting. "It's the power that drives me, that makes me tick." He takes out his cigar and lights it with one or two puffs.

The waiter approaches and swiftly places a crystal ash-tray close to Ray's hand. Ray thanks him by name and orders dinner for the two of us without looking at a menu. "You like white or red wine?" He asks me. I thought he had forgotten for a moment I was sitting next to him.

"Red," I say.

"Good, good. So do I." He orders a French wine and smokes absent-mindedly while it's being poured. He raises his glass to me, barely touching my glass and says, "To the beginning of a most promising friendship." His long, smooth fingers graze mine and I don't remove my hand.

"Cheers," I say and sip the smoothest red wine I've ever tasted.

We feast on paté and Cornish hen and the most exquisite potatoes ever concocted by human imagination. I had no idea potatoes could ever taste like that. Smooth and creamy and crunchy and delicate. Heavenly. I hesitate briefly—very briefly—before digging into dessert, a marvelous mango mousse. Made with fresh mangoes. Amazing. And amidst Ray's stories and poems and jokes we polish off two full bottles of that magnificent red wine. With a few more meals like this I'll soon be looking like Ray. Funny thing is, though, that the longer we spend talking and laughing, the longer I listen to his tales, the slimmer he appears to become. After a while his enormous girth has almost disappeared from my consciousness. Nevertheless, tomorrow I'm spending at least an hour working out in the gym. No excuses.

"Well, Sugar," he says to me at the end of the meal, wiping his mouth with a white linen napkin, "you must agree this wasn't half bad."

I smile at him. "No, Ray, not half bad at all."

"Well then Sugar, you'll have to allow me to escort you around town and show you the true highlights of D.C. The ones that really count. Like this one." He takes a sip of his port—I begged off on this one as my head's spinning—and pats my hand. "Two things you must do for me. First, I know you're involved in the fund-raiser for Children's Hospital. It so happens that my wife is the chairman of that fund-raiser this year and I want to make sure you make it the greatest triumph it's ever been. Come to the house. Please. Talk to her. Set it up. Make it succeed. Second, next weekend we'll have our annual party at our place on the Maryland Eastern Shore. You'll amaze the people there, I'm sure. With your voice and your graceful body, and with that hair of yours the color of burnt cinnamon. Bring some girlfriends along if you want. Don't bring a boyfriend, even if you have one. It's a whole weekend, so come prepared. Boating, swimming, tennis, horse-back riding, skeet shooting. Lots of food and drinks and good music and dancing and interesting people. Don't worry. I'll make sure you're back at the station in time for your Sunday interview show. I won't accept no for an answer. You'll make the whole weekend shine."

He takes my breath away. I feel I'm swimming near a whirlpool and with every stroke I take, every word from Ray's mouth, I get closer to the vortex. But I'm flattered by his attention and I merely nod.

"Sugar, it's almost ten. A promise is a promise and I have to get you back to your place."

"I need to get back to the station. My car is still parked there. I'll need it for tomorrow."

"Forget about your car. You're in no condition to drive." *He's right.* He pulls me gently from my seat, places an arm around my waist—it feels more protective than seductive—and we walk out slowly to his waiting car. I never see a bill brought to us.

"By the way," he says quietly as we are both seated in the back of his shiny black Mercedes, "how is your little friend doing?"

"What little friend?"

"The pretty blonde girl, the one who works with you."

My slight intoxication evaporates instantaneously. All my senses come to the fore and I sit up straight. We've been keeping Renata's attack very quiet while the police investigate.

"How do you know—"

"Sugar, D.C. is really a small town," he interrupts. "Isn't it? People hear things." He notices my discomfort and pats my hand. "So, how is she?"

"She's hurt," is all I'm willing to say. He doesn't press for more.

We arrive at my apartment building and it occurs to me that nobody bothered to ask me for my address. One of his "friends" walks me silently up to my apartment and stands by the door while I fumble with my key and walk in. I say goodnight and he tips his hat.

I walk over to my small balcony, throw it wide open and inhale the aroma of the honeysuckle. I look around at the unusually quiet Sunday night in Adams Morgan and suddenly gasp in amazement: my little blue Escort is parked in its usual spot right underneath my balcony.

CHAPTER 3

P EOPLE SMILE AT ME WHEN I WALK INTO THE STATION ON Monday afternoon. "Great show, Gloria," they say. "Way to go." I'm feeling very good about myself and yesterday's program even though, if truth be told, it was all Ray's doing. I only needed to introduce him and he took it from there. But he made me sound very good indeed.

As I sprint past Sue's office—I'm not walking today, I'm sprinting—she comes out and, in a grim voice, asks me in. A frown creases her creamy brow.

"Hi, Sue," I sing to her as I take a seat near her crowded desk. An enormous bouquet of ivory-colored roses is sitting on the teak credenza where she displays all the station's awards and citations. "Oh my, Sue," I gasp. "Those are gorgeous. Who are they from?"

"They're for you," she answers quietly. *Oh, I see. That's why the long face.*

I jump from my seat and rush to grasp the card. The envelope has been opened. I look up at Sue and she's hiding her eyes. Even though she's my friend and we've worked together for years—ever since my college days—I don't think she should have looked at the card.

"I'm sorry. I opened it before I realized the flowers were for you. I was sure they were for me from Ron."

I slide the card out of the small envelope. There are only two lines: *She was a phantom of delight, When first she gleamed upon my sight.* No signature. My heart takes a vault. I know they're from Ray. It's part of a poem by William Wordsworth. I briefly mentioned to him last night that I love Wordsworth's poetry. He remembered. I'm very touched.

"Gloria, those flowers are from Raymond Velasco, aren't they?" Sue asks quite brusquely.

"I don't know, Sue. You saw there's no signature on the card."

"Who else would send you an expensive bouquet like this? There must be at least three dozen roses there." *That's a really nice question to ask.*

"Why do you ask me, Sue? What difference does it make?"

"Gloria, I heard the interview yesterday. He had you mesmerized, just like he's mesmerized half the city..."

"The interview was great!" I interrupt forcefully. I'm still standing by the credenza and I look down upon Sue, sitting at her desk.

She blushes. "It was great. Indeed it was. But that's where it should end. Why the flowers? What do the lines he wrote to you mean?"

"Sue, why on earth would that make any difference to you?" *Why don't you just stay away from my life?*

"He's dangerous, Gloria. He's a dangerous, powerful, wealthy man. It's well known around the city that his lust for power and women knows no limits. He conquers, destroys, and then moves on. I worry about you."

"Well, you have nothing to worry about. He was nothing, if not charming, with me."

"I know. That's just the trouble."

"I've got a show to put on." My voice is too high and my tone is too haughty. "I thought you would be pleased by yesterday's show. Everybody's talking about it."

"And well they should be. He was close to inciting the Latin community to form a revolutionary movement."

"He was not," I reply much too quickly. "He just wants all the people to get equal treatment." The reply sounds childish, even to me.

"You're naive, Gloria. But I'm sure you'll learn. Just be careful. You're my friend and I care for you and I really don't want any more ugly incidents happening at my station. Besides, we want interviews that will bring us clients. Revenues. I'm not interested in raising the social consciousness of the masses. This is a business, I'm sure I don't have to remind you. This is not your own little soap box where you can espouse all the social causes you believe in. I can just imagine how many advertisers will cancel after last evening's display. Please try to be more circumspect about the people you invite to your show."

I take a few slow breaths to stifle my anger. "My show is very successful," I manage to mutter.

Sue shuffles some papers and doesn't answer.

"Anything else?" I ask as I turn to walk away from her office.

"Yes, have you heard from Renata?"

"I saw her briefly yesterday morning. No change."

"O.K., just be careful Gloria. Have a good show."

I don't even answer. I grunt involuntarily when I pick up the heavy flower vase and waddle to my cubicle. The bouquet takes over my entire desk. Sue's right, there have to be more than three dozen very long stemmed roses. They're close to bursting into bloom and seem to be made of porcelain and silk. I can't stop looking at them.

I'm startled when I hear my name being paged by the receptionist and hunt for my phone hidden amidst the roses whose wonderful aroma has filled my tiny cubicle.

"Gloria Berk here," I bark into the phone, Sue having got me so mad.

"Well, do you like them?" It's Ray's smooth voice.

"My God. They're spectacular. I've never seen roses like these."

"They're called Pascali roses, Sugar. I had them flown in from a nursery in New Orleans. I thought they'd make a nice thank you for giving me the pleasure of your company last evening."

"You shouldn't have. I mean, it was really a very nice evening. But you're married. It was just a business dinner. There was no need to..."

"Of course there was. How else do you tell a woman, a lovely woman, you're thinking of her?"

I feel myself blush and I know the people around me in the programming office, where I have my cubicle, are listening intently to my end of the conversation. I face the wall, almost burying my face in the flowers, and say, "Thank you." I don't want to say his name, even though everybody probably knows by now who sent me the flowers and who's on the phone. You can't have many secrets around here.

"Was the car in good shape?"

"What car?"

"Yours, of course."

"Oh, yes, yes. Who took it to my house? How could they start it? I have the keys."

"Oh, Sugar. We have ways." He laughs a warm, friendly laugh. "About the meeting with my wife, I asked her to expect you tomorrow at our house at ten a.m. I hope that's all right for you. Oh, and try not to be late. She appreciates punctuality. The address is 3532 Mass Avenue, near the Brazilian embassy. You needn't tell her of our dinner last night." He hangs up the phone without even a goodbye or a response from me about tomorrow's appointment. I whisper, "goodbye" into the phone and hang it up gently while I turn to see who has been listening to me. Sue's standing at the doorway. I quickly pick up the script I prepared for my afternoon contest, walk past her and enter the studio without looking back.

✣ ✣

I TALK MY WAY INTO RENATA'S HOSPITAL ROOM AFTER THE ICU visiting hours are over. She looks somewhat better tonight. At least her bandages don't look as tight around her face. I put a bunch of yellow tulips in a vase and set them close to her bed, straighten out the covers, pour a glass of water, anything to keep me busy so as not to look at her too long. It scares me to look at her. It scares me even to think what's underneath those heavy bandages.

She follows my every move with her piercing blue eyes. The red rims appear less swollen, look less angry.

"Sit by me, Gloria. I've been lonely all day." Her voice sounds softer and more childish than usual. "I listened to your show yesterday. It was really good."

I pull up a chair next to her bed and take hold of her pale, thin hand. Her fingers immediately intertwine with mine, grasping me with a strength I didn't expect.

"Thanks. Ray Velasco is an interesting man," I say. " I talked to the police. They still don't know who did this to you."

"I know," she whispers. "I don't think they even have any leads."

"I'm sure they'll find them, Renata. You'll see." I try to sound positive. "You look better, you know."

"They changed my bandages today. I couldn't bear to look. I asked the nurse how I looked and she said 'better'. Better than what? Oh, Gloria." She starts whimpering. She sounds lost, like a scared little girl who has suddenly found herself in an unknown place. Her body is so thin, so lithe, it barely shows through the thin hospital covers. "What am I going to do?"

I start massaging her hand and her fingers, one by one, "It's going to be O.K., Renata. I'm sure you're going to look fine."

"It's the only thing I have going for me—my face. That's what gets me in the door, you know, when I make my sales calls. I've got nothing much else. I know it. Now people will be afraid to look at me. He'll be afraid to look at me."

Her beautiful eyes start welling up and I gently pat them dry with a tissue.

"There, there, Renata. Don't cry. Even if you are scarred you know that plastic surgery can work wonders now." I say that while I'm looking at a picture someone brought her and placed near her bed. It's a picture of some of us taken only a week ago, in one of our remote broadcasts benefitting the Cystic Fibrosis Foundation. Renata's leaning against the car a sponsor donated for the auction and her shoulders are almost totally engulfed by his arm. Her smiling face is beaming. Her long hair is carelessly tied back in a pony tail, her snug jeans hug her long slim legs and her tank top barely covers her braless breasts. All the rest of us, attired in our "remote wear" of chinos and polo shirts with the station's logo that make us look like mannequins, merely fade into the background. Sue would have a fit if we didn't appear in our professional uniforms while at a public function. But Sue's strictness about the way we look doesn't seem to extend to Renata. Her charm has captivated all of us at the station, including the steel-hearted manager, Sue. "I know you'll look just as wonderful as you always did," I say.

I know she doesn't believe me. I don't believe it myself.

"Gloria, I need to ask you to do something for me. It's very important." Her voice suddenly takes on an urgency I've never heard in it before.

"Anything I can, I'll do for you."

"I have no one here. My father's dead, you know, and my mother lives in Sweden with her parents."

"You want me to let her know what happened to you?" I gulp hard. *Oh, please God, let her say no. I'm just terrible at delivering bad news.*

"No, it's not that."

Thank you, God.

"My mother isn't well and I don't want to disturb her. She had a bad drinking problem after my father died. She needed help and I

26

couldn't help her. So her parents came for her, took her back to her childhood home. She's getting better, but I know that news like this could send her back to where she started. Please don't let anybody get in touch with my mother. I'll let her know later on."

She pauses for a long time. I don't want to interrupt her melancholic silence. Suddenly a nurse bursts into the room. I watch as she checks Renata's IV, adjusts her needle. She looks sternly at me.

"You need to leave now," she says. "This patient needs her rest. Who let you in so late? Are you family?"

"Please," Renata says. "Nobody's been here all day today. She's my friend. She's been my only visitor."

"Five more minutes. No more." The large nurse blocks the entire doorway as she stands there looking at me. "Only five."

"Gloria," Renata swallows hard and grasps my hand again, her nails dig into my skin, but I don't flinch and I don't move my hand away. "The man I told you about, the man I was going away with...." she looks at me expectantly.

"Yes? What about him?"

"He hasn't come to see me. He hasn't called at all. It's so unlike him. He loves me. I know he loves me. I'm very worried about him. I'm afraid something's happened to him." She starts weeping and holds my hand tighter.

"Have you told the police?"

"I can't. I'm afraid."

"Renata, that's silly. What do you mean?"

"Nobody knew about us. Nobody. I don't want to tell anybody. You know, in case he changed his mind about us. Maybe he wants to stay with his wife. I wouldn't blame him now. Especially the way I look." Tears well up in her eyes. "I don't want to hurt him."

"That's ridiculous," I say. "If you think something's happened to him you've got to go to the police—"

"You don't understand. He's..."

A gust of air reeking of alcohol rattles Renata's IV line as the nurse pushes the door open. "Young lady, I don't want to take you out of here by force. Renata needs her rest. Leave now."

"Please, Nurse Brown. Only two more minutes. I need her."

The nurse stands guard by the door, her thick arms looking like overstuffed sausages under her tight uniform. She doesn't budge.

"Come close to me," Renata whispers.

I lean towards her face, careful not to graze her bandages.

"My lover. Help me find him. I'm so worried. I'm sure something's happened to him," she whispers.

"I'll try," I whisper back. "Who is he?"

"Alan White. You know, Raymond Velasco's son-in-law."

CHAPTER 4

"MRS. VELASCO'S WAITING FOR YOU. PLEASE FOLLOW me." The maid is a beautiful young woman, olive-skinned with shiny black hair gathered in a long braid that falls halfway down her back. Her voice is softly accented and very appealing. She almost seems to be singing. She's wearing a starched black-and-white uniform, one of those uniforms from the Hollywood movies of the forties. There's even a lacy white cap that offsets the ebony of her hair.

The maid opens the mahogany door wide and gestures grandly at me. I follow her into a hallway of marble and mirrors. An enormous chandelier is hanging at the entrance and the breeze drifting in through the open door gently swings the hanging crystals into a murmur of Japanese chimes.

There's a center table in the middle of the large entrance foyer with a breathtaking bouquet of fresh cut flowers. I don't see any Pascali roses among them, and I smile to myself.

I've dressed up for the occasion. A navy blue skirt, white shirt, gold belt and a navy and green silk scarf tied jauntily around my neck. I think I look quite good. My high heels, however, are making so much noise on the marble floor it embarrasses me. It seems my clacking is the only sound being made in this expansive house.

We walk through hallways filled with art and family portraits. But the maid's walking so fast I have no time to stop and look at them. I cough a little, trying to attract her attention. I would like to ask her questions about the house, about the Velascos, about Linda, their daughter. She doesn't even turn around. We finally stop in front of a large double door. She knocks gently and opens the door for me.

"Please go in. The señora will be with you very soon. She's just finishing her morning prayers." She closes the door behind her.

It's a beautiful, sun-filled room in shades of gold and brown that bathe it in an aura of gentility. It's lined with books and pictures. Two large, brown velvet sofas face each other and there's a small desk, it looks like an antique, off in one corner. I step onto a soft oriental carpet that glistens in the sunlight. I bend down to touch it. *My God, this is all silk.* I steal a glance at the pictures and manage to see Alan White's smiling image. He looks very different here than the way he looked at the interview with Senator Clark. In the picture he's dressed in white shorts and a white T-shirt, his blond hair carelessly arranged. Both his arms encircle a petite, dark-haired, unsmiling woman. I'd like to look at all the pictures on the desk and the bookshelves, but I don't want to appear nosy. Instead, I walk over to the French glass doors that lead out to an astonishing garden.

"Lovely, isn't it?" A gentle voice, sweet and mellow, greets me.

I turn around and face an elegant woman, dressed entirely in black. She comes towards me in measured, dignified steps, her large gold cross bouncing heavily against her chest.

"Welcome, Ms. Berk. I'm Miriam Velasco." She takes my hand and moves her hand up towards my wrist. It's an unusual gesture, one of superiority, but also of friendliness, and it fills me instantly with a gnawing regret about Sunday night's dinner.

I smile at her while she's still holding me by the wrist. "This view is just so beautiful."

"Thank you, my dear. I had my landscapers design it to bring me peace and contentment. It relaxes me just to look at it. There's something spiritual about the garden, wouldn't you say? I'm so glad you like it." A hint of a Spanish accent is fighting to get through, but she has it well under control.

"It's magnificent," I say.

She leads me by the arm to one of the couches, motioning me to sit by her side. "Since this is the room where I spend so much of my time, I thought I should bring in nature, and with nature I have God here with me." Her voice is soft and cultivated, her manner is gentle. Every movement she makes is slow and deliberate.

"Thank you so much for coming here, Ms. Berk. And for being so prompt." She looks at me with liquid brown eyes flecked with gold. Warm, soft eyes. "Raymundo spoke to me about you. He said you were smart and knowledgeable. He didn't tell me you were so young and pretty." She purses her red lips—the only make-up I can detect on her face—and she seems to pick some lint off her black skirt.

"Well, thank you, Mrs. Velasco. It's a pleasure to finally meet you in person. Please call me Gloria."

"Oh? Have we seen each other before?"

"I've seen you at some of the Children's Hospital gatherings."

"Well, I certainly hope you'll be able to help us as much as Raymundo thinks you will."

"I'll certainly try my very best. I've done these fundraisers before. And we have enough time to plan it."

"Yes. We have time. It's good that it's at the end of July, before everybody takes off for the summer."

Well, not everybody. "We'll be able to plan a wonderful auction and radio-thon. We'll make a lot of money for the hospital."

"I want you to explain all that to me. But first, would you like some tea?"

"I'd love some."

31

She rings a little silver bell that she's picked up from the wood-carved cocktail table in front of us. A different maid appears instantly, as though she was standing just outside the door.

"Bring two teas." Curt, forceful, imperious.

The tea is brought promptly in a lovely silver tea pot. Mrs. Velasco lifts the lid and a cloud of steam rises, permeating the air with a delicate aroma. I inhale deeply and close my eyes.

"Like it? It's lemon tea. From my garden. I brought the seedling from my ranch in Puerto Rico and now we have an enchanting bush in the atrium, right outside my bedroom. I missed it so much, but now I can enjoy it and remember my childhood. Isn't it silly?" she pours tea gracefully into fine, translucent china cups. "Would you like some sugar? It really tastes much better plain."

"No, no sugar. Plain is fine." She hands me the cup and saucer, holding them with well-manicured hands, and I notice a very large emerald-cut diamond on her right hand—a very large diamond. On her left hand she's wearing a thin, plain gold band. I sip the tea and let it linger on my tongue. It's tart, but it has a fresh sweetness to it, as though a freshly cut lemon had been dipped in honey. "Extraordinary," I say.

She merely smiles. I notice she's staring at me and I question her with my eyes.

"Oh, please forgive me. I didn't mean to stare. It's really so rude. It's so impolite. But I just cannot get over something."

"Is there something wrong?"

"Wrong? Oh, no. Nothing's wrong, bless my soul. It's just that you remind me so much of my friend, Carina. My best friend. You look like she looked twenty-five years ago. The same slight build. The same russet hair and hazel eyes. The same fair complexion that everybody seems to envy. And the proud chin. It's uncanny. You have to meet her. She won't believe her eyes."

"I'd love to." *What else can I say?*

"Ms. Berk, before we start working together, I really would like to get to know you. To know something about you. You know, to feel comfortable with you. And you with me, of course," she adds. She's fingering the huge gold cross hanging over her black blouse. "You don't mind, do you, Ms. Berk?"

So I tell her about my work, about the radio station, about the evening course on evidence I'm taking at the local law school.

"No, no. Tell me about you. About your life. About your family," she insists.

While I talk about my parents, their move to Boca Raton, about my childhood filled with music and love, she sits back on the sofa, closes her eyes, crosses one black-stockinged leg over the other, and absent-mindedly caresses her knee. When I'm finished with my not-too-exciting life story she opens her eyes, sighs, and appears satisfied with me.

"Count yourself lucky, Ms. Berk, and very blessed. You seem surrounded by love. Your parents love you and they love each other. Some people are not so lucky."

I can't bring myself to ask her about her life. She sounds so wistful and melancholic it feels like I would be intruding if I asked her anything.

"No husband?" she wants to know.

"No."

"Serious boyfriend?"

"No."

"Strange. Pretty girl like you."

"I still haven't found the man of my dreams." *I wish I had. How I wish I had.*

"I understand Raymundo has invited you to our place at the Eastern Shore." She picks up some lint again. I see no lint.

"Yes, he has. I hope it's not an inconvenience for you."

She waves her hand rapidly, as though fanning herself and brushes some more lint off the skirt. "Of course not. We're used to having many people at our gatherings. My whole family will be there. You'll meet them all."

"Oh, I'd love to meet them all. I had your son-in-law, Alan, as my guest last week."

Color seems to disappear from her face. She lowers her eyes, but she quickly looks up at me, smiling. "Alan. Yes, yes. He's always involved in something."

"Will he be at the party too?"

"You can never tell with Alan," she tells me, tapping the velvet arm rest gently. "You can never tell. Will you be bringing someone?"

"Mr. Velasco was kind enough to tell me to bring a girlfriend." She nods several times. "So I thought, if you don't mind, I'd bring along my general manager, Sue Hamilton. She'll be instrumental in our radio-thon I imagine you'd like to meet her."

"Of course, of course. It'll be our pleasure."

I glance at my watch surreptitiously. I have a show at two p.m. and need to prepare for it. She notices.

"You need to leave already?"

"Not quite yet, but I have to get back to the station soon."

"It's a pity. I wanted you to stay and have lunch here with me, to get us started in our project. But if you have a few minutes before you leave let me take you around my garden. It's a beautiful day. Let's enjoy it. We can have lunch together another day."

The telephone rings, but Mrs. Velasco doesn't make a move to get it. Still another maid comes in after knocking softly.

"Sorry to interrupt you, Mrs. Velasco. But Ms. Carina is on the phone and I thought..."

"You thought! I've told you so many times never to interrupt me when I'm with a guest."

"But Mrs..."

"That's fine. You can leave. I might as well take the call." She turns toward me, "It won't take more than a minute," she says with an apologetic tone.

I busy myself looking at book spines—a lot of biology and herbalism—so as not to appear to be eavesdropping.

"...yes, Friday night is in my house. I'll have hot hors d'oeuvres ready. Seven sharp. That's right. No, no, I couldn't make it last Friday. I was busy helping out at St. Matthews. Yes, there were a lot of people there... O.K. I'll see you for lunch tomorrow. At the Club. Twelve sharp. Goodbye." She turns to me. "That was my friend—your double."

We walk out through the French doors into a haven of magnificent plants and flowers, most of which I've never seen.

I'm speechless. She notices my enchantment and seems very pleased.

"I call it my Eden on earth," she says as she caresses a small pine tree that seems to encircle itself.

"It fits."

A young Hispanic man is working in the garden, pruning some branches. She stops suddenly and stares at the man. "Are you deaf?" she demands, bearing down on him. "Are you an idiot? How many times have I told you not to prune the branches of the hydrangea? You'd better learn fast. Otherwise you won't be working here too long." She turns to me before the young man has a chance to answer, takes me by the arm.

"Well, Ms. Berk, would you like to meet with me next week? Shall we say Tuesday at ten? I can meet you right after I come back from church."

"That sounds fine."

"We can have an early lunch. I'll invite Carina. She won't believe her eyes. Bless my soul. She just won't believe her eyes."

"Thank you for the tea."

"I'm glad you enjoyed it."

We walk together in silence to the front door and when I turn around to shake her hand goodbye I notice she's staring at me with a glassy, strange look, almost dream-like.

"Everything O.K., Mrs. Velasco?"

"Oh, yes. Of course." I turn to the door to step outside into a brilliant day and she calls after me. "Tell me, Ms. Berk, how did you enjoy Jean Luc's?"

❧   ❧

"GLORIA, THERE'S A PACKAGE WAITING FOR YOU. A MESSENGER brought it an hour ago. I put it on your desk," Veronica, the station's receptionist, tells me. She winks at me. "It's about time someone started sending you gifts, girl. This one looks real expensive. Nice going, girl-friend." *My God, does everybody at the station know what's going on with Ray?*

I hurry to my cubicle without looking into Sue's office. There's no need for more lectures. She sees me, though, and calls out to me, "Just be careful."

I trace my steps back, stand at the entrance of her office without stepping in, and with the least irony I can muster I ask her, "How would you like to spend the weekend at the Velasco estate at the Eastern Shore?"

She closes her eyes very rapidly once or twice. "What, am I invited?"

"Yes, I'm inviting you."

She blushes, stammers something and I see her nodding.

"Good, I'll pick you up Saturday at eight in the morning so we can enjoy the whole day there."

"Could I bring Ron along?"

If Sue is busy with Ron I'll have more freedom to wander about and find out about Alan. I answer slowly, as though I'm giving it a lot of thought, "sure, I don't think the Velascos would mind."

"Good. Ron will be thrilled. He's heard so much about that place from Alan White."

I try not to look startled. After all, Ron works in the Senate. "He knows Alan White?"

"Sure. They work in the same place and the play racquetball together once in a while. They've become pretty close," Sue says. "By the way, what was in the package?"

"I don't know. I haven't seen it yet."

Sue gets up from her desk and walks with me to the programming office. I think she's more curious than I. A small box wrapped in gold foil with a huge purple ribbon is on my desk, right under the ivory roses. A note is attached to it. I open the envelope and try to shield the message from Sue's inquisitive gaze. I put it so close to my face I can hardly read it. It's a poem:

> *My somber heart searches for you,*
> *and I love your joyful body, your slender and floating*
> *voice.*
>
> *Dark daisy, sweet and absolute*
> *like the fields and the sun, the poppy*
> *and the water.*
>
> Pablo Neruda (My favorite poet.)

No signature. Not that I need one. I unwrap the box slowly. I'm hoping Sue will be paged, that someone will be looking for her.

"Will you hurry it up, Gloria? What's the matter with you?"

I open the box and take out a gold bracelet encrusted with small stones—rubies and sapphires,I think—and there's a small diamond hanging from a heart on one side. I look at it and spread it out.

Sue lets out a whistle.

"It's way too long," I say, wrapping it around my arm.

"Silly girl, it's an ankle bracelet. It's gorgeous." She's gushing.

Veronica pages me and I pick up the phone, heart beating very fast.

"Have dinner with me tonight," Ray's warm voice sings in my ear.

I turn toward the wall. I don't want Sue to hear. She understands and leaves my little cubicle.

"Ray," I whisper. "This is too expensive. I can't possibly accept it."

"It's yours, Sugar. Do with it what you like. Have dinner with me tonight."

"I can't. I have a law class tonight."

"But Sugar," his voice scolds, "your class finishes at nine thirty. Have dinner with me at ten."

I don't like it that he knows so much about me. I feel invaded. "Ray, your wife knows we had dinner together on Sunday."

There's a momentary pause in our conversation. A slight hesitation on the other end of the line. "Sugar, you're making things up."

"Ray, she asked me how I had enjoyed Jean Luc's. Sunday is the first time I've been there. She knows."

"I'll take care of it, Sugar. Have a good show."

❦   ❦

AFTER CLASS I'M TOO ANXIOUS, TOO EXCITED, TO FALL ASLEEP. Ray didn't call back and I ate alone—a light dinner in my apartment. At two a.m. I get out of bed, walk over to my small kitchen to pour myself a glass of orange juice. As soon as I'm back in bed, the phone rings. *Oh Peter, thank God you're calling.* I snuggle up in bed, ready for a romantic, heart-warming, tingling conversation.

"Sugar," Ray whispers. Strangely, I'm thrilled at the sound of his voice.

"My God, Ray, where are you?" I whisper too.

"Thinking of you, enjoying your voice, imagining you're here with me."

"Ray, I don't think..."

"Sugar, on Saturday, at the Eastern shore, wear the bracelet. Wear it for me. Let me see it on your beautiful leg. I'll know you're thinking of me, wearing it just for me. I wish it were my hand, rather than the bracelet, caressing your velvety skin. Go to sleep now. You're in my thoughts."

I turn off the light and smile into my pillow. The phone rings again.

"Ray?..."

There's no answer. I can only hear breathing on the other side. Then, a loud click.

I pull the covers all the way up to my chin. A cold chill makes my whole body shake.

CHAPTER 5

I

T'S SATURDAY. I JUMP OUT OF BED MUCH EARLIER THAN usual. My exercises this morning consist of five sit-ups and five toe-touches. That's it. I'm rearing to go. The shower feels delicious on my skin and I linger a little longer than necessary, rubbing my legs to a shining buff. I'm feeling great. I saw Renata yesterda, and her spirits got much better once I told her I might see Alan today. Also, she told her mother about the attack and she didn't fall apart. Apparently she's coming to visit Renata soon so she won't be so alone. Oh, and Peter called last night again. I think he misses me.

I'm whistling some mindless tune while I prepare a bag of goodies for the two-hour drive. I pack my overnight bag and get dressed. White denim shorts, very tight, very short—they make my legs look longer than they are—a striped white and blue tank-top and a pair of white sandals. I look like a caricature of a French sailor. I hesitate a moment by my chest of drawers where I keep the ankle bracelet Ray gave me. I look at it, pick it up, shrug and drop it in my handbag. Who knows, maybe I'll wear it. A final light spray of cologne behind my ears and behind my knees and I fly down the stairs on my way to pick up Sue.

It's a glorious May morning. The sun's rays are reflected on the pools left from last night's rain storm, and small pink petals of cherry blossoms are floating on them. Like pink clouds on a golden sky. I'm humming along to a song being played on a competing station—always have to check out the competition. Sue's not outside as she said she would be. I grunt a little, double-park, and dash out to ring her bell. A policeman walks by me, looks at my bare legs and my bouncing breasts, smiles and nods. "Nice, very nice," he says. I smile back and return to my car.

Sue comes out holding a straw hat, hair swinging, tight jeans and a white silk shirt. She looks elegant everywhere she goes. Ron follows her, carrying two very large suitcases—for two days and one night. I suppress a laugh.

I'm surprised to see Ron open the back door for Sue. *What? They're both going to sit in back making out all the way to the Bay?* But he closes the back door after she gets in and he sits in front with me.

"Well, Gloria," he says, pushing his tortoise-shell glasses back, "let's get going."

"Good morning to you too, Ron." I look back at Sue, questioning this arrangement. She shrugs at me and says, "He always likes to see where he's going. He says he knows the fastest route to the Eastern shore."

"O.K., then," I say. "Let's go."

Ron adjusts his seat belt two or three times, moves the seat forward, then back, then a little forward again, looks at his watch. I notice it's a large Rolex. He says crisply, "shouldn't take us more than an hour and fifty minutes to Easton, barring any accidents and if you obey all traffic regulations."

"Thank you," I say. "Have you ever been to the Velasco estate?" I know full well he's never been there.

"Well no, actually. Been invited once. Couldn't make it. Congress was in session."

I look at Sue in the mirror for her reaction to his answer, but she doesn't seem to have noticed. I guess she's used to him by now.

"Ah, then you know the Velascos?" I ask.

"Well, everybody knows Raymond Velasco. Or knows about him. I'm perfectly well acquainted with Alan White, his son-in-law. We've spent long hours working together. And of course, playing together." He makes a sound that could pass for laughter. "I also know Alan's brother-in-law, Enrique. We play racquet ball together some Friday nights." He adjusts his glasses. "Now that you remind me, they both left me waiting last Friday a week ago. We had a firm date. No apologies. No phone calls. I was quite miffed," he sniffs.

"Friday?" I ask. "Last Friday?"

"Yup. It was not like Alan, I tell you. Not like him at all."

"You know anybody else?"

"Well, I've had occasion to see the entire Velasco family at congressional gatherings, but I cannot say with total honesty that I've met them personally."

Oh, brother! This is going to be a very long trip, indeed. "Tell me about Alan," I say. *At least let's make this worthwhile.*

"Good chap. Good racquet ball player. Much better than Enrique, certainly. Alan was a stand-out football player in high-school and also played at Georgia Tech. He's still quite an athlete." Ron rolls up the sleeves of his Ralph Lauren light blue denim shirt. His arms are muscular and tanned. Dark blond hairs shine in the sunlight. He notices me looking. He smiles, smooths down his perfectly groomed hair, and winks at me. *Oh, God.*

"What's he like? Alan, I mean?"

"Why all the interest, girlie? Has he made a pass at you too? Oh, I see, you're not talking. Well, I wouldn't be surprised. Quite a ladies' man. Quite a show-off too. Drives a super car. White Aston-Martin I think it is. A real show-stopper. Wouldn't mind having one of those myself. And, of course, I'm sure you know he's married." He laughs his guttural laugh. "Has three small children and is a hit with all the ladies in Congress. Can get them to do anything he wants."

"Oh?"

"Like filing his papers, fetching him coffee, just about anything. His Southern charms gets him things."

Ron starts playing with the select button on the radio. God, I hate that. It's my car, my radio. But I'm too polite to say anything. Sue's strangely quiet, sitting there in back.

"Doesn't all that attention bother his wife?" I resume my questioning.

"Well," *does he have to start every single sentence with 'well'?* "To tell you the absolute truth, I have no idea. I have my suspicions that they really don't get along swimmingly, but Alan really doesn't talk too much about her, as a matter of fact."

"Does he talk about other women?"

Ron looks at me, puzzled, smacks his lips, thinks for a second or two and says, "Other women. I don't think he's ever mentioned other women to me. Why would you ask such a question?"

"I'm just naturally a very curious person." I smile at him. "Does he get along with his father-in-law?"

"Truth be told, I do believe he's getting quite frustrated by the way Mr. Velasco runs their lives. He apparently exerts an inordinate amount of influence over all the members of his family. Alan has brought that up a number of times."

"How did he meet the family?" I know I'm asking too many questions, but Ron seems more than happy to be the news-bearer.

"Well, I do know he went to law school with Enrique. I think they shared an apartment when they were at Georgetown Law. That's how Alan got involved with the whole clan. They're very tightly knit, those Velascos."

"Did you go to Georgetown too?"

"Oh no, no. I went to Yale Law."

I finally regain control of the radio and listen to different stations, commenting with Sue about the quality of the programming. Ron seems to sulk when the conversation steers away from him and I catch him more than once stealing glances at my legs.

Exactly one hour and fifty minutes later—*damn!*—we arrive at Easton and turn right onto a shaded country lane. We follow the signs to "Villa Marina," the Velasco estate. Ron checks his watch one more time and utters a contented, "HMMM."

Sue says, "He's never wrong. About anything." I think she sounds a little disappointed.

At the end of the long, narrow, unpaved lane, I park in a gravel lot that already has some twenty vehicles in it. Very fancy looking vehicles. My little blue Escort looks like a midget among them. Some of Ray's "friends" are there to greet us. Same black pants, same aviator dark glasses, but this time they're wearing black caps and black T-shirts. Tight black T-shirts that reveal every muscle of their chests and shoulders. One of them rushes over to open my door, tipping his cap. "Ms. Berk," he says very politely as I step out, "we'll take care of your bags."

"Do you know these men?" Ron asks me, eyes popping out in amazement.

"Oh, yeah. We're very good friends." I walk away swinging my hips a little more than necessary.

We walk into a renovated 1920's-type mansion, high ceilings, gorgeous views of the bay. A string quartet is playing a Viennese waltz and a butler greets us with a tray full of champagne glasses. It isn't even eleven yet. We're escorted to a living room that is surrounded by large windows, overlooking the garden and the Chesapeake Bay. Sunlight and blue reflections of the still waters are pouring in. Wherever there's some wall space there are sports trophies and heads of stuffed animals. *God. I hate that stuff. I hate to see those poor things. I hate hunting.* Voices and laughter seem to come out of every corner of the house.

Miriam Velasco breaks away from a small group of people and approaches us with her slow, majestic walk, her long brown skirt flowing. Her brown silk shirt emphasizes the loveliness of her bronze skin.

"Welcome, Ms. Berk." Not even a hint of a smile. She looks down at my bare legs and makes me feel utterly naked. "This must be Ms. Hamilton." Sue nods. "Welcome to Villa Marina. I'm Miriam Velasco."

Sue shakes Mrs. Velasco's hand and in the most subdued voice I've ever heard Sue use she says, "Thank you, Mrs. Velasco. It's an honor to be here." *Wow, she doesn't talk like that even to the owners of the station.* "May I introduce Ronald Douglas, a friend of mine. He works for Senator McIntyre of Vermont."

"Enchanted," Ron bows low, takes Mrs. Velasco's hand, and in a gallant gesture I never would have expected, kisses it.

"Mr. Douglas," she says. "Welcome. We couldn't be more delighted to have you as our guest. You work in the Senate? Then you must know my son-in-law, Alan."

"Indeed I do. Fine chap, Alan. I'm quite anxious to see him and discuss with him a few matters of utter importance to the Senate, if you wouldn't mind and if it wouldn't interfere with your party, of course." *I myself am quite anxious to see this chap, Alan.*

"I haven't seen Alan around the halls of the Senate for a couple of days," Ron says, wiping his brow with an impeccable white handkerchief.

"Oh," Mrs. Velasco starts playing with her gold cross and purses her lips. "I'm afraid Alan isn't here. He took a short vacation to rest up now that Senator Clark is leaving the Senate." *Oh God. What am I going to tell Renata?*

I start looking around and see Ray walking in the garden, holding the hand of a young, dark-haired woman. They seem to be engrossed in deep conversation and I see him caress her arm once in a while. I think I feel a momentary pang of jealousy and I'm glad I didn't put on the ankle bracelet.

We are shown to our rooms to freshen up a bit. Mine is small, on the first floor, with a little window overlooking the bay. "You can open it," I'm told by a maid, "let the fresh air in. And don't worry. They're not alarmed." Charming room, all done in white tulle and pink bows.

A beautiful painting of a Madonna and Child hangs over the bed.

The Madonna strongly resembles Mrs. Velasco. It must be one of the girls' rooms. It has its own bathroom, a small night table with a radio on it, and plenty of fresh air. I don't need anything more.

My small overnight bag has been placed on a bench and I decide to wash up and unpack right away. When I open the drawer to store my things I find a brown packet wrapped in a bright red ribbon. *Oh, a flower sachet someone forgot.* I pick it up to smell its aroma and I almost gag from its foul odor. I throw it out in the bathroom pail and spray it heavily with perfume to mask that stink. I take off my top and go to lock the door, but the lock doesn't work. Oh, well. With Ray's "friends" roaming the premises I don't think I should worry too much for my safety.

I join Sue and Ron and a few other guests for a ride around the bay in one of the Velascos' power boats. The spray of the water is thrilling and I sit all the way in front to get the splash all over my body.

When we arrive ashore I'm drenched, but delighted. Ray is standing at the pier. His gray beard seems to glisten in the sun. The pleated pants and guayabera shirt hide his girth. His eyes are concealed by very dark sunglasses. I'm the last one to exit the boat and Ray helps me off.

"Gloria, nice to see you again." He lifts me by the waist to put me down on land. One of his hands slides down to my buttocks, but he removes it quickly.

"Mr. Velasco, so nice to be here. Thank you for the invitation."

We start walking back to join the group just ahead of us and he murmurs, "You look superb. That T-shirt you're wearing is soaking, you know. I would love to caress your nipples." And he walks away to mingle with the others.

I'm just standing there, flustered and embarrassed, arms crossed over my chest.

"Gloria, are you coming?" Sue calls after me.

※　※

AFTER A BUFFET LUNCH OF GAZPACHO, PAELLA, FLAN AND SOME wonderful Spanish wines, I excuse myself. Ron and Sue look very cozy, both lying on one chaise, his body totally engulfing her. She seems happy. I start to stroll around, exploring, poking, doing a little digging. I'm just approaching the stables when I'm stopped by two very large "friends."

"Can we help you, Miss?"

"Oh, no thank you. I just want to see the place."

"Mrs. Velasco has a tour planned for tomorrow morning. There's some work going on around here. Could be dangerous. Please join the group."

I comply grudgingly. But the rest of the day is very nice. We spend it playing tennis, horseback riding, lying around the pool and sipping martinis. It's a superb, sun-soaked, alcohol-filled, gossipy afternoon. There are at least thirty people here: congressmen, senators, D.C. councilmen. A lot of power and many beautiful people—men and women. The band hasn't stopped playing all day. I learn that the dark-haired beauty I saw walking with Ray this morning is Linda, his daughter—Alan's wife. And Ray keeps appearing at my side to whisper in my ear. I love all of it.

After a short nap and a long shower I dress for dinner. My skin is tingling from the soap, from the sun, from the excitement of the day. I put on a white strapless dress, white high-heeled shoes, and long dangling earrings. With my short hair, the earrings emphasize my neck. I spray a perfume that smells like gardenias that I find intoxicating—my mother thinks it's much too sweet—and emerge from my little room feeling devastating. My dress sways with my every step and my skin shimmers. Or at least that's what it feels like.

A new music group is playing a slow bolero. Couples are dancing on a wooden floor in the middle of the garden. The boards are gleaming and reflect the tall trees above us. They erupt into small popping noises when people step on them and sound almost like old wood crackling in a fireplace. Glittering lanterns have been hung among the branches and the whole garden smells like the sea and like lavender. It's magical.

A dark, tall, slender man approaches me. "I've been watching you all day. You ride horseback very well," he says. "You haven't noticed me, though. I'm Luis Velasco." Brooding eyes bore into mine. Not a hint of a smile. I don't know how to react, so I look back at him. "Come, dance with me," he says and takes me by the hand. We glide onto the dance floor and start dancing slowly, sensually. An old, silver ankle bracelet my father once gave me glints with the lights of the lanterns every time I move my left leg. I keep catching sight of the glints out of the corner of my eye. Ray's ankle bracelet is hidden in its unopened box. "I noticed my father looking at you," Luis whispers into my ear and holds me tight against him. I inhale his cologne, something musky, masculine, and I look up at him. His somber face is still, his arms are strong and his heart is beating very fast.

Suddenly his hand, the one holding me by my waist, starts caressing my bare back.

"Soft," he says. And I feel his lips grazing my shoulders. I close my eyes and enjoy the sensation.

Someone's tapping me in the shoulder. I open my eyes and find Ray, unsmiling, looking straight at me. "May I have a word with you?" he says sternly.

"Not now, Father," Luis replies in the same tone. "Not now." His entire body stiffens, his jaws tightens and his eyes become thin slits of burning coal.

Ray looks menacingly at his son, is about to say something, decides not to do it, and steps away from the dance floor. I don't see him again the rest of the evening.

Luis and I don't stop dancing. I'm enthralled by the elegance of his movements, by the way he sweeps me across the dance floor, by his embrace. I close my eyes again and let myself enter a maelstrom of passions and tantalizing music and perfumed air.

☙   ☙

AT TWO A.M. THE BAND ANNOUNCES IT'S PLAYING ITS LAST SONG. ONLY Luis and I are left dancing on the floor, under the starry sky. The last song is a tango. *La cumparsita.* Sad and nostalgic music. Almost like a sigh. Luis is holding me with both hands around my back and my face is buried in his chest. We are hardly moving now. The rhythmic beat of the music is reverberating in my chest. Maybe it's Luis' heartbeat. He's murmuring something, but I only feel the caress of his breath on my hair. I don't know where I am anymore. Luis guides my body, my arms, my legs, and I let myself go carelessly. I look up at the yellow moon and Luis presses his lips to my neck. I run my fingers through his hair, down his cheek, down to his lips. His soft kisses burn the palm of my hand while the warm breeze in the garden sweeps through my bare legs. It feels like a velvet caress. The powerful smell of the gardenias around us makes me feel drunk. The music stops.

"We have to go," he whispers in my ear and kisses it.

We walk down the corridor to my room, holding each other by the waist. The only sounds around us are those of the cicadas and the crickets. We stand silently by the door of my room. My back is pressed against the wall and I'm enveloped in his arms, his whole body pressed to mine. He slowly bends down to my face and kisses my forehead, my eyes, my neck.

"Luis..." I whisper.

He shakes his head. "No, no, Red. Not here. I don't think it's smart."

He opens the door for me and I walk in. He stands by the door, pulls me to him one more time and kisses my lips with a sweet passion. "Good night, Red." He walks away.

I undress, throw the dress and my briefs on the chair, and open the window to let the breezes of the bay cool my naked body. I raise my arms to my head, close my eyes and let the mist of the night bathe me.

I lie down and put my hands under the pillow. *My God, what's this?* The brown, foul-smelling sachet is under the pillow. I get up in a hurry, go to the window, and throw it out.

Finally I fall asleep.

⚜ ⚜

A STRANGE NOISE SNAPS ME AWAKE. SOMEONE'S AT MY DOOR. IT'S BEING opened carefully, gingerly. I lie there uncovered, naked, excited, very still, just looking at the door. It seems it takes ages for it to open entirely and a figure comes into the room. I can't see the face. It's too dark in the room for me to distinguish any features. It's a man's body though— long, lean, with a strong, determined stride. He takes five steps to my bed, kneels on the floor next to me and places his hands on my breasts.

"God, Red. You're beautiful."

I throw my head back and embrace him by the neck, moaning his name.

His hands travel to my lips and he places a finger inside my mouth. It tastes of salt and soap. I lick it.

Still kneeling on the floor he caresses my neck and my breasts. He kisses my belly. I let out a muffled groan.

"Shh... Shh... They'll hear you. Try to be still. They're sleeping right above us." He kisses my legs and my thighs. I grasp the headboard and arch my back.

"Please..." I whisper. "Please..." I pull him up by the hair and bring him close to my face, close to my mouth.

He climbs onto the small bed with me and holds me tightly against his lean body. I caress his back, his buttocks, kiss his face.

We make love to each other gently, quietly, very quietly. I moan and he quickly covers my mouth with his.

"Shh... Shh... They'll hear."

His mouth is pressed against mine, his body tight against mine. The heat, the excitement, the ardor, enshrouded in a cloak of silence are overwhelming.

When the moans and the sighs subside, he holds my face and tells me he loves my graceful body. I've never felt more beautiful. Abruptly, he presses me very hard against him, almost squeezing the breath out of my body, and hisses in my ear, "Don't do this with anybody else." He brushes my lips lightly and leaves.

I'm warm. And excited. I walk to the open window to feel the coolness of the night. I let out a small cry. Someone's standing by the window looking into my room. *God! Oh my God! Who could it be?* I start shaking with shame and anger. *Dear God, it looks like the same figure I saw standing outside Renata's house the night of the attack.*

CHAPTER 6

SUNDAY'S BRUNCH IS SERVED ON THE VERANDAH OVER-looking the bay. Exquisite. Fresh orange juice, eggs Florentine, Canadian bacon, heavenly, crusty freshly-made bread and good, strong coffee. There are very few of us for brunch. I guess most guests are still asleep after last night's revelry. Luis doesn't put in an appear-ance. Neither does Ray. Mrs. Velasco, in a flowing, chic blue robe, pre-sides over the meal. The perfection and silkiness of her skin is striking even under the harsh glare of the morning sun. She looks resplendent. *How does she do it?*

There is a stark contrast between yesterday's gaiety and excitement and this morning's almost dispirited mood. I don't dare look anybody in the eye. I don't know who saw me last night making love to Luis and I cannot stand the thought that it could be one of these people.

As soon as brunch is over, I announce to Ron and Sue that's it's time to leave. Both of them grunt their objection.

"It isn't quite one o'clock," Ron says stifling a yawn. *I wonder how much sleep they got last night.*

"I've got to get back. I have a show at six and I need to prepare for it. You two can stay longer and get a ride from somebody else," I say. I can't wait to leave this place.

I thank Mrs. Velasco for her hospitality.

"You're welcome, Ms. Berk. Glad you could make it. Don't forget we have an appointment on Tuesday, at ten. I'll be waiting for you." I feel diffident in her presence. Her dark eyes are looking through me, her unsmiling face shows no emotion.

"I'll be there, Mrs. Velasco," I say.

"Good," she says, fingering her large gold cross.

"Please thank Mr. Velasco for the weekend. It was really wonderful."

"I'm sure he'll appreciate your kind words." She turns from me and approaches a group of guests.

I watch her for a few seconds. Her walk is slow, controlled, majestic. She surprises me as she turns, looks at me, and her eyes narrow to small, dark slits. I pick up my small night bag and sprint to my car.

We hardly talk on the return drive to D.C. The music on the radio is playing softly and Ron and Sue nap on and off.

I look at the young corn plants on both sides of the road, swaying gently, almost to the rhythm of the music. The traffic is very light this Sunday afternoon and I'm glad I don't have to fight my way back to D.C. Instead, I'm immersed in thoughts about last night. Luis' body, his essence, his kisses, fill my every pore. I can think of nothing else, feel nothing else. Suddenly the song being played on the radio reminds me of Peter's sweet smile and I feel infinitely sad that I never had a strong, passionate relationship with him. I never felt his body on mine. Never enjoyed his kisses. I felt more romantic towards Peter, but less feverish, less hungry, and certainly much less desired.

After dropping off Sue and Ron I go by the hospital to visit Renata. Her eyes are dancing today, alert and curious. Her bandages—freshly changed—are covering less of her face. I can actually see patches of pink, new, unburnt skin.

"Well, did you see him?" is her greeting. "Did you see Alan? What did he say?"

She's sitting up today, which I'm sure is a very good sign. *How do I break it to her without making her suffer? What do I tell her?*

"He wasn't there, Renata. I didn't see him at all."

"Not there?" She practically shrieks. "Weren't they all there?"

"Except for Alan. Mrs. Velasco said he's on vacation."

"My God. That's not true. He wouldn't have left without me." She starts sobbing. "He loves me. I know he loves me." I can hardly understand what she's saying to me, she's crying so hard.

"Calm down, Renata. If he's on vacation we'll find him. Freddy, my friend in the police department, could help. Please let me talk to him. He'll help us find Alan, you'll see." I'm patting her on the back, patting her arm. I don't know what to do to calm her down.

"No, no. They hate him, Gloria. They did something to him. They all hate him."

"You're blathering. Who hates him?"

"The Velascos. All of them. Especially Enrique, that horrible jerk."

I saw Enrique Velasco yesterday. He's anything but horrible. Luis' older brother, taller, fuller, darker, more somber. The women at the party couldn't stop staring. I certainly wouldn't describe him as horrible.

"Why do you say that?"

Renata grabs a tissue, dabs at her eyes, adjusts her nightgown—I notice she's now wearing her own—and says, "This is going to hurt the Velasco family. But I swear to you, Gloria, if Alan doesn't show up soon, I'm going public with this. Nobody will be able to keep me quiet about this."

"What, what is it?"

"Alan knows a terrible secret about Enrique. And he told me that Enrique has always been worried that he'll slip and give it away. He told me that's the reason Mr. Velasco was so intent in marrying off his spoiled, silly daughter to him. To make sure he was always being watched and that he kept his mouth shut. Jesus. I'm afraid."

She starts crying again and her narrow shoulders hunch over, quivering. She's breaking my heart and I don't know how to help her.

"Please, Renata. Please start at the beginning. I can't follow what you're saying."

She takes a sip of water, rearranges her flimsy nightie, and sighs with exasperation, as though I should know everything she's about to tell.

"Alan and Enrique went to law school together," she begins. "Alan was a very good student and Enrique asked him for help. He paid him, of course. Alan comes from a very poor family, farmers in Georgia, and he needed every cent he could get. After a while, they decided to share an apartment. Apparently it was very fancy. Near here, in Georgetown. Enrique paid most of the rent and Alan repaid him by tutoring him. He taught him everything. Enrique didn't even attend classes. He spent his days drinking and doing drugs and screwing every woman he could lay his filthy hands on while Alan went to school and took notes for both of them. Then, just before exams, Alan would tutor him."

She looks at me questioningly.

"Yes," I say. "I understand the scenario. Go on."

As if in a trance now, without any show of emotion, Renata continues with her story.

"Enrique would go out driving drunk, even though Alan always tried to prevent it. Well, one Friday night, after an evening of bar-hopping and who knows what else, after dropping a girl off, he backed up in an alley without looking and ran over and killed a man. An undocumented Hispanic—from El Salvador, I think. And what did the jerk do? He called Alan. The sissy was so afraid to call his powerful father that he called Alan, the poor boy from the farms of Georgia." She turns to me. "Can you please tell me, Gloria, what could Alan do?"

I shrug.

"That's right. Nothing. Nothing." Her voice starts to rise. "Alan rushed over, called Mr. Velasco, and Velasco arrived on the scene with his goons. According to Alan he never goes anywhere without his goons. I wonder if they sleep in the same room with him. One of the goons grabs Alan by the arm and whisks him away—I guess they didn't want any witnesses there, even though Alan already was a witness. And then the wonderful Mr. Velasco arranged everything for his darling son. Alan thinks they paid the poor man's family a huge amount of money to keep them quiet. The accident was never reported. So Enrique Velasco, the great lawyer, the president of the Latino Bar Society, killed a Hispanic. Isn't that just a wonderful irony? Couldn't you just die laughing?"

She dabs at her eyes. I'm afraid she's becoming hysterical. I offer her a glass of water, to help calm her down, but she pushes my hand away, spilling some water on her covers.

"But Alan knows," she continues. "He knows. So the father introduced him to Linda, that spoiled brat always dressed in Dior, and the whole family courted Alan, the whole group of them. Of course he was captivated—who wouldn't be? With their wealth, and their parties, and all that attention they gave him. And oh, yes, the power. He fell under their spell, he fell into that horrible web they all wove and they caught him. And they swallowed him. And so he married Linda and they thought they buried their dirty secret within their family. But Alan was always the outsider. They really never accepted him. He told me that until he met me he never really knew what love was."

Don't they all say the same thing?

"He was ready to give it all up. For me. Give up their filthy wealth, and their lies, and their conspiracies. For me."

Well, at least that's what he said. I wonder what he would've done after your little tryst.

"And now, oh my God." Deep sobs rack her slender body again. "And now this. How is he going to stand looking at me? Oh my God." She falls into my arms sobbing disconsolately. I try my best, murmur to her, pat her, embrace her. Nothing works. Her sobs don't subside.

"I know something happened to him, Gloria, " she says between hiccups. "They've hurt him too. Find him for me. Find him soon."

She seems to calm down a little after my solemn promise that I will look for him and try to find him. She warns me not to talk about him with the family. "Any one of them is capable of hurting him. Anyone." Those are her parting words to me.

※　※

MY INTERVIEW SHOW TODAY ON "LET'S CHAT" IS AN ABYSMAL failure. I can't concentrate. My guest, Rhoda Sokolov, a classically trained violinist who just joined a jazz band, is going to start touring as an opening act with Madonna. The reviews of her jazz performances are fabulous. Rhoda is charming during the interview, talkative, amusing, tantalizing. Unfortunately, it never clicks. I can't come up with the right amount of enthusiasm to ask the questions that would energize my audience. I pray the phones will start ringing soon, but it just doesn't happen. I pick up the receiver several times to see if the lines are functioning. They are. People just aren't calling in. It's my fault. I have to make it up to Rhoda and have her over again soon. When there's less going on in my head. I hope she'll accept my invitation.

On my way home I stop at the local Greek restaurant to get myself a gyro. Nikko, the owner, has become friendly and listens to my show. He always has sweet words of encouragement for me, delivered in his musical, deeply accented speech. I notice he doesn't even look at me this evening. He busies himself with the other customer in the shop and waves at me only when he sees me leave. I don't blame him. The show was a fiasco.

I walk up the three flights to my apartment, lugging my overnight bag and the gyro bag that has started to sprout huge grease spots. I put everything down on the floor and unlock the two safety locks my father installed for me just before he moved to Florida. God, if feels as if I left the apartment years ago, not just one night ago. I sit at my table, near the balcony, and bite into my gyro. I look around and have the feeling that something is not quite right. I'm not exactly sure what it is. I put down the gyro, start walking around the living room of my very small apartment. Small, but intimate. And mine. Nothing's missing. Everything's in its place in the living room. When I walk into my bedroom I stop dead on my tracks. Next to my bed, on the night table, there's a small leather-bound book. I'm sure I didn't leave it there. I don't even own a book that looks like that. I go look at it, my heart skipping a beat. It's a book of poems. *Goddam it! What's going on here?* I open it and a note comes flying out. I pick it up angrily and read it.

> *My hands*
> *Open the curtains of your being*
> *Clothe you in a deeper nudity*
> *Uncover all the bodies of your body*
> *My hands*
> *Invent another body for your body.*
> Octavio Paz

Sweet God. Ray again. This has got to stop. I have to tell him this has to stop. I feel invaded. I have no privacy, no serenity. I've got to get all the locks changed first thing in the morning. *Sure, as though that's going to deter him.*

I've got to figure out what's happening here. Is this a cat and mouse game between father and son? Ray saw me dancing with Luis last night. Maybe it was even one of his goons he sent to peek into the window and observe our love-making. If this is a contest between the two of them I don't want to be in the middle. I don't want to be the prize or the prey.

However, if I keep my wits about me, if I play my cards right, I can keep the friendship of both and not alienate either, and I might be able to help Renata find her Alan. It's walking a tight-rope, I know. It's risky. But then, so is life. So I'll just go with the flow. Let's see what comes up.

I go back to the dining room to finish my gyro and a glass of cold Zinfandel. I start looking at the book of poems. The loud ringing of the phone startles me.

"Red, how was your drive home?"

"I didn't see you this morning, Luis."

"I didn't want to face you in front of my parents."

"Why not?"

"I was sure they would be able to see in my face how much I want you when I'm around you."

So, we're afraid of mommy and daddy. "Well, that's smart, I guess."

"Yeah. You bet it's smart. I want to feel you Red. Caress your body. Right now."

"Where are you?"

A few seconds of silence on the other side. "At Villa Marina, still with the family. We're driving back tomorrow. They all went to dinner and I stayed behind to call you."

"Thank you."

"Red..." The tone has become more sensual, softer. "You're incredible, you know? You have the sweetest little body I've ever seen."

"Seen many?" I tease, not really that interested.

"A few," he whispers. "How about you?"

"How about me what?"

The voice takes a more serious tone now. Huskier somehow. "How many men have you had?"

It's none of your business. "Luis, I don't think..."

"How many?" he fairly shouts into the phone, belligerent, angry.

"None," I lie. I don't want an argument this late at night.

"Good, my sweet little virgin. Good." The voice is kind again. Softer. "Let's keep it that way."

"Good night, Luis. I'm really tired. I've got to get to work early tomorrow."

"I'll come see you tomorrow night. I'll bring dinner. You provide the dessert." He laughs a short, friendly laugh. "Good night, Red. I'll be seeing you in my dreams."

I fall into bed and get to sleep almost immediately. The sound of the phone wakes me with a jolt.

"So, did you like the book? They're the greatest poems of the twentieth century."

I look at the alarm clock. *It's three in the morning. Don't these people ever sleep?*

"Ray, how dare you —"

"Read them carefully. They're erotic poems. Listen, Sugar. There's going to be an important political rally on Tuesday night. You come with me. I'll introduce you to everybody who's anybody in D.C. politics."

"Ray," I interrupt curtly. "Why did you come into my apartment? How dare you? Do you know about Luis and me?" I'm fairly shouting into the phone.

"Sugar, there's very little that happens in this town that I don't know about. And you really have to be more careful about the security in your apartment. See how easy it was."

"So..."

"And look, if my boy wants to have a little fling what's the harm? Let him. If he wants to try to beat me, let him try. I always let him think he's winning. In the end, though, I'm always the one who walks away with the big trophy. Good night, Sugar. See you Tuesday."

CHAPTER 7

Luis arrives at seven with a large bag from the gourmet shop down the street. "Here, dinner," he says, handing me the bag, and he picks me up in a hard embrace. I almost drop our dinner.

He kisses me on the lips, runs his hand down my chest. "Umm," he says, "What I've been dreaming about all day." He walks me to the small kitchen and opens the bottle of champagne while I arrange the caviar, salmon, brie and bread on cut glass platters. *I'm going to be hungry by ten.*

He walks toward me, stands behind me and holds me tight while I prepare our "dinner." He smooches my neck and puts his hands on each breast. I can feel him getting excited almost instantly and move slightly away from him. He turns me around, looks at me, and kisses me hard for a long time.

"I missed you, baby," he says. "Let's eat quickly and go to bed."

I light the candle, put on a Bach Brandenburg concerto, and go to sit by his side.

"Oh, jeez. The same music my father likes. Who died here? Let's hear something alive."

He riffles through my collection of CDS, grumbling all the time under his breath.

"What kind of music do you have here? There's nothing sexy, Red."

"Try Scheherezade. That's sexy," I say. I look at him and smile. His slender body is tall and graceful under the tight black turtleneck. His shiny, slightly disheveled hair makes him look like a young boy and his eyes are black coals with a fire still burning within. He looks delicious.

He returns to the table, sits very close to me. "Well Red, how do you like our little feast?" he asks, munching on a piece of toast laden with black caviar. Imperial Beluga. He says it's the lightest, smoothest tasting caviar there is. It's O.K., I guess. But I like the red salmon caviar much better. He feeds me a bite of his toast with caviar. When I open my mouth he inserts a finger and I lick it. He laughs out loud. We're having fun.

"Tell me about your family," I say to him, pouring more champagne into his still almost full glass. He caresses my bare arm and kisses the inside of my elbow.

"We're just like everybody else. Just as nutty as the next. I'm the sanest of the lot, if you want to know the truth." I don't know if he's serious.

"Tell me about Linda, I hardly had a chance to talk to her."

"She's very spoiled. She's also the apple of my father's eye. The oldest and the brattiest."

"She's beautiful," I say in total honesty.

"She's had help."

"What kind of help."

"You mention it and she's had it. Not natural, like you." He rubs my thigh. I'm wearing jeans. "Don't you want to change? Wear those sexy shorts you were wearing the other day? Show me your legs?"

"They're in the wash. I'll change later."

"I want you all the time, you know." He lowers his voice. "I could hardly concentrate at work."

"What do you do?"

"I'm a lawyer. My brother and I have a law firm. We do a lot of contractual work for Latin American clients. But I couldn't work today. I had you on my mind, just kept thinking about Saturday night. Wanted to feel you." He puts his hand inside my thigh and I remove it gently and kiss his fingers.

"Let's finish the champagne first, and then we'll go to the bedroom."

"Whatever my lady wants," he says.

"Tell me more about Linda."

"She's an old married lady. Why the interest? She has three girls. All brats like her. Her husband can hardly stand her and I don't blame him. She's such a princess."

"Does she love her husband?"

"How the hell would I know, Red? I suppose she does. She married him, didn't she? Anyway, he's always busy—with the senator, with his sports, with the women."

"What women?"

"I don't really know. But if you're a man in the Velasco family, you always have women in your life. And I can't imagine Linda being the kind of woman who'd inspire a man to great acts of devotion."

"Does he love her?"

"Why so many questions?" he asks me, tracing the length of my arm with his finger. "Enough questions. Enough about Alan and Linda."

"Well, the more I know about your family, the more I'll know about you." *A likely story.* He seems perfectly satisfied by the answer.

"I think he does love her. At least he seemed to love her when they just got married. He couldn't stay away from her for a second. Always glued to her."

"How come he wasn't at the estate last weekend? With the family, I mean?" I'm trying to sound as guileless as possible.

"Linda said he left her a note saying he was taking off for a few days. I guess he needs a vacation from her. Hell, we all need a vacation from her. She's tough to live with."

"Do you think he left by himself?"

Luis looks at me hard, shifts in his chair, smacks his lips and says, "I really don't know." *And I don't believe him at all.*

"I need to find him, Luis. It's important. It would mean a lot to me if you could help me find him."

"Why do you need to find him?" He puts his arm around my shoulders and lightly strokes my arm. "Why?" He squeezes my shoulder a little harder than necessary.

"I did a show with him and the Senator a little over a week ago," I say truthfully. "And people have been calling me with questions about the Senator." That's a bold lie. "As you know, the Senator left on a farewell junket to the Middle East and he can't be reached. Believe me, I tried. So I thought that Alan could help. It's really important." His fingers start caressing me again, the squeezing stops.

"Well, Red, if it's important to you, I'll help you. I'll do anything to make you happy. Try calling his former girlfriend. She's been calling the house a lot. Maybe she knows something."

I gulp hard. I thought Renata said nobody knew a thing about them. "His girlfriend?" I ask softly.

"Yep. Some bimbo he knew in high school in the hinterlands of Georgia. Another farmer girl. Just like his kind. She may know where my dear brother-in-law is hiding."

I relax. It's not Renata.

"Who is she?"

"A nurse of some kind. A nurse's aide, maybe. I don't know what the difference is. She works at Children's Hospital, I think."

"What's her name, do you know?"

"If I answer you, will that be the last question? Will you then go to bed with me? I'm salivating."

"Yes, I promise."

"It's Anne, or Anita. Something like that."

"Her last name, Luis." I'm growing impatient.

"I don't know, Red. Let me think. He once told me about her. He said she was a real nut. Let's see. Anne Simms. No, no, Anita Simons. That's it. Or something like that. Come on, let's go. Hurry with your champagne, Red. I can hardly wait."

I swallow the last drops of my drink and he lifts me up in the air, and carries me in his arms. "Lead the way, my lady," he says while kissing my neck and cheeks.

Even though I'm fighting it, there's something about Luis that unnerves me—perhaps his brooding eyes. But I'm also very excited by him, by his touch and his looks and his eagerness.

We make love openly, freely, hungrily, with all the lights on. He's not concerned with the noise we make and he covers my face, my body, my mouth, with damp, hot lips. I've never been made love to with so much passion. It's lust and excitement. He inflames all my senses. I want him to touch me everywhere, kiss me everywhere. There's no sense of shame. Just pleasure and passion. It feels as though I just woke up to sex.

"What are you thinking, Red?" he asks me as we lie next to each other. The neighbor's cat, Honey, has climbed up on the balcony and joined us in bed. I'm caressing her fur. Even that feels different with Luis at my side.

"This is great," I say.

He turns his body to me, embraces me, making Honey jump out of the way, and he curls his legs around mine. "I think so too. Want to do it again tomorrow?"

"I can't tomorrow."

He stiffens up immediately, unfurls his legs and tightens his embrace around me. It's not a friendly move. "Why not? I thought you had no other men." He's squeezing me hard. Too hard.

"Luis." I manage to free myself from his arms and prop myself on one elbow. I feel too exposed, too bare. I sit up, cover myself with the sheet, and face him. "I'm not sleeping with anybody else," I say. "But I have a lot of friends and a lot of commitments. I cannot drop everything just to please you."

His dark face becomes even darker. His eyebrows seem to have been drawn with one long black stroke. "I'm not sure I like that," he says.

"Well, take it or leave it. I can't change it."

He uncovers my body, pulling the sheet back in a violent movement and I sit, looking impassively at him, not moving a muscle.

"I'll take it," he says finally. "I like you, Red. You have spunk." And he kisses my throat and caresses my thighs. I shudder.

⚜ ⚜

MRS. VELASCO DIDN'T FORGET ABOUT CARINA. BOTH ARE WAITing for me when I arrive on Tuesday morning at ten sharp. I'm amazed at what I see. Mrs. Velasco wasn't kidding when she said Carina and I look alike. This woman, dressed in a smart white pants suit, seems to be my double—somewhat older, somewhat more distinguished. But we have the same slight build, similar red hair, fair skin, hazel eyes. I walk over to her and she extends her hand to me. *My God she even smiles like me.*

"Well, Gloria," she says without waiting for an introduction. "Look at yourself twenty-five years from now. Like what you see?"

Mrs. Velasco says, "Ms. Berk, this is Mrs. Lozano."

I smile at Carina, shake her hand and say to her, "Indeed I do, Mrs. Lozano. Indeed I do."

"Come now, girl. You have to call me Carina. Forget the Mrs. Lozano part. It makes me feel even older."

Mrs. Velasco, dressed in a navy blue suit, looks sober and elegant, her gold cross nestled between her ample breasts. She looks at the two of us without comment, without a trace of emotion.

"Well, let's get started with the fundraiser plans," she says. "Carina's a board member at Children's Hospital. She'll be my co-chair and we want everything to be perfect. Carina's a very good photographer and has an eye for every detail. She'll be very helpful, I'm sure."

"How did you like the preamble?" Carina laughs. "Let's have some tea first, Miriam. And maybe a smile might help too. After all, dear, this girl is here to help us. She doesn't have to do it. And you're not paying her to do it."

"You're right. I'm not being a very good hostess. I'll get us some tea. Same as last week, Ms. Berk?"

"Please," I say and find a seat close to Carina.

"I can't get over this," she says. "It's like floating back in time. I love it. I hope we become good friends and you tell me about your life and I can relive my youth. What fun."

The tea arrives promptly and we start planning the radio involvement in the fundraiser. I propose a whole day of raising money, a day of music and dedications and short interviews with doctors, nurses and young patients. And of course, a plea for donations. "If you'd like," I add, "we could ask our best advertisers for free merchandise in exchange for a couple of free commercials on the air, and then we can give away those prizes for donations."

"I love it." Carina's very enthusiastic. "We have a lot of rich friends. We'll force them to donate money and gifts."

"We can't force anybody to do anything," Mrs. Velasco says.

"Very well, then. We'll ask for the money and gifts and if they don't come up with it, we'll erase their names from your social register and we'll sic Ray's dogs on them."

"Carina, you're not funny. Ray will have nothing to do with this affair. It's strictly ours."

"Where's your sense of humor, Miriam? It's going to be very hard working with you if you don't lighten up a bit."

I couldn't agree more.

The doors to the library swing open and Linda walks in. I think she looks gorgeous despite what Luis told me about her. Every hair is in place, her face is fully made up and the hot pink suit she's wearing looks very expensive. She herself looks expensive.

Carina bolts up and immediately sits down again, and Linda pales visibly. She stops close to the door, holding on to the handle. She seems to be shaking slightly.

"Excuse me, Mother. I didn't know you had company."

"Come in, sweetheart. Say hello." Miriam's voice seems to caress Linda. Her smile widens and she follows Linda's movements with obvious delight.

Linda walks in and hugs Carina. "I haven't seen you in a while," she says somberly.

Carina answers in the same serious tone. "I've been busy. How have you been?"

The two get involved in a short conversation about their lives, totally shutting out Mrs. Velasco and me. I feel as though I'm seeing them through a keyhole. I'm a witnesses to their exchange, but don't belong in the picture whatsoever.

Finally, Linda turns to me. She says, "You're the disc jockey, aren't you?" She barely touches my fingertips with her tanned, manicured hands. "Nice meeting you." And she leaves.

⁂

AN EARLY LUNCH IS SERVED IN THE DINING ROOM ON A BEAU-tifully set lacewood table. The faces in the old-fashioned portraits peer at us from the walls. I feel like tiptoing in this dark, solemn room. The Venetian chandelier is lit, the curtains are closed, and we eat our chicken salad and croissants on very fine bone china. Just Mrs. Velasco, Carina and I. The maids come and go quietly, serving the lunch without looking at us and without uttering a word. Mrs. Velasco has a small silver bell by her side, but she doesn't need to ring it. The service is smooth and flawless.

Mrs. Velasco hardly touches her food. Instead, she helps herself to leaves and capsules that overflow the vials and small bowls set in front of her. I see her take a handful of capsules and swallow them down with a sip of the mango and orange juice we were served.

I look with amazement at Carina who has finished her salad in three forkfuls and has already asked for seconds.

"Eat," she says to me. "Enjoy it. Miriam has a superb cook. Too bad she doesn't enjoy any of her cooking. Instead, she's always eating her herbs. Or drinking them. Or rubbing them on her body and her face." She turns to Mrs. Velasco. "What are you having today, dear?"

Mrs. Velasco, who has been silent throughout lunch, hesitates for a second and then decides to answer. "These are a few drops of Echinacea; it boosts the immune system. This," she says, showing us a few leaves, "is Glucomannan; it helps me curb my appetite. And this is Hawthorn, good for my heart."

"Miriam, dear, you know very well there's nothing wrong with your heart."

Mrs. Velasco's eyes cloud with a veil of anger. "Carina," she says in a very low tone, "you don't know everything that's going on in my heart."

"All right, dear. Please forgive me. Let's drop the subject." She turns to me. "Doesn't Miriam's skin look magnificent? It's like porcelain. Like delicate porcelain, wouldn't you say, Gloria?"

"It's absolutely perfect," I gush.

"It's all due to her herbs. She's an accomplished herbalist. She learned it from her Indian nanny in Puerto Rico." Carina reaches for her third croissant and eats it while she continues talking. "Miriam prepares her own potions, her own facials, and then she applies them to herself. She's a magician. Oh, Miriam, I'll tell you what..." Carina's face lights up suddenly. "I have a great idea. Why don't you give the girl one of your marvelous facials? Let her see how you do it—from scratch. Then maybe she can interview you on her show, make you famous."

"I don't think so," is Mrs. Velasco's curt response.

Carina makes a pouting face. "Oh, Miriam, at least it can be a sort of pay-back for the time this girl is putting in here. Wouldn't you like to have one, Gloria?"

"I'd love to."

"Don't you have to get back to the radio station, Ms. Berk?"

"It's still early," I say looking at my watch. "I'm prepared for my show this afternoon." *I'd do anything to have skin like hers.*

"Very well then," Mrs. Velasco says grudgingly, rising very slowly from the table. "Follow me."

Carina pats me lightly on the back. She takes hold of my arm as we walk behind Mrs. Velasco. "Hold on to your seat. You're in for a treat," she whispers to me.

We walk into a small room, very white, very clean—spotless. It must be next to the kitchen because I can hear voices and smell something cooking. There's a long, narrow table next to the wall and shelves filled with tubes and containers. There's also a small bench facing a window. Outside, in the garden, azaleas are in full bloom, magnolia trees sway in the light breeze. This is a tranquil space.

"Please sit," Mrs. Velasco says, pointing to the bench. When I have complied, she comes very close to my face. I can feel her warm breath on my cheek. I close my eyes.

She spends a minute or two examining the skin of my face, touching it lightly, "Hmmm... Hmmm..." she's saying. "Dry, it's very, very dry." I open my eyes and look at Carina standing near the bench, looking at me.

"Now, girl, don't be nervous. You can relax. This won't hurt a bit."

Mrs. Velasco reaches for a container, then another, humming under her breath. She takes out a mortar and pestle and starts mixing all the ingredients.

"Tell us what you're doing Miriam. Listening to you is half the fun."

"I'm mixing fresh pineapple—it has a natural acid that will balance your PH—carrots, chamomile, honey and vitamin E. I'll add a few drops of vetivert, to give it a fresh, clean aroma. That's all. It's very simple and natural. And Carina's right, you have to relax. If you're not relaxed it won't have any effect."

She cleans my face with a damp cloth that smells of mint and cucumbers and applies the mixture. It feels glorious. It's cool and creamy and luxurious.

"That's it," she says. "Now we have to cover it and let it penetrate."

She carefully wraps my face with a warm, moist towel, starting at the chin and working in fast, confident, knowing strokes—my forehead, nose, mouth, until she covers my eyes. The towel stings my skin and I wiggle in my discomfort.

"Just relax," she whispers and I hear both of them quietly shuffling out of the room. I'm bound. Blind. Powerless.

CHAPTER 8

I FEEL DEVASTATINGLY BEAUTIFUL. GORGEOUS. MY SKIN HAS never looked this smooth, has never been this radiant. I walk into the station turning this way and that, making sure everyone sees my glowing face. Maybe someone notices, but nobody says anything. *Oh, well. Who cares, as long as I feel good.* And I do. Mrs. Velasco herself seemed very pleased with the results of the facial and invited me for another session. I thought I even saw a hint of a smile when she said goodbye.

My daily music show is a breeze today. The song selections are warm and happy and easy going. I find myself whistling along once in a while. And, best of all, I have a thousand-dollar winner for the new afternoon contest I recently devised. I made a young mother very, very happy. Also, every time I have a big winner, my listenership increases. Sue's happy and so am I. The only thing weighing on my conscience today is how I'm going to break the news to Renata about Alan's girl-friend. Or former girlfriend. I'm sure Renata has suffered enough and now I will inflict more pain on her. Before I do that, though, I have to find the former girlfriend. Let's see if she knows where Alan is.

At six o'clock, after ending my show with a dazzling song by Celine Dion, I walk down the eight floors to the basement garage—I don't have the patience to wait for the elevator. Ray never called back about the political rally. So, I'm going to miss my first truly political experience. Oh, well. I'm just as glad. I don't want to miss my law class. I look forward to Tuesdays and Thursdays. I love law school. It will take me three more years of evening classes before I get my law degree, but the effort is well worth it. I'd like to become a public defender and I know my parents will be so proud of me. Meanwhile, I'm greatly enjoying my Evidence class with Professor Bennett. He's not Peter, of course, but he's so totally in love with our legal system that he makes the class intellectually stimulating and a lot of fun. Besides, the class takes me away from the craziness of the radio business, of the bruised egos, of the relentless pressure to be better than the rest. So, it's O.K. if I don't go to the rally with Ray.

I walk toward the far wall in the garage, near the spot where I usually park my car—there are no assigned spaces here—but I can't find it. *Could I have parked it somewhere else today?* I'm about to turn around, to look somewhere else—it wouldn't be the first time I forgot where I've parked it—when I see one of Ray's "friends" coming out of the black Mercedes, parked in the spot where I'm now sure I left my own car. The guy's dark glasses are two blanks on his face and the ominous sound of his clicking heels makes my stomach take an unwelcome turn.

"Ms. Berk," he says in a deep, slow slur. "Mr. Velasco is waiting for you. Please follow me."

He approaches me and I retreat a few steps. I don't want him too close to me. He lengthens his stride, reaches me and grabs me by the elbow. "He's waiting," he says, pulling me to the car. He opens the back door and fairly pushes me in.

"Jesus, Ray," I say. "How did you get into the garage? It's a secure place, you know? You need a special card to get in. What are you doing here?" I'm babbling, I'm so angry.

"Hello, Sugar. You look good. The facial agrees with you," he says, caressing my cheek and then carelessly letting his hand graze my breast.

76

"Or is it really the facial that's giving you such a radiance?" He smiles broadly and then smacks his lips.

"Ray, for goodness sake. You have to stop doing this."

The car leaves the garage and we enter very heavy traffic in the middle of D.C.

"Doing what, Sugar?" He takes out a long cigar and starts lighting it in small puffs.

"Surprising me like this. If you told me you'd be here, I'd have gone down the street and met you there. There was no need for..."

"Sugar," he interrupts. "Isn't it better that fewer people see you climbing into my car? Especially someone close to my wife?"

He has a point there.

"Where's my car?" I try to sound indignant, but the anger has gone out of me.

"Don't worry." He pets my hand. "It's safe in its own little spot outside your apartment. Now, don't fret any more Sugar and tell me if you enjoyed the book of poems. Which one did you like the best? Erotic, aren't they?"

A Beethoven string quartet is playing softly on the car's stereo. Ray's two "friends" are sitting very still in front. I can only see the well-trimmed backs of their heads and Ray's cigar glowing in the darkened car. The windows are so heavily tinted that although it's still light outside, we're immersed in gloom.

Ray slides his arm over to me, holds me by the waist and lightly strokes the skin under my sweater. "Smooth all over, Sugar. Very nice."

I wiggle away from him. I feel uncomfortable having him touch me.

"What, Sugar, are you shy? Fine, fine, I understand. Let me know when it's O.K. with you. We're not going to do anything you don't want."

He turns away from me and smokes in silence.

"Ray," I say without a preamble. "Do you know where Alan is?"

He turns his face toward me slowly, deliberately. The hand holding his cigar seems to tremble slightly and I feel warm ashes falling onto my lap.

"In what way does that interest you?" he asks, blowing cigar smoke in my face.

I cough a little and give him the same explanation I gave Luis. He doesn't accept it as readily, presses me for more details. I'm making them up as I go along. He finally relents.

"Look, Sugar. This is a family affair. We don't want anyone involved in this. He left a note saying he was leaving for a couple of weeks, that he's tired. The Senator's retirement was a chance for him to unwind and think about his future. He asked us not to try to contact him, that he would be in touch with us in due time. We're following his request. We're leaving him alone. Everybody needs time for himself once in a while. I understand that very well. Hell, I'd like to do it myself, if you want to know the truth. Just leave for a while, no responsibilities, no family, nothing to worry about. So, we're lying low. Don't you make any waves, Sugar. I wouldn't recommend it. You can ask him whatever you want whenever he comes back. Now, we just don't do a thing. Understand?" He pats my thigh lightly.

"Tell me about him. What kind of person is he?"

"I don't know, Sugar. You met him. He's a man. He's driven, ambitious, a very hard worker. Really wants to succeed. He's climbing the ladder to success one rung at a time."

"Do you like him?"

"He's the father of my three granddaughters. Of course I like him. And he has power. He works in the seat of power here. And best of all, he has aspirations. He'd like to run for the Senate himself. He's discussed it with me and asked for my support. And as long as he doesn't disappoint me, well..."

I'd like to discuss his former girlfriend with Ray. I'm sure he knows about her, but I don't know how to raise the subject.

"I'd like to know..." I start, and hesitate.

"Sugar," he seems to be reading my thoughts, "Alan is a busy, complicated man. You'd better leave it be. Here we are in the innards of the city. In the very heart of what makes this city tick. I'll show you tonight what D.C. is all about."

Ray's guardians jump out of the car, dark jackets flapping in the light wind and hold the doors open for us. Ray struggles getting out of the car and one of the companions holds his arm gently, carefully, almost tenderly. The breeze ruffles Ray's gray hair and he smooths it out carefully. He arranges his blue-and-gold-striped tie and places his impeccable blue blazer over his shoulders. His gold and diamond cufflinks glimmer as he gently tucks his arm under mine.

"Come, Sugar. This is going to be fun," he says. His walk has taken on a lighter quality. It's jovial, easy-going. He's pulling me by the arm.

"You look happy, Ray." I smile at him while I try to keep pace with him.

"Wait till you see it, till you feel it. This is life. This is really what I love."

Dusk helps Anacostia hide her homeliness. The usually littered streets seem to glimmer under the fading light of the reddish sunset and the old, yellowing street lamps seem to add a touch of glamour to the crumbling townhouses and decayed buildings. The shimmering Anacostia River looks like a silver arrow puncturing the horizon. Children's voices seem to come from everywhere. I bend down to pick up a stray ball and give it back to a little girl in braids. Ray's smiling broadly.

Ray's bodyguards hold open two heavy-looking steel doors into what must have been a warehouse at the river's edge. The moment I step inside a heavy cloud of smoke envelops me. Ray seems to inhale the smoke and lets out a small chortle. His smile broadens and he walks into the large, noisy crowd, keeping me close to him, holding me by the shoulders in a gesture that makes me feel protected and almost invulnerable—a warm, friendly sensation. Ray uses his free hand to shake the hand of every person who crosses his path.

"Is the mayor coming, Ray?" I ask.

"Sugar, the mayor wouldn't be caught dead at one of my rallies. He hates me. Hates everything I do and stand for."

"Why?"

"Because we're trying to put a new mayor in here. And people better not oppose us. They wouldn't like the consequences. Because we want power. Because I'm really working for the disenfranchised and the needy; unlike him, I'm not working for myself. So, tell me, how do you like being the only Anglo here?" He's smiling. His eyes are full of light and excitement. We're engulfed by people. Some come over to Ray wordlessly, apparently just to be close to him, to look at him, without uttering a word. One slight, dark-skinned, intense looking man approaches us and stands eye-to eye with Ray.

"Raymond," he says in a heavy Spanish accent and without even noticing me. "We need to talk."

"Sure, sure, Oscar. Here, meet Gloria, the secret weapon I talked to you about."

Oscar looks at me, bows his head slightly. "Miss," he says unimpressed and continues to gravitate towards Ray. "It's important..."

"Sugar," Ray cuts him short, "please meet Oscar Acevedo. He'll be our next mayor."

"Ray, I don't think..." he says.

"It's O.K., my friend. We can trust Ms. Berk, here. Isn't that right, Sugar?" He grips my shoulder. "She'd never betray us. I'm sure of that." He grips me harder. "Oscar is the head of our movement, GUERRA."

I blink and gulp hard. "My God," I say under my breath.

Ray notices my discomfort. "GUERRA, that's right. It means war. But we're not for war. Of course not, are we Oscar? GUERRA is merely an acronym, Sugar. It's really quite innocent. It stands for Give Us Every Right and Representation Association. Mild, very mild, don't you think?" He takes a puff from his cigar. "We would never advocate a war, nor a revolution, nor any violence. Unless it was absolutely necessary, of course." He finishes his sentence with a chuckle. Oscar joins him and surprises me by the sound that comes out of his mouth. He sounds like a turkey.

"Why do you have to call it GUERRA, though?" I ask in a voice much louder than I intended. I notice people around us get very quiet, many looking at me with unfriendly stares. "And Ray, why am I here?"

"Because I wanted you to see this. I wanted you to understand a real political grass-roots movement. Because I need you and because my movement needs you."

"Why? Why do you need me? I don't know anything about politics. I've never been involved in a political movement."

"I'm quite aware of that," Ray says, wiping his shiny forehead with a fancy looking handkerchief. It's getting very hot in here. It's humid and smoky and I feel uncomfortable, cornered. I want to leave, but Ray has me firmly by the arm and his protectors are standing guard by the door. "And Sugar, that's why you are perfect. Unbiased. Apolitical. Young and female. Exactly the kind of person who can spread our doctrine in D.C. without being called a partisan. And," he smiles, flashing perfect teeth that I have never noticed before, "you have a nice little radio show that can be used by us without attracting attention from the mayor."

I decide to keep my mouth shut for the time being. I'm looking around, listening, absorbing. Ray seems to be revered by all the people here. They approach him with a certain reverence that I find disarming. They listen to his every word with great interest, nodding in assent to everything he says. But he doesn't leave my side. Any time I take a step to look around, I notice him watching me from the corner of his eye. *Is there something or somebody here he doesn't want me to get close to?*

My eyes are burning from the heat and the smoke. I need some fresh air. Now. Or at least I've got to splash some cold water on my face. I gently disengage myself from Ray's arm and get lost in the crowd, looking for a bathroom. I push my way into the corner of the room, where the smoke seems to get heavier. I imagine the bathrooms should be located around here. There's one door with no signs on it. I try to open it, but it seems to be stuck. I give it a harder push and it finally surrenders to the weight of my shoulder. I walk in. It's dark in here. I take two steps inside and start hunting for a light switch on the wall. Suddenly I touch something hard and cold. The lights turn on in an abrupt flash and I see I'm standing in a room full of guns, and rifles, and cartons of ammunition.

"Get the hell out of here. Now." Oscar Acevedo hisses at me. "If you ever mention this to anybody..."

I don't let him finish the sentence. I step back, hitting my head on the wall. I turn around quickly and close the door behind me. Ray's standing outside the room, smiling.

"Come with me, Sugar," he says. "It's time to go." Ray starts on his way back to the door, jovially patting everybody on the back. "It's getting late, Sugar, isn't it?" It takes us a long time to reach the door. People are crowding Ray, asking for advice, holding onto his hand, kissing it. I don't seem to exist for any one of them.

Back in the Mercedes, Ray exhales, removes his coat, unknots his tie. Between deep puffs of his cigar he reaches for my arm, pats it and asks, "Well, Sugar, what did you think?"

"Interesting, Ray. I'm very impressed by the way they all treat you."

"It's because I give them the respect they deserve. And provide them with housing and jobs when they need them. Even if it costs me money. Even if others don't like it. My people know I'll work for them. I'll do whatever it takes to get them what they deserve."

"Ray..." I take a deep breath. "I can't use my radio show to promote your political movement. I'd have to do the same for all the other political parties in the city. I just won't do it. I won't use my show as a political platform." I'm adamant.

"I'm not asking you to do anything of the kind. We have writers among us, and lawyers and artists. You only need to invite them to your show. Show my people and others that we Latinos are productive members of this community. That we make a contribution. That we're smart and capable just like the rest of them. Just like you. I'll take care of the rest. You won't let me down, Sugar, will you?" There's no mention of the cache of guns I just witnessed.

Ray turns to me, holds me by the arms, suddenly pulls me towards him and hugs me tight. Very tight. I feel the hard butt of his pistol jabbing into my ribs.

CHAPTER 9

THERE'S A GLOOM IN CHILDREN'S HOSPITAL, A CERTAIN feeling of despair that emanates from the walls of the place. The gloom clings to the air and to my clothes and to my nostrils. The pictures of clowns and of colorful balloons in the waiting rooms, and elsewhere in the hospital, don't seem to help at all. Parents sitting with their children cradled in their arms look forlorn, children so pale and drawn they break my heart. I want to reach out to each one of them and assure them it's going to be all right. The cold, quiet efficiency of the nurses makes the place even more somber, sadder somehow. There are no smiles, I hear no laughter, no childish sounds anywhere except for the occasional wailing or sobbing that seeps out through closed doors.

I have to find Alan's former girlfriend. I haven't told Renata about this yet. No reason to upset her if this lead doesn't pan out. *Maybe the girlfriend is just an invention of Luis, to steer me away from... from what?* I may be chasing my own tail, but I have to follow any clue that comes my way.

I'm sitting in the outer office of the staff administrator, Mrs. Walker. This may be the only way to get the girlfriend's name. The appointment I was given was for nine-thirty a.m. and it's already after ten. The white-haired receptionist typing busily at an old computer keeps stealing glances at me. I'm sure she's seen me here before. I've done so many remote broadcasts from this hospital that some people walk by me and greet me like an old friend. The white-haired receptionist, however, can't place me. It happens a lot. I look at her every time she glances up and I smile my most polite smile. Maybe that will make Mrs. Walker see me sooner.

Finally, Mrs. Walker emerges. "Sorry to keep you waiting," she says. "It's always one emergency after another." Her hand is warm and her handshake is firm. "Please come with me."

I follow her silent footsteps—she's wearing white nurse's shoes—and I feel self conscious of the tap-tap-tap of my own high heeled shoes.

"So," she says as she sits heavily by a massive desk filled with papers. "You're here to help us with the radiothon. Ms..." she puts her round tortoise-shell glasses on and glances at a pink piece of paper. "Ms. Berk. Is that right? How can I help you?"

"Well, someone on the Board of Directors told me there's a nurse here who's volunteered to help out. In her spare time, that is. We really need a coordinator between the radio station and the hospital, and it would be great to have someone who knows what she's doing and is willing to put in the necessary effort to make our radiothon collect a lot of money." I'm making this up as I go along.

"And who's this angel we're talking about?"

"That's the problem, Mrs. Walker. The board member just couldn't remember her name. She could only tell me that she's a nurse or a nurse's aide, that she's from the South—Georgia I think—and that her name could be Anna Simms."

"Well, my dear, my nursing staff here is very large. And I certainly don't know all their names. You'll have to be more precise if you want us to find her for you."

"I'm sorry, but that's as precise as I can get. I have no more information."

"Well, then, I'm sorry…"

"Mrs. Walker," I interrupt, "if it wouldn't be too presumptuous of me to ask, could you let me look at your staff registry? Perhaps I could…"

"Oh, no, no, no. That's not information we give out to the public, my dear. I'm sure you understand."

"Of course, I understand. But without the hospital's involvement it'll be close to impossible to carry out a successful radiothon." *God, I hope she doesn't call the station and finds out this is totally untrue.* "And if I have a volunteer who's enthusiastic, well…"

"Who did you say the board member is?"

I bite my lip slightly. "Carina Lozano."

"Oh, Mrs. Lozano. I know her. Lovely, lovely lady. You said she's a friend of yours?"

"Yes." I nod.

Mrs. Walker hesitates a few moments, taps her pencil on the only clear spot on her desk and then reaches down to her left, opens a metal file cabinet, riffles through it and finally takes out a thick folder. "Here. This is a list of my nursing staff. You can look at it in the outer office. Don't take it out of there and be quick with it. Please bring it back here in less than fifteen minutes."

I thank her effusively and leave her office in a hurry, carrying the folder under my arm. Sitting in one of the corners of the small outer office I open the folder. It has more than twenty pages. I go to the S's and look for Simms. There are two Simms, but no one named Anna or anything similar to Anna. So I start looking for whatever Anne, Anna, or anything resembling it there are in the list. Fifteen of them. One of them is Annette Simmons. Sounds promising. It lists her address and her social security number. No other background. I can't be sure if that's Alan's girlfriend, but it's the most promising. I take the folder back to Mrs. Walker, who's busy on the phone. *I just hope she's not calling Carina.* She motions me to sit down. And I wait.

"Any luck?" she asks me when she's finished with her call.

"Yes, thank you. Annette Simmons."

She pulls out a list hidden in a mountain of papers, looks at it and says, "Well, you can find her right now on the third floor with our little heart patients. She's on duty right now."

"I don't know how to thank you," I say, standing to leave.

"Just collect a lot of money for the hospital and for our kids. That's enough thanks."

She shakes my hand warmly and flashes me the friendliest, sweetest smile I've seen in a long time. *They need more of those smiles around here.*

I take the elevator to the third floor trying very hard not to look at the little girl in the wheelchair who's riding with me. Blond hair in a pony tail, sad blue eyes. *It's for you, little girl. I'm doing the radiothon for you.*

❧ ❧

IT'S QUIET HERE ON THE THIRD FLOOR. THERE'S A BUZZ OF monitors and humming from other machines. Doors to the rooms are partially open, but I don't dare look inside. The theme music of some television show is wafting out of some rooms and the air is thick with smells of alcohol and antiseptics. I keep walking straight ahead, my eyes glued to the wide blue line painted on the linoleum floor, to the nurses' station at the end of a wide corridor. The wall behind the desk is brimming with pictures of smiling children, little ones and teenagers, all saying thank you. They make a cheerful backdrop to the all white environment of the nurses' desk.

I approach the desk on tiptoes. Everything is so quiet around here, I'm afraid the sound of my steps will disturb the hushed rhythm of the third floor.

"Yes? What can I do for you?" A middle-aged, very heavy nurse with her cap askew speaks without looking up.

"I'm looking for Annette Simmons. Is she here now? Mrs. Walker told me I could find her here."

"Did she do anything wrong? She's under my supervision. I haven't heard any..."

"No, no," I interrupt quickly. "It's nothing like that. I'm with WVVV, the radio station that's going to have the radiothon to benefit the hospital."

"So?" She turns now and looks at me briefly.

"Mrs. Walker, the staff administrator, thought Annette would be a good liaison person between the hospital and the station."

"Annette?" There's genuine surprise in the question. "Mrs. Walker thought Annette would be good? Why?"

"Well, I really don't know why. Maybe I could talk to her and see if she'd like to do it? Where can I find here?"

"She's very busy right now. She's helping the patients with their mid-morning snacks. If you wait a while, she'll be coming around here sooner or later. Please have a seat in our waiting room. I'll send her to you."

I find a small chair in a corner, grateful to be able to sit down. The smells and sounds of the place are making me dizzy. I've got to concentrate on something if I don't want to pass out. I start making an inventory of the toys and magazines lying around. Coloring books. Broken crayons. A few dolls. Trucks tucked in a corner. They look lonely. I've got to bring these kids some interesting toys, something that will fire up their imaginations.

I've been sitting on that little chair for the better part of twenty minutes, when a thin, blonde woman dressed in blue scrubs printed with small animal figures comes tentatively towards me. She looks to be in her mid-thirties, but her brown eyes look so tired, so drained, they make her look much older. They're riveting eyes because of the sorrow they reflect, because of the depth of their sadness.

"Vera told me you wanted to talk to me." Her slow, deep Southern accent sounds peculiar to my northern ears. "What can I do for you?"

"Miss Simmons? Miss Annette Simmons?"

I stand up and am surprised at having to look up at her. She's almost six feet tall, but her slow, stooped walk made me think she was much shorter.

"That's right," she says impatiently. "What can I do for you?" She jangles a ring of keys dangling from her wrist.

"I'm... Hmmm... I'm Gloria Berk. I work for the radio station that's going to broadcast a radiothon to benefit your hospital."

She looks uninterested and unimpressed. She starts playing with a loose strand of her blond hair that has escaped from under her nurse's cap. I notice that her nails are badly chewed.

"I thought you might be willing to help us in some way," I say.

"I don't know anything about radio and besides, I don't have any spare time." She turns and starts walking away down the hall. I can't lose my chance to talk to her.

"Ms. Simmons—Annette," I call after her. "I need to talk to you about Alan."

She stops abruptly, as if she's hit a wall. I actually see her head thrust backwards, as though something had pushed her back. She doesn't turn around, though. She's standing quite immobile, except for her hands, which slowly close into tight fists.

"Alan White," I say.

"How do you know him? What do you want with him?" She's not facing me and she speaks softly, but I can hear her.

"Please talk to me, Ms. Simmons. This is very important. You see, I've been looking for him for a couple of weeks now and he seems to have disappeared without a trace. Couldn't you please help me?"

She turns around with a fierce look on her face. Her eyes, so dead, so veiled before, are now burning and her mouth is mumbling something I can't understand. The keys fall out of her hand and I quickly bend down to retrieve them and give them back to her. She grabs them from me. *Could she be the one who attacked Renata? She has access to all these drugs.*

"How do you know about me?" Hissing sounds escape from between her clenched teeth.

I take a step towards her. "Can we go to the cafeteria? I'll buy you a cup of coffee. It's a long explanation."

"Can't you see I'm working? I don't have time to go to the cafeteria in the middle of the morning."

"Then can we please meet after work today? I finish my shift at six o'clock. Let me buy you dinner. I'll meet you wherever you want."

"I'm not sure I can. I'm busy tonight. I... go..."

"Annette, please. Please. Just for drinks, then. For just half an hour."

"OK," she says without much conviction. "There's a bar close to my place in Capitol Hill. It's called Sweet Carolina. Meet me there at six-thirty. I can't give you more than half an hour."

"Thank you, Annette. Thank you."

She turns around and leaves without saying goodbye.

❧ ❧

ON MY WAY TO THE RADIO STATION I STOP AT VIET PLACE FOR A bite to eat. The smells of the spices, the fresh limes, the mouth watering aromas assail all my senses and I'm filled with a strange feeling of nostalgic pleasure. I was with Peter the last time I ate here. His presence overcomes me. The memory of his blue eyes, of the gentle stroke of his hand, of his friendly smile, fill my eyes with tears and make me forget for a moment why I'm here.

"Miss... Miss, can I help you?" The young waiter is asking me repeatedly.

I feel like running out, like escaping from... I don't know from what. "Oh, oh, just a Summer roll, please. Steamed. To go," I manage to stammer.

I get in the car and start munching on the delicious treat. Bits of lettuce and shrimp are dropping on my black skirt. My cell phone rings and I don't answer it. I let it ring. *I don't care who it is.*

⚜ ⚜

AS LONG AS MY SHOW GOES WELL, SUE DOESN'T COME INTO MY cubicle or the studio any more. There's a chasm between us now that didn't exist before, a separateness that bespeaks more than the boss-underling relationship. We were never very close. After all, she's always been my supervisor ever since college. I really have never had any other bosses. But we were always friendly. We ate together once in a while. We drank together certainly more than once.

But ever since my involvement with the Velasco family and my pursuit of Alan's whereabouts, Sue has become aloof, reticent even. Today, however, she's following me around, smiling, friendly, obsequious. *What could she possibly want from me? I have nothing I can give her.*

I've been worrying all afternoon about the meeting I'll have with Annette Simmons and how I'll approach the subject of her relationship with Alan. So my show has suffered a bit. I've been distracted. I've missed a few cues and mentioned the wrong artist's name twice. I know tonight I'll hear from Sue.

But she surprises me with a broad smile as I step out of the studio when my shift is over. She's standing by the receptionist desk, her dark hair, as always, in a perfect pageboy, her gray suit with not a wrinkle on it. And this after a whole day of dealing with unhappy advertisers and bruised egos from her staff.

"Gloria, let's have a drink, shall we?"

"How about on Friday, Sue? I can't tonight and I have a class tomorrow night."

"Maybe Friday. I'll walk you to your car."

Sue walking me to my car?

We wait together by the elevator door, Sue making small talk while I stand quietly wandering when it's going to hit.

"So, Gloria..." she looks at her nails absent-mindedly. "How's everything going?" Her tone is friendly, easy going.

"Fine, fine." I'm distracted. I don't want to be late to my meeting with Annette. I keep glancing at my watch.

We take the elevator down, Sue chatting away amiably and me looking up at the numbers. Perhaps that'll make it go down faster.

"Uhmm..., Gloria, so, are you going to the ball at the Spanish Embassy on Saturday?"

"Yes. I'm going with Luis."

"I thought so. Uhmm... It's supposed to be the social event of the season. Everyone will be there, I've heard."

"I suppose so."

"Gloria, uhmm... Could you...? I mean... I've heard Ray Velasco is a very good friend of the Ambassador's. I heard Ray donated a huge amount of money for a new museum being built in Spain and that the Ambassador is awfully beholden to him."

"I heard that too." I'm walking fast now, reaching my car. Sue's trying to catch up to me.

She suddenly stops, holds me by the arm. "Please wrangle an invitation for Ron and me," she says vehemently. "We're dying to go. Ask Ray or Luis to get us invited. I'll always be grateful to you."

"I'll talk to Ray, Sue. I don't know what he can do, but I'll try."

Sue hugs me hard. "Thank you, thank you." She walks back quickly toward the elevator. There's a spring in her step.

CHAPTER 10

I'M SURPRISED THAT "SWEET CAROLINA" IS SO CROWDED on a weeknight at six-thirty. It takes me a while to get used to the dim lighting and clouds of smoke. The place is not large and the noise and the dark-paneled walls make it oppressive. The only bright spot in the whole place is a long, narrow mirror on the wall behind the counter, running the whole length of the bar. I walk to the end of the bar and back twice, and I don't see Annette. My heart sinks. It was too good to be true. Well, I have her home address from Mrs. Walker's list and I plan to pay her a visit this weekend if she doesn't show tonight.

I take a seat at the bar, suddenly feeling very thirsty, and order a glass of Chardonnay, Peter's favorite wine. His image has not left me the whole day. I sip the wine slowly, relishing its taste and my memories. *Can it be possible to be in love with two men at the same time?*

I munch on some stale peanuts and start looking around, ready to leave. In the mirror, to my left, I see a very tall blond woman with big hair and dark glasses approaching me. She's wearing a revealing black halter top and very tight black jeans, and her lips are the color of dark cherries. So are her short nails. I look at her and she smiles at me. *My God, it's Annette.* She slithers close to me and sits on the empty stool I've been saving for her.

"Let's go sit over at that corner table," she says. "We'll be more comfortable there."

I pick up my drink and follow her to her table. It's certainly quieter.

"I thought you weren't coming," I say as I sit on a small bench opposite her.

"I've been here since six." I can tell. Her breath is rancid. "I didn't want you to see me until I was sure you were alone."

"I almost left."

"I saw you. I would've followed you."

"Why all the intrigue?" I'm annoyed.

"I wanted to make sure you weren't followed. I don't trust the Velascos."

"Do you know the Velascos?"

"Sure, everybody knows them and I, for one, don't trust them one little tiny bit."

I play dumb. "Why? I hear they're nice people. They're helping with the fundraiser for the hospital."

"Yeah, sure. It's good public relations for them. Nothing else. They'll have a great time at the fundraising ball. They don't even think about the poor little children. Not one of them ever comes to see them or sends them balloons, gifts—nothing. It's just a social occasion for them. But they're dangerous people. I know."

She waves the waitress over and I order another glass of wine and she orders a Jack Daniels with beer as a chaser. She drinks both of them in a few gulps and quickly orders another round.

"Why are the Velascos dangerous?" I want to get back to the conversation, but I catch myself staring intently at Annette. She looks completely different than this morning at the hospital—self-assured, poised, proud, quite beautiful. Loud and brassy and beautiful. Men walk by our table and stare openly at her sitting there at our little corner table flaunting her brazen beauty. She doesn't look back at them.

"They'll do anything to get what they want. Anything at all." She gulps down her beer and cleans her mouth with a crumpled paper napkin she has been holding. She smears her lipstick, but doesn't wipe it off her face.

"How do you know this, Annette?"

She stares at me with dark brown eyes lined in black, the mascara starting to run a little.

"They took Alan away from me. They've left strange messages on my machine. They've poisoned Alan's mind and I hate them for that. And I hate Alan for having left me. By the way," she pauses and seems to concentrate for a moment, scratching her cheek. "By the way, how do you know Alan and why are you looking for him? Are you one of his women?" That thought appears to upset her and frown lines crease her brow. The hand holding the beer glass clenches it more tightly. "Because if you are..."

"No, no," I answer very quickly. She looked ready to slap me one. "Not at all." I tell her the same story I told Luis and Ray, that I need to talk to Alan to settle some questions about the Senator for my radio show—that's all.

She relaxes. She starts smiling slightly, her smeared lipstick giving her a crooked smile. Her grip on the glass softens and she starts playing with her long blond hair.

"Is that the only reason?" She eyes me suspiciously.

"The only reason." I take a sip of my wine so I don't have to look her in the eyes while I lie.

"He's good looking, isn't he?"

"He sure is." This time I'm not lying. "He's a hunk."

"Yeah. God. I loved him so much. He was my life." Big, fat tears start rolling down her cheeks, and black lines of mascara streak her delicate face. She makes no effort to wipe them. She gulps down her beer and motions for another. "Jesus, I'm getting drunk, and I don't care. It's the only thing that makes me feel good. I know I shouldn't drink.

And I really wouldn't if I just had Alan. And God, I never will. I never will." She takes a tissue out of her massive black shoulder bag, dabs at her eyes and then blows her nose noisily. "Hey, what did you say your name is?"

"Gloria. Gloria Berk."

"Nice name."

"Thank you."

"Don't mention it. What do you do, Gloria Berk?"

"I'm a radio disc jockey."

She whistles a low, long whistle. "My, my, I'm honored. I'm in the presence of royalty."

"Not quite," I laugh, but feel flattered.

"Well," she says, "you must be paid a bundle. Are you rich?"

"No, no," I laugh again. "My salary's rather small, actually."

"So, why do you do it?" She stares at me with big, brown eyes.

"It's a fun job. I do it for the prestige, to meet new people. I really enjoy doing it. And when my shows are very good I get such a rush, such excitement, that I would pay the station to let me do it."

Annette looks skeptical. "I'm not convinced," she says. "But if that's what turns you on, who am I to say? For me, though, it's the money. I've never had it, still don't, but I really love it. Maybe some day..."

"So why did you go into nursing? Didn't you know at the outset that the pay would be lousy?"

"Sure I did. But I didn't have any money to go to college to get a fancy degree. A hospital close to Aiken, where I lived with my aunt, was so desperate for nurses they were offering scholarships to people who would pay them back by serving as nurses for at least three years. Slave labor. That's what it was. But it was the only thing I could afford, and I would be close to my Ricky, so I applied and they accepted me. And after the three years, I remained there seven more. And then I came here. Without that scholarship I'd be working in the fields, or cleaning streets. Or worse yet, walking the streets selling my legs. By the way, they aren't half bad." She laughs hard and orders another beer.

"You're spunky, Annette. I admire you."

She blushes hard, slaps my arm and smiles. "I like you, Gloria Berk. I hope you don't mind if I smoke, because I've been restraining myself and I've been dying for a cigarette and I didn't want to bother you. Nobody lets you smoke anymore. Anywhere. Have you noticed? I hope you don't mind."

"No Annette, I don't mind. Go ahead."

She lights up. "Join me," she says, offering me the crumpled box.

"I don't smoke."

"Join me anyway."

I pull out a cigarette and put it between my lips. She lights it with her cheap plastic lighter. I inhale lightly, try not to cough, and she looks approvingly at me.

"Good girl. I like you, Gloria Berk, you're all right. So," she says inhaling deeply, "what do you want to know?"

"Do you know where Alan is?"

"The jerk." Her voice rises. "The goddam, fucking jerk. He left me, you know? And I loved him more than life. I gave up everything for that goddam jerk. Everything."

"What happened?"

"We were sweethearts. In high school." She looks at me and takes a long drag from her cigarette. "I shouldn't tell you any of this. Why should I? Why should you care? But, shit. I'm loaded. And lonely. And might as well talk to another broad. And besides, you're buying, right? Is that right?" I nod. "Well, shit, he's the only boy I ever loved. Ever. He was my next door neighbor. Can you believe it? The boy next door. Oh, my, he was so good looking. Powerful. Amazing. God. I lived for him. I dreamed about him. My life revolved around him." She stops, looks dreamily into her beer glass and strokes her bare arm. "I don't have a life without him. I really sort of stopped living the moment he left Augusta."

Tears stream down her face again. I'm not sure if they're the result of her memories or the beer.

"You went to school together?" I ask. I want to bring her back to her story.

"Yes. He's a year older than me. He hardly noticed me when we were growing up. He was the star of the football team. Their captain. Their running back. I was... just there. There was nothing to me that made me special, except that I was lucky enough to live right next door to him. His parents and mine both had small plots of land behind our houses. We grew peanuts. Can you believe it? True Georgia peanut farmers. Just like Jimmy Carter." She lets out a laugh that sounds more like a groan.

"But you know what we did with our peanuts?" She stops and waits for an answer. I shake my head. "We sold them soft boiled. Every game, every fair, every event, there we would be, at dawn, me and my parents and Alan and his, and we would lug huge vats filled with water and brine and the lousy green peanuts we had picked the day before, and boil them for hours. We had to have them ready for whenever the people showed up. And here I was, a skinny runt in pigtails screaming at the top of my lungs, 'Fresh boiled peanuts, come and get your peanuts.' We sold them in newspaper cones. For a buck. For a lousy fucking buck. It would be hot by then, the sun would bake us. And it was muggy and oppressive. It was truly hell.

"The only thing that kept me going was that Alan was there too. I needed only to turn my face to see him standing there in a sleeveless T-shirt, sweat covering his body. God, he was the most beautiful thing I ever saw. But he hated doing that. He was so embarrassed about it. You could tell. He would sell the peanuts, take the dollar, not even talk to the people buying them. He never looked at them. Just took the money and looked away. He hated that. Hated the little farm, the town, the people. Hated everything around us. Probably hated me too, now that I think of it. I was part of all that. Poor Alan. So he decided to do some-thing, I guess. He was always studying or working out. Became the best student in his class. And at night, I would spend hours watching him from my bedroom window while he was working out in the small gym he had built for himself out back. Just some weights, some dumbbells, nothing fancy. He would work out there for hours and hours. And he ran. And he practiced throwing the football through a spare tire hanging from a tree limb. So he became a star athlete."

"But he was never happy. Never satisfied with what he achieved. Poor Alan. Always so afraid someone would find him out."

"Find what out?"

"What he was. What his parents were. He hid this from everyone. His parents were heavy drinkers. Very heavy drinkers. Beat him up. But good. And believe me, I know about beating. Boy, do I know. So he never invited anybody to his house. Even I, poor and gawky and unsophisticated, had my little parties with my girlfriends, always spying on good old Alan. All my girlfriends thought he was so gorgeous. God, how I loved him."

Annette goes silent. She seems to have spent herself. She looks drawn and pale under the black mascara streaks.

"Annette, would you like something to eat? You look exhausted."

"No, no. I don't have time. I have to go to another job."

"Now?" *Dressed like that?*

"At eight."

"Where do you work so late?"

She hesitates, draws some wet circles on the plastic table top and sniffs. "An abortion clinic."

I'm taken aback. After helping the little children in the hospital she goes to an abortion clinic at night. Dead drunk. "Why?" I ask. "Why an abortion clinic?"

"Because they need my help, that's why. Because I see life and death every day and neither one matters to me. That's why." It's a curt reply, the wistful tone of her memories vanishing completely. And it fills me with an incredible sorrow for her. We need to get back to Alan.

"So, when did you and Alan become sweethearts?" I ask brightly.

Her face lights up again. Those brown eyes take on a dreamy quality and she lights up another cigarette. A stream of smoke comes softly out of her half-parted lips.

"He never had really looked at me, you know? I wasn't much to look at then. Thin, mousy, scared. Flat in front and flat in back. But one day, a Saturday, when I was a junior in high school, a few months before Alan's graduation, my parents left for a day at the fair in Augusta. They asked me to clean the attic. So I went up to clean it and I heard the most horrible noises there. I mean they were just horrible. Screeching, scratching, shrieks. I ran down out of there and stumbled and broke the last step down the ladder. I was petrified. Petrified of the noises and of what my father would do to me when he returned and found that broken ladder. I ran over to Alan's house screaming, crying, in a total panic. He was working out when I found him in the back and he smiled when I told him what happened. 'Come with me, girl,' he said, 'I'll help you out.' I swear to you that's what he said. 'I'll help you out.' He dropped his weights, took my hand, and we walked into my house. With him there, you cannot imagine how everything changed. God. The house looked lighter, more cheerful. Everything around us looked brighter, nicer. It was the first time he held my hand. His hand felt rough, but sweet at the same time. You know what I mean?"

I nod. I don't want to interrupt.

"There he is," she continues. "In my house. That beautiful boy with the shining blond hair and those blue eyes looking at me. At me. I wanted to sing, to dance. He looked at the damage I'd done to the ladder and fixed it with a hammer and some nails. It took him five minutes."

She holds up her hand to show me her five fingers spread wide apart. "He then went up to the attic and came down holding two little owl chicks in his hands. 'Do you want me to take these away, girl? Look, they're just babies,' he said. He was holding these two little furry, scared things in his big tanned hands. 'No, no, put them back there. They must have a nest there.' So he went back to the attic, very slowly, holding the little chicks very carefully, very gently, so as not to alarm them more than necessary. I kept looking up at him, at his bare feet gripping each rung of the ladder, and my heart was breaking up with all the tenderness that filled it. I though it was going to explode. When he came down he found me sitting at the bottom of the ladder crying buckets. I didn't know what was the matter with me. I swear. I wanted to die of embarrassment. Here is my darling in my own home, alone with me, and I am bawling, my eyes red and swollen and my nose dripping. What a sight I must've been.

"But he sat down next to me, took me in his arms and cradled me there. He cradled me. Like a baby. I don't remember anybody ever cradling me before. Alan cradled me. I swear to you that never in my life had I been happier. And I just couldn't stop crying. So he caressed my hair, whispered to me that everything would be fine. Kissed my forehead, kissed my eyes and oh, God, how I wanted him. I put my arms around his shoulders which were moist with sweat, I inhaled his smell, his sweat, his soap, and I kissed him on the lips again and again. I couldn't stop. I was like crazy, you know? I could hear him whispering 'easy now, easy girl,' but I couldn't stop myself. I bit into him, dug my nails into him, clung to him. He picked me up, held me in his arms for a while. He took me to my room, slipped off my sundress and made love to me. I'll tell you, Gloria, never, never, never..." Her voice trails off and the tears stream down again.

I reach out and pat her hand. She pulls it back violently. It looks as though my touch scorched her skin. She takes another gulp of beer, it's her fourth bottle since I've been here, and she looks around aimlessly.

"What happened next?" I ask.

She sighs. "After that afternoon we would sneak around whenever we had a chance, secretly. Nobody knew we were sweethearts—he wanted it that way. We would make love, always in a hurry. He was always in a rush. Always had to get somewhere. But those were the sweetest months of my life. I treasured my moments with Alan.

"Finally, one day I discovered I was pregnant. Great, huh? A sixteen-year-old in rural Georgia, pregnant and unmarried. Just the stuff novels are made of. My father would've been so thrilled with my news, he probably would've killed me. Honestly. But can you believe I was actually happy? Idiot me. I though Alan would be happy too. A baby. Born from the two of us. I was so in love I actually started laughing when I found out.

"When I told him he just grunted. Told me we needed to find a way to get rid of it, quick. Get rid of it, he said. Get rid of my own little sweet baby."

She goes quiet and smokes for a while, without saying a word. I just stare at those sad brown eyes.

"So," she continues after a long pause, "he took me somewhere. I don't even know where it was or how long we traveled. I was crying all the way there. He thought I was scared. The fool. I walked into that dark, foul-smelling room after Alan had paid and they got me ready. But I couldn't do it. I bolted from that table and cowered in a corner for a long time. I finally got out of there and cried all the way home. Alan thought I was crying because they had hurt me and he kept his arm around me, comforting me, telling me the pain would soon go away. That all happened just a few weeks before he left for college. He told me to keep our love affair a secret. 'Our secret,' he said."

"My God. He ..."

"That's right. Alan never knew. He left and so did I. In shame. To live with my sainted Aunt Clara in Aiken, South Carolina, not too far from my parents. And I studied there, with the help of my wonderful aunt, bless her dear and gentle heart."

"And?"

"And I had a little boy. Ricky. My Ricky. Aunt Clara helped me raise him. He's eighteen now. My parents have never cared to meet him. Isn't it sad?" She takes a long drag from her cigarette and shakes her head. "He just started college. Big boy. He thinks his daddy died in a motorcycle accident. And he looks just like him." She wipes some tears from her face.

"And Alan?"

"He left for college. Left right after graduation from high school. He promised me he would be back and would you believe he never did? Eighteen years passed and I hadn't seen him at all. The Velascos kidnaped him, I tell you. They bewitched him. I came up here when his poppa told me where he was living. Do you know his parents have never even met his wife and children? Can you believe it? He's bewitched. I came up here to take him back. To save him from that damned family. To get him to get acquainted with his son."

She stops abruptly, as though the well has run dry.

"Annette? Annette!" She looks at me as though she were seeing me for the first time. "So, have you seen him since you got here?"

"Yes. I've seen him."

"When?"

"Couple of months ago."

"Where?"

"Here."

I'm astonished that Alan came to see her.

"Don't be surprised, Gloria Berk. I called him several times and told him if he didn't come see me I'd tell his wonderful wife about us, about our secret." She looks at me with glassy eyes and lets out a howl. "Ha!" I jump in my seat. "Imagine, Gloria Berk, just imagine how that stiff-backed, ass-licking family would react if they knew their lovely Alan had a bastard son. Ha! I can just picture it. What would they do to him? Cut off his dick? And what would they do to me if I opened my big trap? But I won't say a thing. I'll let Alan handle it. I only want him to meet his son."

"Why now, Annette? Why didn't you let him know earlier?"

"Because I only found him six months ago. I didn't know where he was. All this time I wasn't living at home. My parents didn't want me, so since I started living with my aunt I didn't have any contact with them. Six months ago my poppa died and my momma let me come to his funeral. Alan's parents were also there. After the funeral I went to visit Alan's parents and they told me where he was. That's when I came here and got me a job. I wanted Alan to know about his son."

"I see."

"Yeah, I guess you do. So did he. He promised me he would go back and see the boy. But he just kept putting it off." She frowns at me. "His own son."

"It's hard to imagine..."

"Yeah. It's hard. It was also hard raising my boy without a daddy, without money, and without a family. Though Aunt Clara made up for some of that part. But he's O.K., my boy. Bless his heart. And I wish I were too."

"Annette, do you know where Alan is?"

"I'll tell you something, Gloria Berk." She doesn't seem to hear me. "I hate him for what he did to me. And he's also changed, you know?"

"We all change in eighteen years."

"No, not that way. He's really changed. He's not the same at all. His eyes look different. I don't know exactly how. Mean, you know? Like sort of dead?"

"Why do you say that?"

"I was just talking to him, about his life and the great Senator he works for..."

"Oh? You know Senator Clark?" I'm amazed.

She looks at me with a sad look and a crooked smile crosses her face.

"Well, Gloria Berk, don't be so surprised. No, I don't know him personally. I've just heard about him. And I asked Alan if he was involved in the baby-selling business with the Senator."

"The what?" I'm having trouble understanding her. She's slurring her words and her tone is low and conspiratorial.

"Pay attention, Gloria," she says. "While I was at the hospital down home, we had young unmarried mothers giving away their babies. For money. I worked in the nursery. Our babies would be born to some young poor mother and leave the hospital with someone else. Usually in a very fancy car. We were never told. And we never asked. But we knew. And then, just before I came to D.C., someone told me the Senator was being investigated. I can put two and two together." She raises her eyebrows and looks at me. "So I asked Alan if he was helping the Senator."

I let out my breath. "What did he say?"

"He looked so damn cross I thought he was going to hit me. Honest to God. And then he said I shouldn't be talking like that. That talking like that could get me killed." She looks around surreptitiously, as if to check whether anyone has heard her. "The bastard. I hate him."

"I can see that."

"And then I saw how he lives. I went by his home in that fancy neighborhood, and I saw his in-laws' house, and how his little wife is all gussied up. Look at her and then look at me. Just look at me. He was mine. He was my entire life. And they took him away from me. He was all I had. All I wanted. And I hate them all. All the Velascos. And that means Alan too." She stops herself, reaches for another cigarette. "No, I don't know where he is," she says when she has lit it.

She inhales deeply, rubs her eyes.

"Man, I'm beat," she says, and her face shows it. "What a God-awful day. Hate it so much when we lose a little one. Just can't get used to it." She gets close to me and I smell the alcohol and cigarette reek of her breath.

"She was just three," she says.

"Who?"

"The little girl in the emergency room. Nothing we did helped. Nothing. Her parents are going crazy. I'm lucky, you know," she says suddenly smiling brightly. She looks different when she smiles. Prettier. Younger. "My Ricky was fine. He was a little devil. Got into everything, broke a bone once while playing football. Had more scrapes than I can remember, but he was always healthy, thank the good Lord. Always fit and happy and healthy. He made my life hell with his pranks and wild streak, but all in all we had a good time together. Good kid. Love him to death. And he loves his momma." She inhales again and crushes the cigarette into the overflowing ashtray.

She wipes her mouth with the back of her hand, stands up shakily. "Well, you invited me," she says, "so I guess you'll pay, right? Leave a nice tip for the waitress. She was good. And then I need a lift to the clinic. I'm in no condition to drive."

I pay the bill and help Annette to the door. She's staggering. We walk the two blocks to where I parked my car and I drive her to her clinic a few blocks from the Capitol in one of the poorest neighborhoods of Washington. The radio is on, Manny's dedications hour.

"I hate that love gunk music," she says as Manny is playing Elton John's "Don't go Breaking my Heart." "It puts me to sleep. Have you noticed that all those songs sound alike? Like love songs for the dead. Mind if we listen to country?"

"Feel free."

She finds one of the country music stations at once and we listen to Patsy Cline's "I Fall to Pieces." Her eyes close, her breathing becomes deeper and I'm not sure if she's asleep. When I park the car she opens her eyes. She pulls the visor mirror down, wipes at her black streaks with a little saliva, applies a fresh coat of lipstick and turns to me.

"If you see that son of a bitch, just tell him... Oh, forget it. Just fucking forget it."

I watch her disappear into a dark, narrow entranceway littered with paper cups and sandwich wrappers and cigarette butts. The remains of those waiting for the procedure to be finished.

꙳ ꙳

MY ANSWERING MACHINE IS BLINKING. I DON'T WANT TO HEAR any messages. I'm exhausted and famished. But I turn it on anyway.

"Red, where the hell are you? I've been trying to reach you all evening. What's happened to your cell phone? I hope you've bought yourself a sexy dress for the Saturday dance. I want you to look hot. Call me the minute you walk in."

"Hello, kiddo." *Oh, my God. It's Peter, sweet Peter. You've been in my thoughts all day.* "Just called to check in. Miss you, babe. I hope you're well. I'll call you again soon."

My heart melts at the thought of Peter. I listen to the message again and again. Just to hear him say "Hello, kiddo."

And then I settle down in front of a piece of cold chicken and dial Luis' number.

CHAPTER 11

MY FIRST STOP TODAY IS A VISIT TO RENATA. HER HOSPITAL room is brimming with flowers: roses, orchids, dahlias. The drab gray room is festooned with flowers.

She's sitting up cradling the phone with her shoulder when I walk in, her blue eyes smiling, her long fingers caressing her half covered thigh. There are fewer bandages on her face, and her golden hair has been fixed up in a braid that falls gently by her left shoulder. Her small, hard-looking breasts show through her sheer blue nightgown. She looks good. Very good, indeed. I smile at her, sit by her side and start looking at all the get-well cards she has put on display on the small table by her bedside.

"No, no," she's saying into the phone, "I'm really doing much better. There's no reason for it. Honest. Honest. Thank you so much. The flowers are beautiful. Yes. Yes. I hope to see you soon too. Bye." She hangs up with a giggle and turns her shimmering gaze at me. "Hi, Gloria. Isn't it amazing?" She sweeps her hand in the air to let me take it all in.

"My goodness," I say. "Very impressive. From Alan?"

"No, no," she shakes her head adamantly. "I haven't even heard from him. I'm really worried about him." She doesn't look it.

"So, who are all these flowers from?"

"You won't believe me."

"Try me."

"It's a little embarrassing." She hesitates and I wait. "Enrique Velasco," she finally says.

I blink once or twice. "All of them?" I ask stupidly. "I didn't even know you two knew each other."

"Oh, yes. We knew each other," she says in what I take to be a meaningful tone. But I don't get her meaning.

"When?" I ask.

"Right after his divorce. We dated a few times. Well, we more than dated. We were sort of intimate, you know." She winks at me. "But it really didn't mean anything much to me. I had a lot of boyfriends then, before I met Alan..."

She's talking very fast, gesturing with her hands, moving her body right and left, as though suddenly the bed has become lumpy, uncomfortable.

"Slow down, Renata, I can't follow you. Tell me the whole story."

"I met Enrique at the Presidential Country Club. You know, the club where senators and congressmen belong..."

"I know," I say.

"Well, I had a friend who was a member there, and he would take me occasionally to play tennis. One day I didn't feel like playing and I was waiting for my friend at the bar while he was playing with one of his friends, and this tall, dark, handsome man came over to me and said 'you know, you're very beautiful.' So I giggled, what else could I do?" She looks at me and I smile at her. "He said he'd like to take me out someday, and I asked him if he was married. Can you believe it? Here I am, pining away for a married man, ready to run away with him, and the first question I asked Enrique was if he was married." She giggles and covers her lips with long, pale fingers. "He said 'no, I'm not married,' so I gave him my phone number. He called me that very night and we went dancing till dawn. Funny thing was he never drank any-thing, and was very serious the whole time. I really don't think he was having a lot of fun. I invited him over to my house and we made out a little. I'm not the kind of girl who has to wait till the third date if I like the man. And I thought he was awfully good-looking. We went out a couple of times after that. Then, at a dance he invited me to, I think it was the D.C. Bar Ball, Alan came over to say hello to us. Enrique intro-duced us and I fell for Alan instantly. You know what I mean? Head over heels. Immediately. That night. I flirted a little with Alan and when we said goodbye I pressed a card with my phone number into his open hand. I think Enrique noticed that. He never said a thing, though. And when I told Enrique once or twice that I was busy and couldn't go out with him, he stopped calling me. He was still in mourn-ing or something after his divorce, and he couldn't stop talking about it. He was boring me to death, you know? And Alan did call the day after we met. It was wonderful going out with him, making love with him. Better than with anyone else I had ever had..."

"Renata, I think this is too..."

"Oh, Gloria, you already know so much about my affair, you might as well hear the whole thing. After all, you're my friend. You'll under-stand. There's no one else I can tell this to, and it's so beautiful, so romantic. Want me to go on, please?"

"Sure," I say. "Go on."

"Well," Renata continues after taking a small sip of water. "Alan was so gentle, sweet, tentative, you know? I think he was a little embar-rassed of sex when we first started dating. He wouldn't let me see him naked at first. We would make love in the dark. He wasn't free at all. Once," she giggles again, "you're going to think I'm just terrible Gloria, but you know me so well, what the hell, here goes. Once, when we were making love he accidentally came all over me and he couldn't even look at it. I took it in my hand and spread it on my leg and made him look at it and said to him 'look, it's shiny. There's nothing wrong with it.'

113

And he held me so tight I could hardly breath and that's when he told me, for the first time, that he loved me. And I knew he meant it. And that's when we both knew we were made for each other. We understood each other. And I haven't seen anyone else since then."

She stops and takes another sip of water and looks at me. I nod at her and she continues with her story.

"It's amazing to me that Enrique is reacting like this, though. I think he really loves me. That he always did. And he doesn't seem to care about my scarred face. It's so fantastic." She's clearly delighted by the attention she's getting and starts humming softly to herself.

"I didn't know Enrique had been married," I say.

"Yes. Just for a short while. Nine or ten months, I think. Not even a year."

"Who was he married to?"

"Some very wealthy Puerto Rican girl. Apparently she was a real knockout. A beauty. An amazon, by the way Enrique described her. He told me his parents knew hers and they wanted them to meet. The parents arranged the match. The girl was much younger than Enrique. She was still in her teens, maybe she was twenty. And Enrique had already finished law school, but, as he tells it, he had never been in love. Lots of hunting, and fishing, and drinking, and riding with his father, lots of one-night stands, that sort of thing. And then the girl's parents came to D.C. for a visit and their daughter met them here after a year of finishing school in Switzerland. The Velascos hosted a party for them and Enrique saw her and he was a goner. They married six months later. She spent her life at the gym and shopping, you know? And according to Enrique, making love to him every night. So be it. Then, one day, his racquet ball game was canceled, his partner got sick or something, and he came home early, ready for a shower and a little kiss from the wife. And what do you think he found?" Renata looks at me expectantly.

"What," I say. It's not hard to guess.

114

"His sweet little wife, the love of his life, in bed with her trainer. In their own bed. How could she be so stupid?"

"Did he tell you all that?" I ask in amazement.

"No. Alan did. The family wanted to keep it a secret. They were all very embarrassed about the whole thing. They wanted to sweep it under the rug. But Enrique didn't want her any more. I guess his male pride was hurt more than he could bear."

"So what happened?"

"He sent her back to Puerto Rico in a flash and somehow managed to get their marriage annulled. So, in fact, he really isn't a divorced man. What is he, an annulled man?" She laughs at her joke. "God, that's something. And isn't he just great to look at?"

"He's a very good looking man," I agree.

"I'd say so. And now, after my accident, all of a sudden he's at my door again, visiting me, concerned for me. Go figure. But I'm not complaining. So be it."

"I thought you hated him. How come he's coming to see you now?"

"I asked him that and he said he'd heard about my accident and was concerned about me. God knows why. He said he missed me all this time. That he was just waiting around for the right moment. So I don't hate him any more. He's been sweet to me and I don't think he would harm Alan. And just look at all these flowers and all the attention he's paying me. I really need it now. I feel so alone."

"Did you ask him about Alan?"

Renata's eyes cloud and she looks at me reproachfully, as though I am stepping into forbidden territory.

"No. I didn't. I don't know whether he knows about our affair. Alan and I were always very careful. I thought I shouldn't mention it."

"Has he mentioned Alan?"

Renata adjusts one of the bandages covering her cheek, plays with her golden braid. "Not directly," she says softly.

"Meaning?"

"Well, he just said he hopes the 'obstacle' that was keeping us apart no longer exists and that we can become better acquainted now. He didn't mention Alan, but I'm sure he was referring to him."

"So, he probably did know about you and Alan. Didn't you press him for details?" I ask irritably. I've been losing sleep over Alan's whereabouts and she lets potentially important facts slip through her fingers.

Renata senses my anger and she focuses on her own quest for Alan. Her eyes lose their shimmer, she covers her slim body with the hospital blanket and clutches at her bosom with both hands.

"Oh, Gloria. I'm so worried about my poor love. Have you been able to find out anything at all?"

"Well, Renata..." I hesitate for an instant. I guess it's time to let her know about Annette.

Her hands tremble a bit. "What, what is it? Is he hurt? Oh my God." Her hands fly to her mouth.

"No. I mean, I don't know. This situation is more complicated than we thought."

"Why? What do you mean complicated? What have you found out?" She lets out a whimper and wrings her hands.

"It's possible that Alan ran away by himself. That he needed to escape some responsibilities he just couldn't face."

A large nurse bursts into Renata's room and starts taking Renata's blood pressure. I keep quiet while she busies herself.

"And...?" Renata asks, without paying any attention to the nurse.

I don't dare say too much in front of the nurse. Who knows if someone's paying her to spy on Renata and me. I pour myself a glass of water and walk over to a spectacular orchid arrangement. I turn over leaves, inspect the basket, pluck out a piece of lint stuck to a bud.

"Beautiful arrangement, Renata. Very original."

She appears to understand my concerns and follows my lead. "Yes, yes. Very original. It's from the Nikkito Flower Gallery around the corner. They make beautiful designs."

It seems to me the nurse is lingering, taking much longer than necessary.

"Are you allowed to walk, Renata?" I ask. "Can you leave your bed?"

"Yes, yes. You want to go to the solarium? It's very pleasant there, if you can describe any room in a hospital as pleasant. Have you seen it?"

"No. I'd like to see it, though."

"Just a minute, little Miss," the nurse chimes in. "I'm not finished with you. I need to get a blood sample. Got to make sure all those antibiotics aren't affecting your system too much."

"Aw, not now nurse Higgins," Renata whines. "I hate it when people draw blood. And I have a visitor now. Can't we do it later? Please?"

"O.K., then, but let me listen to your heart and take your temperature."

I know for sure the nurse is lingering now. I notice her eyeing me carefully for no apparent reason. "Are you going to visit very long, Miss...?"

"No, not very long." I'm not going to give her my name. "Maybe ten more minutes."

The nurse finally gathers her instruments and walks out slowly. She turns around when she gets to the door, glances at Renata and grunts, "Don't overdo it, little Miss. And cover yourself up. This is not a dance hall."

"Wow," I say. "Friendly!"

"All the other nurses are really nice. This one has it in for me. I don't know why. She's always around, looking at all the notes I get, skulking. She spooks me." She's putting on a blue silk robe and ties its satin sash around her slim waist. Despite her bandages she looks positively stunning.

We walk down the hallway, Renata's gown billowing with every step, and we take the elevator to the top floor, to the solarium. There's no one there now, despite the cheery surroundings. There are large windows all around that seem to glow with the sun that's bathing them in a golden light. Large pots of birds of paradise and banana plants are all around, a few blooming azaleas and some card tables and wicker chairs. Very tropical. There's juice and a coffee machine in one corner and I go get coffee for the two of us.

"My mother's arriving tomorrow," Renata says when I hand her the styrofoam coffee cup. "It makes me nervous. She doesn't know anything about my relationship with Alan and it's going to freak her out when she finds out. And I really want to tell her. I'm so worried about him and I'd like to talk about him with somebody else besides you. I mean, you're great for trying to help me and all that, but I see you very little and I need to discuss it with somebody else. I just hope my news doesn't make my mother start drinking again. I'm terrified of that. She's so worried about what happened to me, and the police haven't found any leads whatsoever. And she's going to stay at my place and I have alcohol there."

"Even if you didn't, if she wanted it she would go get it. It's good she's coming to keep you company."

"Please tell me what you found out about Alan. I miss him so much," she sighs.

I gulp down my coffee, burning my tongue in the process. "He had a son out of wedlock," I blurt out. "There's no other way to put it and I'm really sorry to be the one giving you this bad news."

Renata's hands are shaking. She puts down her coffee cup, takes a tissue out of her robe pocket and starts wringing it. "With whom? When? How did you find out? Oh my God. My God."

She's twisting her tissue with such frenzy, its falling in shreds onto the card table.

"Take it easy, Renata. Let me tell you. Luis Velasco told me Alan had a high-school sweetheart who's been calling him lately. Luis thought she might know where Alan is. So I contacted her and we had drinks."

Renata nods a few times and begins to calm down. The tip of her tongue is dabbing her lips and her shoulders sag a little. I'm sure she's heard of Annette and I wait for her to say so, but she says nothing. She's just looking at me, very pale, very still, waiting for me to continue.

"We met for a couple of hours and she told me the story of their love affair," I go on. "A sad affair, very one-sided. But it resulted in a baby. A boy. Alan's son. The former girlfriend came here to Washington to confront him and to have him take some responsibility for their child. After Alan agreed to go visit the child, he disappeared. So I thought there might be a connection between those two events."

Renata's sipping her coffee calmly now, very composed. The nervousness and excitement of moments ago have disappeared completely. She looks at me with a cold, piercing blue stare.

"Oh, so that's it," she says. "That's her game. Very clever. And she has you ensnared."

"What do you mean her game? Do you know her? Have you heard of her?"

"Sure I've heard of her. Alan told me about her. And no, I don't have the pleasure of knowing her. And I don't want to meet her."

"But why?"

"Because she's a nut. Alan told me all about her craziness. As soon as her phone calls started he told me the whole story."

"Did he tell you about his son?"

"Listen, Gloria. She has you completely fooled." Her voice has turned chilly and she's hardly looking at me.

"What do you mean?" I really don't appreciate the high-handed tone Renata has suddenly taken with me.

"Alan told me she's a nut. A certifiable crazy. He said she used to live next door to him in Augusta and that she spent her days and nights just looking at him, at everything he did. He said it was spooky."

"Didn't he tell you they were sweethearts?"

"Not at all. He said she even brought her girlfriends over and they would all stare at him while he was working out and practicing for the football team. He hated that. He didn't even look at them."

119

"But she said..."

"Listen, Gloria. I don't give a damn what she said. Alan told me he hardly spoke to her and I believe him. She was this skinny, ugly girl who was always staring at him. He said she was a first-rate nut. He was happy to get out of Augusta to get away from her spooky stares."

"And the boy? Did he mention his son?"

"Don't be ridiculous. He doesn't have a son. He said they never dated. They never went out. He said he never touched her. Never spoke to her if he could help it. Not only was she ugly, but she had the meanest daddy in the world, who would've killed Alan if he ever thought the two of them were making out. So, please drop the subject, will you?"

I walk Renata back to her room and promise to come back to see her soon. She seems relieved to see me leave. On my way out, in the corridor, I see Enrique walking towards me. He's carrying a large bouquet of white tulips. He looks straight at me, unsmiling, points his finger and thumb at me, imitating a gun, and walks away without saying a word.

꙳   ꙳

THERE'S A GIFT WAITING FOR ME AT MY CUBICLE AT THE STA-tion. People are getting used to the presents and the flowers and the phone calls, so no one's making a great fuss over it anymore. This one's flat and thin and wrapped in an opalescent wrapping paper and tied with a wide maroon velvet bow. The wrapping is so pretty, it's almost a shame to open it. Another book from Ray? *I haven't seen or heard from him in two days—since the rally. I'd like to stay away from the Velascos for a few more days.* I open the colorful wrapper with little interest, thinking about the show I'm about to put on. I haven't had much of a chance to prepare and I'm afraid it'll be just an average show. Not up to my standards. I know I'll feel sad and disappointed about my performance by the end of the evening.

I'm astounded at what I see when I peel the wrapper off the gift. It's a glittery frame, it looks like it's made of gold—it has such a rich, deep shine—and in one of the corners it has an ornate G, encrusted with pearls. *Is it a G for "Gloria" or a G for "Guerra?"* I wonder. Inside the frame there is a poem, written in Ray's elegant script:

Give me your body, Gloria. I'm
    Lusting for your breasts and loin. An
      Odd, strong desire runs throughout my blood.
        Return to me and take me, make me whole again.
    I dream of your sweet scent, querida. You're
      Always in my soul.
R.V.

I read the poem quickly, take it out of the frame, and stuff it into the pocket of my jeans. I don't want to explain myself to anyone. The phone rings on my way to the studio.

"Gloria Berk."

"Sugar." I just knew it would be Ray on the phone. "Do you like it?"

"It's gorgeous, Ray. But please stop sending me gifts. It's enough."

"There are not enough gifts for a beautiful woman. I wanted to let you know I've been thinking of you."

"Ray, I need to..."

He interrupts me, "I wanted you to know that I miss your sparkling voice."

"I'm late..."

"That I dream about you. Do you like the poem, Sugar? It spells your name. I wrote it for you."

"It's hmmm... sensual."

"Well, I'm glad you like it. I wrote it to fit the circumstances."

"What circumstances, Ray?"

"Our friendship, Sugar."

"Ray, can we talk later? I'm late for my show." I glance at my watch. *God, I only have three minutes.*

"Sugar, you know you still have a couple of minutes. You have time for everybody but me, it seems. But if I must, I'll call you tonight."

"Please don't. You know that Luis..."

"My boy's not staying the night now, is he?"

"Well, no."

"So, I'll call you tonight."

He hangs up before I can answer and I walk into the studio just as Tim finishes delivering the two o'clock news. He looks at me sternly, his glasses half-way down his nose.

"Take it, Gloria. I thought you wouldn't get here."

"Sorry, Tim," I adjust my earphones. "Good afternoon ladies and gentlemen, Gloria Berk here. We have an exciting show for you today filled with good music, fun and all kinds of prizes. Please stay tuned."

I'm not doing a very good show. I can't concentrate. I've been missing cues and playing the same record over and over. I'm lucky nobody's called to complain. I'm wondering if Annette really is as crazy as Renata says she is or did Alan lie to Renata in order to cover up his past? I don't know who to believe and there's no one I can ask. If Renata is right and Alan does not have a child with Annette, whose baby did she carry? Did she in fact have a baby? But why would she lie about that? Why would anyone?

I don't do much better in my evidence class. It's merely a mirage for me tonight. I can't pay attention to Professor Bennett. I sit way up in the last row of the auditorium to avoid being called on. My mind is not on the law tonight, but rather on my meetings with Annette and with Renata.

❧ ❧

I CAN SEE LIGHTS BURNING IN MY APARTMENT WHEN I PARK my car. I don't remember leaving them on. I sprint up the stairs to the third floor, heart beating fast. I'm panting hard by the time I reach my door. I can actually hear my own breathing. The door is closed. I rummage in my large handbag for the mace can my father gave me before he and my mother moved to Florida. The door is ajar and I push it slightly with my foot. Luis is standing in the middle of the room, wearing only tight jeans and holding a white rose in his hand.

"Luis..." I gasp. "How did you get..."

He picks me up, hugs me hard, kisses me even harder.

"Dinner is ready for my lady," he says. "And I did it all by myself."

"How did you get in here, Luis? This is ridiculous. You scared me half to death."

"Red, you just have to be more careful with your keys. I made a copy of it when you left it lying around."

"In my own house? I have to be careful about my keys in my own house?"

"Ssh, ssh, Red. Don't get mad at me. Let's eat."

I walk into the small dining area, hungrily searching for anything to bite into, and Luis pulls me gently into the bedroom. "Dinner is served in bed, my lady." He playfully pats my butt.

I let him drag me into the bedroom. On top of the bed I see a silver tray, candles, and another white rose in my blue Grecian vase. The only food I see are two large dishes of caviar and toast and two glasses of champagne.

"What do you think of your own private chef?" he asks with a glint in his eyes.

If he only knew that I'd rather bite into a good juicy hamburger or a sloppy joe, he wouldn't be so proud. I'm starving to death. I haven't had anything to eat all day. *I can always have a ham and cheese sandwich as soon as he leaves.* I sit on one side of the bed and gobble down the small pieces of toast lathered with caviar and crushed pieces of hard-boiled egg.

"Hey, Red, take it easy. Enjoy it. Savor it."

"It's good, Luis. It's really good." I say with my mouth full. "Any more of this?"

"Here, have mine. I ate something before coming here."

I finish his portion in about a minute and look up at him. It always surprises me what a good looking man he is. His dark hair shines and his chest is smooth and strong-looking. He's smiling at me and seems to have enjoyed my eating frenzy.

"You're electric in everything you do," he says, licking his lips. "I guess that's why I like so much. Your excitement, your attitude, your mouth, your body." He lifts the tray and places it on the floor and wipes the crumbs off the white quilted bedspread. It's an Amish bedspread. My parents brought it back for me from one of their trips. They traveled a lot without me, but always remembered me with a pretty gift. It really wasn't a good idea to have dinner on it. I love that bedspread. According to my mother it was a wedding gift to a young Amish girl who ran away from her husband-to-be on the eve of the wedding and is now living in New York. Under an assumed name, of course. My mother said she bought it from the girl's parents who didn't want anything else to do with their daughter and had declared her dead in their eyes. Well, at least that's the story my mother told me.

Luis pulls the bedspread down and holds me tight. I feel exhausted. I snuggle up against his warm body, kiss him lightly on the neck, and promptly fall asleep.

※　※

I'M ALONE IN BED WHEN THE PHONE WAKES ME UP. I FEEL groggy and don't even know where the sound is coming from.

"Sugar, it's me. Like I promised. Had a good time?"

"What time is it?" I say in a hoarse whisper.

"Three."

"When do you sleep, Ray?"

"I need very little sleep, Sugar. I have too many things to do."

"Why are you calling me?" I sound as rough as I feel.

"Because I promised you I would. And because I need a little favor."

My eyes are wide open by now and I sit straight up.

"What?"

"This Sunday's show, I have a Mexican painter I want you to interview."

"No, Ray, I told you I can't do that. Besides, I already have a guest lined up for this Sunday."

"Cancel your guest."

"No. I won't do it."

"Sugar, nobody says no to me." His voice is a growl. Menacing.

"I just did."

He lets out a laugh. "Sugar, Sugar. I don't know how my son puts up with you. Some temper you have there. Very well, then. Schedule her for Sunday after next. Her name is Leonora Siqueiros. I think she's a distant relative to the famous painter Siqueiros. I want you to hear her. The whole community will hear her. Your phone lines will be exploding. I guarantee it."

After that, I can't go back to sleep.

CHAPTER 12

L
UIS AND I ARE TWIRLING AROUND ON THE DANCE FLOOR, HIS
hand caressing my bare back. I'm aware of the many stares following his graceful moves.

The ballroom at the Spanish Embassy is glittering. It looks like the walls are made of mirrors. The dim lights, the thousands of flickering candles give it a dream-like quality, and everyone seems to be floating.

There must be over three hundred people here, but the ballroom is so grand that it feels both spacious and cozy. There are round tables for ten encircling a large dance floor, and on each table there are spectacu-lar flower arrangements, different ones consisting of the native flowers of the various regions of Spain. A large painting of the king and the queen dominates the entire salon and right underneath the painting an orchestra is playing a Viennese waltz.

"You look lovely, Red. Really lovely," Luis whispers into my ear, his warm breath sending shivers up my spine. "You look like a movie star in that dress. White becomes you. It makes you look so... so..."

"Virginal?" I offer.

"So hot. So yummy. I could make love to you right now, right here." His embrace tightens around me and he slides his hand a little lower down my backless gown. I raise it back up and murmur, "Thank you for getting an invitation for Sue and Ron. They really wanted to be here."

"Hey, don't mention it. What are friends for? I just asked my father and he called the Ambassador's secretary. It was as simple as that."

The music stops playing and we return to our table. Miriam Velasco, whispering to Linda, looks lovely in a simple, dark silk gown. She bows her head slightly as I take my seat between Luis and Ray. She's playing with a very large diamond-encrusted cross hanging from a heavy platinum chain. The high neck of her gown accentuates her glowing skin, and her dark, shining hair, gathered loosely at the nape, bounces slightly every time she stirs. Her hair seems to have a life of its own. I smile at her and take a sip of champagne.

"Beautiful earrings," she says to me. "Very becoming."

I touch the small diamond and sapphire earrings dangling from my ears. "Thank you, Mrs. Velasco. They were my grandmother's. My mother gave them to me when I turned twenty-one."

"They're very pretty. They do look like antiques."

"I love them. I just wish I had more opportunities to wear them."

"Well," Ray says. "Pretty soon we'll have the Children's Hospital benefit. That's also a nice affair. You can wear them then too."

As he speaks, he turns to me, leans close and whispers, "your breasts look like ripe peaches under that dress, ready to be picked. My mouth waters just at the sight of you." He slides his hand under the gold-colored table cloth and squeezes my thigh. I look at him and promptly remove his hand. He then just grabs my hand and places it on his thigh. My right hand. I get it loose as fast as I can.

Mrs. Velasco pales a little and lowers her eyes. She picks up a spoon, removes a speck from her water glass, and turns back to Linda. I cannot take my eyes off Linda. She's spectacular in a beaded royal blue gown. She shimmers when she moves. Her waist looks tiny and her olive complexion seems to have absorbed the last glowing rays of an afternoon sun. She looks buffed, regal, as though she had been raised to shine at moments like these. She hasn't even acknowledged my presence at the table. She's been talking mostly with Enrique. I look across the table at him—dark, quiet, apparently aloof from what's going on around him. But I notice that his dusky, arrogant eyes keep coming back to me. I think I detect a smirk, a derisive smile whenever our eyes meet. *This is going to be a long, long night.*

"So, Ms. Berk," Enrique says, putting down his glass of water with a thud and boring his dark eyes into me. "I understand you've been asking questions about Alan's whereabouts."

The whole table becomes very still, all eyes on me. Nobody seems to be eating or drinking. Ray even stops puffing on his cigar. Luis slowly places my hand, which he was holding and caressing, on the gold tablecloth. I see my fingers are shaking a bit. I bite my lower lip and pick up the linen napkin from my lap and dab carefully at my lips. No one says a word.

"Well, isn't it so, Ms. Berk?" Enrique insists, in a louder, angrier tone. "I understand you helped solve a murder at your station last year." He laughs out loud. "Do you think you have license to get involved in other people's lives and affairs because of that?"

I remain very quiet.

"Well?" he goes on. "You don't know what to say?"

I turn to Luis to get a clue about how to answer his brother, but he's looking straight ahead, not willing to help.

"It really is a radio matter," I finally say. "The station needs corroboration on some facts and figures Senator Clark gave out during my show. We thought that Alan, that is, Mr. White, would be the correct person to approach on that."

"Any luck locating him?" Enrique lights a cigarette and speaks through the smoke.

"No so far," I say, looking straight at Enrique.

"He's gone away you know, my dear," Miriam Velasco interjects, interrupting the staring contest. My heart goes out to her in gratitude. "He has asked us to protect his privacy. I'm sure you understand. Families need to stand united, protect each other as much as they possibly can. Don't you agree? But as soon as Alan returns, I promise you, we'll ask him to get in touch with you." Her tone is calm, reassuring.

"Thank you, Mrs. Velasco. That's very kind of you."

She turns away from me and continues her conversation with Linda. Ray starts puffing on his cigar again and Enrique excuses himself from the table to greet some 'old friends.'

I have gone back to my appetizer of cold gazpacho and mussels when Sue, lovely in a black, flowing gown approaches our table dragging Ron by the hand. She looks chic and flushed with excitement. Her usually pale skin is tinged with pink making her appear young and fresh. Ray and Luis spring to their feet to greet them. Sue's hand remains entwined in Ray's for several long, intense moments. Miriam Velasco notices it and she sighs when her husband's large figure bends down and kisses Sue's hand.

"Thank you so very much for getting an invitation for us, Mr. and Mrs. Velasco," Sue gushes after the proper greetings. "This is so fabulous. So incredible. The place is beautiful and just about everybody is here. Absolutely everybody." She's addressing herself only to Ray.

"My dear, it's my pleasure you could join the rest of us here. Your presence is a glittering addition to the beautiful women among us. You honor us with your words of gratitude."

Sue blushes a deep crimson and lets out a small, girlish giggle. She tosses her head back in a flirty movement I've never seen her do before and adjusts a thin strap on her naked shoulder. It didn't need adjusting.

"Mr. Velasco, you flatter me," she says touching her lips with the tip of her tongue. "It's just wonderful to be here. I'm sorry I interrupted your meal. Please, please go on eating."

Luis sits down immediately and Ray lingers a little longer, bows his head, picks up his glass of champagne and says, "To your fall ratings. May you continue being the queen of the radio world in D.C."

Sue giggles again and turns to leave and then comes back to me and says, "Oh, Gloria, do you remember Bernie Rich? Our former news guy?"

"Sure, I remember him."

"Well, he's at our table. He's working at the Press Relations Office at the State Department. He says he loves it there. I told him you were here and he's dying to see you. He says he always had a crush on you."

"Oh, I'd like to see him too," I say. I know he had a crush on me. "I'll go say hello to him after dinner."

"I'll tell him to wait for you." And she's gone.

As I'm finishing my gazpacho I notice that Luis has dropped his spoon and the muscles of his jaw are protruding under his glossy skin.

"What's wrong, Luis?" I ask in surprise. "Anything the matter?"

"You better believe it," he says through clenched teeth.

"What?" I say tiredly.

"Who's this Bernie guy?"

"Bernie Rich. We used to work together in North Carolina and then here. Sue hired us both and brought us with her to D.C."

"Well, I don't think you should go over to his table. You're here. With us. You came with us and you stay here."

I say nothing, but I plan to go over and say hello to Bernie when dinner's over.

The band plays softly while we feast on lobster tails, wild rice, and asparagus with some fancy cream sauce. It's all delicious and I concentrate on my food instead of on Luis' simmering anger. But I can feel it radiating from him. I can sense it in his rigid posture, in the pallor of his complexion. He hardly touches his food. He sits almost motionless, sipping his whisky and soda.

As the waiters move softly to the music of de Falla carrying Baked Alaskas to each table, the Ambassador gets up, walks over to the podium right under the painting of his king and queen, adjusts the mike, and the band goes silent.

Ambassador Salazar-Alva, tanned, urbane, is the perfect image of a Spanish Ambassador. In softly accented English he thanks all of us for attending the dinner-dance and asks us to join him and Lady Salazar-Alva in honoring don Raymundo Velasco and his lovely, lovely wife Miriam for the large gift they have bestowed for the building of a new museum in Granada. That museum is going to bring Spain to the forefront of art and architecture and will make Spain an even greater force to be reckoned with in the world of art, he says. All of Spain owes a large debt of gratitude to the marvelous Velascos for their selfless love for art and for Spain. It's his honor, he adds, to announce that the wing dedicated to Latin American art will be named after them. He raises his glass of champagne and asks us to join him and his wife in a toast to these wonderful, philanthropic people.

We all stand up, raise our glasses, and cheer loudly for Ray and Miriam. They both stand, Ray beaming, Miriam with eyes downcast, and he drapes his arm protectively around her shoulders. Her cross shudders faintly at his touch. He kisses her cheek and sits down smiling broadly. Then he turns to me, face flushed, eyes shining, and whispers, "This was well worth three million dollars." *I hope he's as generous at the Children's Hospital benefit.*

People start milling around after dessert, many well-wishers approach the table to shake Ray's hand, and the band starts playing louder. I get up to find Bernie. His curly, flaming red hair makes him visible from afar. He's sitting at the table closest to the band, his back to me. I walk quickly to him, stand behind him and put my arms around his neck. He turns around, green eyes as clear as ever, encircles my waist and pulls me down onto his lap.

"Gloria, woman of my dreams. How the hell are you?" He screams. My arms are still around his neck and he's holding me tight around the waist, nuzzling my neck. We were great friends at the New Bern station, mostly sticking together as the two new kids in town. We became even better friends when we followed Sue to D.C. But we were never more than friends. We went drinking on a "date" a couple of times, we necked a bit, but my heart wasn't in it. He was too tall, I said to myself, or maybe he was too eager. I never understood why there was no passion there for me. I liked him so much otherwise.

But he was a dear, wonderful friend, a constant in my life and I missed him terribly when he left the station. I haven't seen him now for a couple of years.

"Bernie," I scream back in his ear. "You look terrific."

"Not as good as you, my darling. Not half as good as you. Let's go outside. It's impossible to talk in here."

From the corner of my eye, amidst couples gliding on the dance floor, I see Luis walking determinedly towards me. His dark eyes are blazing and his lips are stretched into an ugly grimace. When he's nearer I can see his lower teeth jutting out. He reminds me of the way a bulldog I once had looked just before he pounced on his prey.

I slowly get up from Bernie's lap and extend my arm out to Luis, to welcome him into the group of radio junkies sitting at Sue's table. He grabs my arm and pulls me toward him.

"Let's dance," is all he says as he drags me to the dance floor.

I look at Bernie who sends me a kiss with his open hand. "Stay well. I'll call you," he shouts at me.

Luis holds me much too tightly as we start dancing. My breasts are being crushed against his tuxedo suspenders.

"You're hurting me, Luis," I say as I try to loosen his grip.

He doesn't answer and holds me tighter, dancing slowly and looking me straight in the eyes. There's not a hint of a smile in those eyes.

"You're hurting me," I repeat firmly.

"Good. I want you to hurt."

I stop dancing in mid-floor and look up at him."Why? Are you crazy?"

"No," he says as he gathers me up in his arms and starts us moving again. "I'm not crazy. But no broad is going to make fun of me. No bitch is going to make me look ridiculous in front of my family. Understand, Red? Am I clear?"

As he's talking, he pushes his right fist deep against my back, knuckles burrowing into my spine. I gasp. I can hardly breath. But we're standing close to Sue's table and all my friends there are looking at us. I can feel their eyes on us.

I'm not about to make a scene. I swallow hard, start moving to the sound of the music.

"I'm going home now," I whisper in his ear, as if I'm caressing it with my lips. "Don't you dare follow me or I'll call the cops on you. You understand? Make my apologies to your parents. Tell them I got sick. And don't you ever call me again."

I pull away from his arms, wave a small goodbye to Sue and her cohorts, and walk out of the Embassy without my wrap, without my evening bag, without any friends.

* *

I ALWAYS KNEW THE EXTRA KEY MY FATHER HID FOR ME UNDER the Chinese pot at the entrance would come in handy someday. I let myself into my dark apartment with a sigh, get some money and rush down to pay the taxi waiting patiently on the busy street in Adams Morgan.

"I hope you don't forget your money again, lady," he says gruffly as he pockets a very large tip. I was lucky to have found a free taxicab on Embassy Row on a Saturday night.

* *

MIDNIGHT. I POUR MYSELF A GLASS OF WHITE WINE, THROW OFF the silver sandals, slip out of my very expensive gown—it cost me one month's salary—and sit down heavily on the living room couch. The only light in the apartment is the yellowish cast of the neon sign on the Café Cuba across the street. Everything around me has a sickly pale tone to it.

The phone rings. *No, no, no. I'm not going to answer it. Can't stand to hear Luis' voice tonight. Nor Ray's. Enough for one night.*

"Hi, this is Gloria Berk," the machine says in a cheerful voice I can hardly recognize as mine right now. "Please leave me a message."

"Kiddo, hi." *Oh my God. It's Peter.* I rush to the phone in the semi-darkness and pick up before he can hang up.

"Peter," I moan into the phone. "Oh, Peter, I'm so glad it's you."

"Kiddo, are you all right? You sound out of breath."

"I'm fine now, Peter. I'm fine now that I hear your voice."

"Anything the matter, babe? You don't sound like your usual delightful self."

"I guess I'm just tired. I've been working very hard."

"On a Saturday night?" Peter's friendly eyes flash before me, smiling, tender. "Kiddo, give it to me, what's happening to you?"

"I think I'm involved in a matter that's too complicated and I think I'm in too deep. I'm trying to find someone who has disappeared and I keep running into a stone wall, no matter where I turn. That just about summarizes my situation."

"Who has disappeared? Can I be of any help from here?"

Sweet, sweet Peter. I wish I were in your arms right now.

"No, I don't think you can help me right now, but thanks for asking. I'm looking for a friend of a friend. I think he may have just run away from his responsibilities, but I'm not sure. I have to dig a little more. I'll fill you in when I know more. Tell me about you now. I've missed you." I walk over to the couch and lean back, cradling the phone with my shoulder.

"You do?" he whispers into my ear. I close my eyes to let the sound of his voice caress me. "Do you think of me once in a while? I miss you, kiddo. It's bleak here without you."

"Oh, Peter, do you know how good it feels to hear you?" *How warm and moist and tender my body becomes at the sound of you.* "I think about you so much."

135

"That's good. Do you think you can come visit?"

My heart skips a beat. "I'm going to try, Peter. I promise. Please call me back soon."

"Very soon, sweet girl. Very soon. I think of you, you know. I think of you a lot."

After I hang up with Peter, I take the phone off the hook and walk slowly to my bedroom. I throw the window open and inhale the air of a chilly night. I undress, pull the covers off the bed, slither into crisp sheets and let the cold breezes graze my naked body.

CHAPTER 13

BEETHOVEN'S SEVENTH SYMPHONY HAS ALWAYS SOOTHED my soul. I love the intertwining melodies of the moody, melancholic second movement. I'm sitting by my open balcony, the sun bathing me in a pale warmth. The morning coffee is exceptionally good and I'm enjoying the music and feeling the terry cloth of my bathrobe rub against my naked skin. Peter's voice, his image, still lingers in my mind. The phone is off the hook. I want to luxuriate this Sunday morning doing nothing, just listening to Beethoven, thinking about Peter. I'll prepare for my evening show after lunch.

A loud knock on the door startles me and makes me spill some coffee on myself. "Shit," I say out loud. "Who'd come bug me on a quiet Sunday morning?"

"Gloria, open up." Sue's urgent voice accompanies her persistent knocks on the door. *When is she ever going to learn to use the door bell?* "Are you all right? Open up."

I get up slowly, smooth out my hair a bit, and open the door. Sue's standing there in her white shorts, her tight white T-shirt and sneakers, an Oriole's cap over her dark hair.

"I was worried sick about you," she says as she pushes her way into my messy apartment. My evening gown is still laying crumpled over the couch looking like a sad rag, and my sandals are scattered in the middle of the living room floor. "I thought something happened to you. You left so suddenly last night. I called and called and your phone was busy. So we just drove over." She twirls around the room a bit, apparently her concern for me evaporating at the sight of me. "What a fantastic night. You're all right, aren't you?"

"I'm fine. I had to leave suddenly. I had a horrible stomach ache."

"What? And the debonair Luis couldn't take you home? You're sure you didn't have a little fight over Bernie? He felt awful about the way Luis grabbed you away from him."

"I'll call Bernie and explain. And I asked Luis to stay at the party and enjoy himself. No sense both of us missing out on the fun just because I wasn't well."

"Are you O.K. now?"

"I'm fine."

"So why aren't you ready? Ron's waiting downstairs. He'll be furious we're making him wait so long."

"Ready for what?"

"Gloria," she uses the same tone my mother used to use when I had made a terrible mistake. "We set up this tennis date at the Presidential Country Club weeks ago. We're playing doubles. Ladies against men. It isn't easy to get reservations for a court on a Sunday. Hurry up. Ron's double parked."

"I'm sorry, Sue. I can't go."

"Nonsense." She takes me by the hand and pulls me into the bedroom. "Get dressed right now. You can shower at the club."

"I can't go." *God. How could I possibly have forgotten about this date? Why did I agree to it in the first place?*

"I won't hear of it." She starts opening drawers and pulls out a pair of white shorts and a white tank top and hands them to me.

"Now, move it."

I obey like a robot. I have no strength to argue. I slide off my robe and obediently jump into my makeshift tennis outfit. I'm only hoping

I don't have to see any of the Velascos at the club. We leave the apartment with Beethoven's Seventh sadly playing for no one.

 ✻   ✻

"WELL, WELL, WELL," RON GREETS ME. "LOOKS LIKE SOMEONE just got out of bed." He looks happy, relaxed, and spiffy in his white Izod shirt and an Orioles hat identical to Sue's.

"Good morning, Ron. Glad to see you too." I run my fingers through my hair and dab a little lipstick on. Maybe it'll help hide my pallor.

"Left pretty abruptly last night, didn't you?" he asks as he pushes his dark glasses up and glances at me in the rear-view mirror.

"Just a stomach ache. I'm all better now."

"I see," he says skeptically. "Thank the Velascos for us, won't you? That's some family. I'll never understand why Alan doesn't like them. Did you take a look at Linda?" He blows a long, low whistle. "What a dish. You'd never guess by looking at her that her husband would be taking a long vacation. I wonder who the other woman is."

My ears perk up and I start listening to Ron's jabbering.

"What other woman?" Sue asks.

"Well, I'm not sure. I just can't imagine dear old Alan without a woman by his side. Women fawn on him. He's been gone now for a good two weeks, hasn't he? Can't fathom that he just went away to a deserted island, cut off from all his friends and family, without somebody to keep him company. I'm positive there must be a woman involved somehow. I just don't know who she is. She'd have to be hot stuff when you look at what he has at home." Another low, long whistle. "He's really secretive about his private life, you know. Who would leave that gorgeous Linda behind, I don't understand."

"What has Alan told you about the Velascos?" Sue changes the topic from Linda.

"He seems to think that all in all they're good people. Apparently Miriam Velasco was the last child of a very wealthy Puerto Rican industrialist. The mother died giving birth to her and the father never forgave little Miriam for it. He would leave her alone for days on end while he took his five sons hunting and fishing. Mrs. Velasco was always left in the care of this Indian nanny who knew all the magic of herbs and potions. She was the one who taught Mrs. Velasco all the beauty secrets. Alan told me she has a whole laboratory in her house. Be that as it may, she's in pretty good shape, isn't she?"

"Oh, she looks fabulous." Sue says. "Is it all due to the herbs?"

"Yes, according to Alan." Ron's driving Sue's BMW using just one hand and gesturing grandly with the other. "And then," he says with a flourish, "when she was maybe ten or eleven, she was sent to a convent. After that, she wasn't home much, just during holidays. It was evidently the convent that made her so religious. According to Alan she's very devout, goes to church every day, and I believe they have some kind of shrine or chapel somewhere in the house."

"Then how did she meet Ray?" Sue asks.

"He was her father's hunting buddy. He met her when she came home for some holiday. She was maybe fourteen or fifteen. Ray was then in his twenties. A wealthy bachelor, the only son of a radio and television magnate. He saw her and was smitten. She apparently was a stunner. He told her father he would wait for her until she turned eighteen, and the father agreed."

"Oh my God," Sue whispers.

"When she turned eighteen the father arranged for them to be married, never even asked her. I don't think she knew Ray for more than a month before the wedding. She went from the convent straight to the marriage bed."

Sue groans, "these things actually happen?"

Ron smiles and pats her bare thigh. "Evidently."

Sue looks back at me, but I pretend I don't notice.

"Was she upset? Did she mind? Did she love Mr. Velasco?" Sue is very taken by the story.

"I don't know. I'm sure Alan doesn't know it either. This isn't something you discuss with your son-in-law—or even with your own children, I imagine. But," Ron continues, "they're still married after all these years and I think she lives a good life. Did you notice the jewelry she was wearing last night? All those diamonds. Carats and carats of diamonds."

"Diamonds aren't everything," Sue says heatedly.

"I'm sure not," Ron answers, letting out a high-pitched giggle. "But I'm sure they don't hurt any, either. Well, girls, we should be arriving at the club in exactly twelve minutes. How's your backhand, Gloria? You get in much practice?"

"No, not much. My tennis game isn't very good. I'm afraid I won't make Sue look good as her partner."

"Oh, don't worry," she says, "I'd rather lose anyway. If Ron doesn't win he pouts all day and then he goes to sleep as soon as we walk into the house."

"I'm afraid you exaggerate a bit, my dear," Ron says, adjusting his glasses. "But I'd rather win than lose. That's a fact."

Ron and his partner Frank, also a legislative assistant, roundly beat us in two straight sets. Ron was definitely playing to win. He sprints back to the showers humming a tune under his breath.

"Take your time, girls," he calls out, waving at us. "Come out looking like a million bucks. I'll be waiting for you at the bar."

Huffing and puffing I strip and walk over to the saunas. Sue doesn't join me. She prefers to take a quick shower and then a long, relaxing dip in the whirlpool. I need a few minutes in the very hot, wet steam to let all the tensions of the last couple of weeks melt away from me.

I grab a bottle of water and wrap my hair in a towel and push the heavy door of the sauna. It's moist and dark inside and I inhale the dense air. I step on the hot wooden floorboards and then I stop dead in my tracks. In the far corner of the small, dim enclosure, the bodies of two women are entwined in an intense, erotic embrace.

"Oh my God, so sorry, so sorry," I whisper and turn to step out, but not before I catch sight of the two women—Linda Velasco and Carina Lozano.

"Sorry," I say again, as I close the door as fast as I can and bolt towards the showers. I want to escape, to bury my head, to erase the image I just witnessed.

"Hey, Gloria." Sue stops me by the shoulders as she steps out of the shower. "You finished so quickly in the sauna?"

I cannot answer.

"What's the matter? You're as white as a sheet. God. Are you feeling sick again? You're not going to throw up now, are you?" She looks so panicked at the thought of my throwing up that I want to laugh out loud.

"No, no, no," I stammer. "I'm fine. I need to get in the shower."

"Need my help?"

"No, thank you. I'll be fine. I'll meet you at the bar in a few minutes." I need time alone, time to let my feelings of shame subside a bit, and to understand what's happening.

I stand under the shower for a long time, scrubbing myself till my skin feels raw. I stand there, looking at the twirls of water and foam forming small eddies at my shriveled toes. I don't want to leave the shower. I'm petrified I'm going to run into Linda or Carina and we would have to face our mutual discomfort.

Finally, when I can no longer feel the tips of my fingers, I leave the shower. I dress in the least conspicuous area of the locker room.

Ron and Sue are sitting at the bar, arms around each other's waists. They're sipping Bloody Marys. They look clean and fresh and suntanned.

"Join us, dear girl," Ron says with a wide smile. "You smell good." It really is the only compliment he can pay me since I look like hell.

"Want a Bloody Mary? You'll find no better in the whole city and surrounding suburbs."

"Sure," I say.

"You put up a good fight, indeed, I have to say. It was pure pleasure beating the two of you beauties. We have to do it again next Sunday, Gloria. Are you up to it?"

"We'll see." As I bend down to take my first sip of the drink, I feel a tap on the shoulder.

"Can I talk to you for a moment?" Carina, standing behind me is smiling at Ron and Sue. She looks beautiful with her short, red hair combed casually in an upswept do, her lips colored a soft peach, her white T-shirt and white jeans showing off a trim figure with firm, well-rounded breasts.

"Can we talk for a few moments?" she asks again.

"I... I'm going to have lunch with my friends here."

"Have lunch with me instead."

"Go ahead, Gloria," Sue says. "We'll catch up with you later."

I dismount the stool nervously, almost spilling my drink on Carina's white outfit. She grabs my arm, steadies me, and we stand, nose to nose, eying each other. I'm amazed again at how much we look alike.

"Wow," Ron says. "You two look a lot alike. Did you know that?"

Carina, without letting go of my arm, walks me into the dining room.

The usually bright, cheerful room seems gloomy today, despite the bright sun pouring into it. It's also very noisy. The clanking of the dishes and the silverware, together with the loud voices of the diners create a deafening sound that's not helped much by the string quartet playing an out-of-tune Mozart minuet.

Carina and I walk the entire length of the dining room amid stares. She doesn't let go of my arm. We must look like a pair of oddly-matched twins marching to two different tunes. We finally take a seat at a small table in the farthest corner of the room, overlooking the well-tended golf course.

She orders for the two of us. I don't even bother looking at the menu. And I don't dare look her in the face.

"So," she says with a sigh. "Now you know."

I'm silent, munching on a tasteless piece of white bread.

"Aren't you going to say anything? Is this so upsetting to you?"

"I don't know what to say, Carina, and I don't know how to react," I say after a very long silence.

"You can say you understand a great passion between two human beings and you don't have to react in any particular way."

I steal a glance at her and quickly avert my eyes.

"Look at you," she says very softly. "You can't even face me. Are you so narrow minded, so judgmental, that this attraction disgusts you?" Her voice is low, without much emotion. But her eyes are burning and her lips are quivering.

"Carina, it doesn't matter to me. It doesn't matter at all. But I'm dying of embarrassment and it's very hard for me to face you."

"Why? You didn't do anything wrong."

Our chicken salad with almonds and orange slices finally arrives and we both busy ourselves, shifting knives and forks and napkins and not looking at our waiter.

I start picking on the salad, eating bits and pieces, but Carina lunges at it, eating with a ravenous appetite.

"Boy, this is good," she says. "The best dish they have here. It's the chef's specialty. He prepares his own mayonnaise. Light, not too creamy. Heavenly. Do you like it, my dear?"

"Yes."

"Dear, there's nothing for you to be embarrassed about. We shouldn't have been embracing in such a public place. We didn't think. We hadn't been with each other in a very long time and we were hungry for each other. Ray has thrown his dogs at Linda, to keep her under surveillance. We have to stay away from each other. Miriam doesn't know about this. She'd hate me if she knew." She glances up at me and questions me with her eyes. I shake my head slightly and Carina smiles at me. "Ray's dogs follow Linda everywhere and so we're not free anymore to meet in my house. So today, after three long months, well..."

"I see."

"I'm afraid you don't. My affair with Linda started a long, long time ago. Before she married Alan. Before she even met him. I went to visit her in Switzerland after she finished high school. I was traveling in Europe and her parents asked me to look in on her. It didn't take long before we were mad for each other. I knew right away that my feelings for her were overwhelming, but I didn't make the first move. She did. In my hotel, a few nights before my scheduled departure. She had gone to an all-girls Catholic high-school and she and her friends had started experimenting with sex while still at school. She was well experienced when she came to me. She came to my hotel one evening after a delightful dinner and a lot of laughter and she climbed into my bed. I was completely scared at first and then totally delighted. Ecstatic, really. I had never had those sexual feelings. She was my first true sexual partner."

"What?"

"Yes. I had been married young, right out of the convent, just like Miriam. We were in the convent together, but we were all watched day and night by the nuns. We were not only virgins when we left the convent, we were also naive and totally ignorant about life. As soon as I left the convent, at eighteen, I was married to a distant cousin. Ten years older than me. A drunkard and a womanizer. And a brute. He raped me on our wedding night and then he went to sleep. I thought that was the way it was supposed to be. I didn't know any better. I dreaded the nights. He would jump into bed, smelly, half-drunk, take me hard and then go to sleep. I cried myself to sleep for two years."

I've put my fork down, unable to continue eating. I'm fascinated by the story of this woman who looks so modern and tells me a tale that I imagined could only have happened hundreds of years ago.

"Luckily," Carina continues as she munches on her salad, "I had a passion. Painting. I got his permission to take some classes. Thank God I met a wonderful woman, my art teacher, a person of intellect and compassion and great vision. I once confided in her and she was horrified by my life. It was she who told me that marriage didn't have to hurt. It was she who gave me the courage to stand up to my husband, my raper, and put a stop to his sexual violence."

"You divorced him?"

"No, no, my dear. In Puerto Rico a good Catholic girl doesn't get a divorce. But I refused to have sex with him. He beat me black and blue."

"My God."

"My mother finally noticed my broken spirit and body and she whisked me out of his house and hid me from him. When my father died I inherited a lot of money and left Puerto Rico and that husband of mine for good."

"Was Mrs. Velasco in the same situation?"

"No. I think she was luckier. I think Ray actually likes her. He certainly treats her with respect. I know she wasn't in love with him when they married, but he took her on a six-month honeymoon around the world. Imagine her delight at everything he showed her. He took her to Paris and bought her the most expensive clothes and jewels. He pampered her for awhile, and then he let her be. He's not faithful to her, I can't even count how many women I know he's had. But he's kind to her. And she's had his children. She lives for them. She would die for them. She's told me so many times they're her treasure, they're her blessing from God. She's been lucky that way. Her children adore her. So, apparently Miriam's satisfied with that. At least she's never complained to me."

"I had no idea that women... that people..."

"That people could live like that?" she finishes my thought for me. "Oh, yes. It's still happening now. It happened to Linda. Ray set her up

to have the same fate. It was Ray who chose Alan for Linda. He wanted
Alan because of his access to power, because of his closeness to Enrique,
because Alan was willing to become Ray's puppet."

"What do you mean his puppet?"

"Alan never, ever makes a move without first consulting with Ray.
About anything."

"Even for this vacation trip he's supposedly taking now?"

"Personally, I don't think it's a vacation trip. I think he's finally tired
of Linda and the Velascos and he's run away."

"Why do you say that?"

"Because of the note he left for Linda. She told me about it and I
don't think anyone else knows about it."

"What did the note say?"

"I never saw it. Linda paraphrased it as saying that she shouldn't look
for him. That he was leaving because the situation at home was intoler-
able. That he had tried very hard to be a good husband and father, but
couldn't take the pressure any more. He said that when things cooled
down a bit he'd be in touch with her, but that she shouldn't send anyone
looking for him because it would be in vain, he would not come back.
He asked her to kiss the children for him. Said he loved them."

"My God. How did Linda take it?"

"Not well at all. She's hurt. Who wouldn't be? And she's humiliated.
She said she'd like to kill him if she saw him." She smiles. "Not that she
loves him. She never did. But it's been a tremendous blow to her. And
she doesn't want the world to know."

"Is that why no one seems to be looking for him?"

"I'm sure Ray's dogs are. They apparently haven't turned up anything yet. Otherwise, Linda would've heard something."

"Why haven't they involved the police?"

"Pride, my dear. Pure and simple. They're too proud to admit to
anyone that one of their own would abandon the clan. They're trying
to do it by themselves. And I've heard, by the way, that they're not
happy about your poking around."

"I know that."

"Why are you, may I ask? Was he involved with you, by any chance?"

I'm startled by the question and somehow feel slighted that she would even think that.

"Of course not," I say in a much too loud voice.

"No, I didn't think so. Ray's interested, though, and so is Luis, from what I can see."

I don't answer.

"Be careful, my dear. That family is very tightly knit. They're fiercely protective. Especially Miriam. They look out for one another. They will maim or kill to protect each other. Even if it seems as though they're competing with each other, it's merely another sport with them. Another game. See who beats whom. Father and sons always competing. Always wrestling to prove who's better. So, for your own sake, be careful."

She reaches for my hand and squeezes it and I pull it away.

She looks at me with a sad look in her eyes. Then she quietly folds her napkin and lays it softly on the table.

"Shall we go?" she says.

CHAPTER 14

L UIS IS SITTING OUTSIDE MY DOOR, KNEES DRAWN UP, HEAD
hung. He looks pale and sad as he stares at me climbing the last
two steps to the third floor landing. He doesn't get up.

"Hi, Red. Please forgive me. I didn't mean to hurt you," he blurts
out.

I stop a few inches from him without looking at him and start
hunting deep in my pocketbook for my house key, as always. *I wonder
why he didn't use my key to let himself in. He has one.*

"Please, Red. Talk to me. Can I come in and just look at you?"

"I have a show tonight and I need to prepare for it. I don't have
time to talk to you now, Luis." I'm curt.

"I won't bother you, Red. I swear. Let me just come in and be in
your house, near you."

He's sitting on the floor, leaning against the wall, gazing at his black
sneakers. His unshaven face, his uncombed hair, give him a forlorn
appearance that softens my heart.

I need to work on this evening's interview of a young D.C. glass
sculptor, Johnny Ellis, who has taken this city by storm. His whimsical
sculptures of mythical figures, especially animals, are being snatched up

by collectors and the Renwick Gallery is going to showcase his art in a ground-breaking one-man show. Johnny and I met a few weeks ago to set up the interview and I was charmed by his down-to-earth attitude, his biting wit, and his obvious talent. He should be a smash with my audience tonight. Nevertheless, no matter how good and quick my guests are, I still have to be prepared with interesting questions. I'm certain that Luis' presence in my apartment, even if he's very quiet, very inconspicuous, will hamper my preparation.

Luis seems to be reading my thoughts.

"I promise you I won't bother you. I'll make coffee for you, sharpen your pencils, get you paper," he says. "Anything, as long as I can look at you. And you let me apologize."

I say nothing to him and slowly and deliberately open the door to my apartment and walk into the foyer without uttering a word. I leave the door ajar.

He springs in after me and walks up close, but doesn't touch me. I can feel his breath on my neck. It's hot. He smells of a mixture of cologne and beer.

"I've been here for hours," he whispers. "I'm so sorry I hurt you."

I go into the small living room, still not looking at him, and he follows me. He sighs heavily. "Thank you," he says.

I busy myself collecting papers, spreading my notes on the dining room table, looking for books on art. He's just standing by the door, eyes downcast, black T-shirt rumpled, hand stuck in his jean pockets.

"I don't know what came over me, Red. I really don't know." He's talking very fast now. "It's like I got this pain, this pang of jealousy when I saw you with that Bernie guy. Like I was about to lose you to someone else and it made me so damn angry. So fucking mad. I couldn't control myself. I wanted to punch out the other guy's eyes because I thought he was stealing you away from me. I just don't understand it. And you so lovely, so happy when I had you in my arms, I wanted you to feel how much you had hurt me. Please forgive me. You're so important to me."

I let him talk.

"Ever since I can remember I've had a jealous streak." He starts walking towards the kitchen. "Do you mind if I grab a beer?"

"Go ahead."

He takes a beer and I decline the one he offers me. He sits on the couch, legs stretched out.

"Am I bothering you with all this chatter?"

I shrug.

"My brother had it all. That fucking bastard had everything. All I ever wanted. And not a shred of kindness in that man. Except for those Salvadoran kids he goes to see every chance he gets. I don't know why. Ever since the accident..."

Luis looks down at his fingernails, examines them with great care, and then takes a sip of beer. "He's always been my father's favorite, they stick together through thick and thin. And boy, Enrique was always in some kind of trouble. And there's papa, right behind him, fixing his problems for him. No matter what. Some pretty big ones. But Enrique didn't have to worry. My father would take care of whatever mess my brother would make and then they laugh about it and go hunting together and all's well with the world."

I'm shuffling papers around without really paying any attention to them and listening intently to Luis' tale. It's getting warm in here and I open the door to the balcony. My neighbor's cat, Honey, jumps in, walks next to my legs, rubbing her soft fur on my skin, and in one swift movement cuddles against Luis. He welcomes her, caresses her gently and murmurs softly into her ear.

"I hated hunting," he continues. "Still do. I don't see the fun in it. My father doesn't even bother bringing the dead animals home so they can be cooked and served to us or the servants. He doesn't give them away to the farmers or his laborers at the ranch. He just leaves them lying right where they were shot dead. The buzzards get them."

I look up at him, finally, and he shows me a wan smile.

"I went with them a couple of times," he says between sips of beer. "More than a couple. I tried. Hell, I really tried hard but I just couldn't do it. I shot one or two small deer to please my father and afterward I puked my heart out. I don't think I ever heard my brother and father laugh harder than when they saw me puking. So I stopped going with them. My mother didn't push me. I think she understood how I felt. She always understands. She has a soft, warm heart. God, I'd do anything for that woman. Anything." He stifles a yawn. "Many times I've wondered how she could have stayed married to him. He's such a brute. And she's a lady. I'll never understand that marriage. What that man has put her through. I'll tell you, Red, you've no idea what that man has put her through."

I look at my watch. It's three o'clock. I have three hours to get ready for my show. I can do it. So, I don't interrupt Luis, but he notices.

"Red, I'm sorry. I'm blabbing like an idiot. You're probably bored stiff but are too polite to tell me to stop. That's why I like you so much. You have class. A fine, fine woman. A true lady."

Great! Any minute now he'll be saying I remind him of his mother.

"But you're different. You're so alive, so much fun. I can relax when I'm around you. Don't have to pretend I'm somebody I'm not. No need to put my guard up all the time like I have to do when I'm around my family. Remember when we made love at the Eastern Shore?"

I nod. *How can I possibly forget?*

"We had to be quiet. Really quiet. You remember? And you know why? Because my mother would have been furious that we were making love under her roof, as she puts it, and my father would have peppered me with questions the next morning, wanting to know every single detail of our lovemaking. Every detail. What you said. What we did. How it felt. And then he'd go and brag about it to his friends. Brag about me, about his sons, and what studs they are. That's why we had to be so quiet. I didn't want anybody to know."

"Somebody did."

"What do you mean?"

"Somebody was looking in the window of my room when you left. Somebody saw us."

He gets up with a jolt, sending Honey scurrying along to find a hiding place in my kitchen.

"Who was it? Did you see who it was? Goddam it." He starts pacing. "Goddam it all. Why didn't you tell me this before? Goddam it, Red."

"I was so embarrassed by it. And I couldn't make out who it was. Just a figure in the dark."

"I'll bet you anything it was my fucking brother, probably mad as hell that you preferred me to him." He looks at me with dark, stormy eyes.

"I couldn't tell who it was."

"Fuck it all."

"What difference does it make? Don't they know we're seeing each other?"

"Yes."

"So what does it matter now?"

"It matters. It just does. It's the story of my goddam life. Of what happens to me all the time. Always spying on me, always following me around."

"Is this the way it is with all of you?"

"Well, my father pretty much knows everything we all do. He has his goons following us around."

"Linda too?"

"Yeah, her too."

"Alan too?"

"Him too. What's this with Alan?" He stops pacing and comes to stand very close to where I'm sitting. "How come you're always asking about him?" The tone of his voice is getting deeper, his eyes darker, menacing. "Don't tell me you had something going with him. If you did I'll... I'll..."

"I didn't have anything going with him, Luis, so you relax and stop the threats. I don't care for your tone either. So, if you want to continue with this conversation," I slap the table so hard my pencils go flying off, "if you want to stay here, you'll sit down, you'll calm down and you'll talk to me in a civil tone. Understood?"

"I'm telling you, Red, you're tough," he says with an easy, boyish laugh. He does as he is told, goes back to the couch, picks up the can of beer and calls for Honey, who happily jumps onto his lap. "So, why the burning interest in Alan?"

"I guess I should tell you. You're probably going to find out anyway, and maybe, just maybe, you can help me."

"Sounds ominous," he says lightly.

"It's not too good. Do you remember that when I first started looking for Alan to answer some questions for my show you told me that maybe his high school sweetheart might know where he is? That she had been calling him incessantly?"

"Yes."

"I tracked her down. She's Annette Simmons, a nurse at Children's Hospital. I went to talk to her."

"No kidding. You're sure a determined investigator."

"Only when I have to be."

"What does she look like? Anything like Linda?"

"Nothing like Linda, the exact opposite of Linda. But she had a very interesting story to tell. She too is looking for Alan," I lied.

"Why?"

"He owes her a debt."

"Money?"

"In a manner of speaking."

Luis starts howling with laughter. "He borrowed money from this woman? He has all the money he can use. Linda has a huge trust fund and she lets her hubby tap into it whenever he has the urge."

"Luis, it's not that. Annette told me Alan fathered her child and she wants him to take responsibility and go visit the boy. Introduce them to each other. She's looking for Alan. She asked me to help her and I said I would. I promised her, and I always keep my promises. Always."

Luis looks stunned. He's staring at me with his mouth half-open, scratching his head, probably wondering how this bit of news will affect his family.

"Does anybody else know about this kid?" he asks.

"Annette told Alan, so he knows. I don't know if she's told anyone else, but what's really strange is that Alan disappeared right after Annette broke the news to him."

"What? He didn't know he had a kid?"

"Apparently not. He thought she had an abortion and then he left town to go to college. Annette also left home to have the baby some-where else. He never had anything to do with the folks back home after college, so he never had the chance to find out."

Luis starts laughing hysterically again. "The golden boy," he says between hiccups. "The boy chosen by my father for his lovely daugh-ter, after such strict scrutiny. The perfect man for his adored daughter has a bastard son—who my father no doubt has known about all along. What a joke. What a funny joke. And here he couldn't give Linda a son. Three little spoiled bratty girls is all he could manage. And my father hungering, salivating for a grandson he could mold to his own image. He probably figured the son was proof Alan could sire boys. And now this, a bastard kid in our family." He lets out a loud laugh. "That's a joke on Ray." He stops suddenly, gets up, starts pacing and looks at me.

He's still chuckling meanly as he gets up and comes over to stand behind my chair.

"Don't tell a soul," he whispers in my ear. He's holding me by the shoulders. "It'll be our secret."

"I have to find him," I say, shaking him off me. "Do you have any idea where he might have gone?"

"No idea whatsoever." He's playing with my hair.

"You know what I think?" I turn around to face him. "I think he found out about the boy, was terribly frightened that your family would discover it too, and he left to a place where he can hide. And now he's away from your family and from the responsibilities to Annette and his son."

"It's possible," he says softly. "Possible. Are you sure he's the father of this kid?"

"I only know what Annette is telling me."

"People do this for money, you know," he says. "It's possible she came to D.C., found out who Alan's married to, and is trying to cash in for having had an affair with him."

"It's possible," I concede.

"We have to find out if the child is really his." His voice is suddenly animated. I turn around to look at him. The color is returning to his face, his eyes are smiling again.

"You want to be involved in this?"

"Red, if you're involved, I'm involved." He sits opposite me at the dining table, hands flat on the table, shoulders squared. "Where was the kid born?"

"In a town near Augusta, where Annette's aunt lives. I thought I'd go there next week-end and do a little investigating."

"I'll go with you."

"But you can't tell a soul. We don't want this to become public knowledge until we find something out. Otherwise it may be blown all out of proportion and we might never find Alan."

"You got it. Not a word to anyone. Can you leave tomorrow?"

"I have to work, Luis. I can't just take off whenever I want to. Friday night, after my show would be good, and I have to be back..."

"Before Sunday evening," he interrupts. "I know, I know. But you know, Red, it would be much better if we left on Thursday. That way we could go to the court house on Friday to do some checking into the kid's birth certificate."

"I understand. I'll try to get Friday off and we can leave Thursday right after my law class. We can drive there in eight or nine hours. Also,

I need an excuse to go visit the aunt. She may be able to clarify a lot of things. Annette was living with her when the baby was born."

"What kind of an excuse?"

"I don't know yet. Maybe I can use my radio show somehow. I'll think about it. I really need to prepare for my show tonight, Luis. It's after four."

He gets up from his chair, walks slowly toward me, takes my face in his hands, and bends down to kiss my forehead.

"All's forgiven?" he asks.

I nod.

He extends his right hand towards me. "Partners?"

"Partners." I shake his hand.

❧   ❧

MY SUNDAY SHOW IS SPECTACULAR. JOHNNY ELLIS IS ALL I thought he would be. Charming, and funny, and informative. The phones don't stop ringing. Mostly women. Young women. If Johnny could sell his art over the phone he would make a fortune. He promises my audience he'll be back soon for another interview and we go for a drink at Max's Bar and Grill, one of my old haunts. We talk about art, D.C., race relations and love. I'm totally enchanted, but I don't feel the exhaustion of the day until I climb the last step to my apartment.

My message light is blinking:

"Sugar, hope the indisposition of last night has been lifted. By the way, I think you stayed out in the sun much too long playing tennis. Your skin is very fair. We don't want to see it get damaged. And Sugar, Max's Bar and Grill is not the place for a sweet young thing like you."

CHAPTER 15

THE DAY AT THE STATION GOES SMOOTHLY—NO upheavals, no downfalls. It's a haven from the mercurial Velascos. I call Renata as soon as I get to the station and she sounds much better. She says she's feeling almost like her old self and is looking forward to going home tomorrow morning to be in the care of her mother.

She's disappointed that the police seem to have lost interest in her case. They told her this morning that they're still looking for the "perpetrator" who burnt her face, but without witnesses and no positive identification from Renata, without any traces or any leads, the investigation will have to slow down. "In other words," Renata says, "they're giving up." The police did find out, however, that the liquid that was thrown at her was a concentrated mixture of drain cleaner and other common household products. "So," the police told Renata, "anybody could've done it." Notwithstanding this bit of bad news, Renata's spirits are soaring. She said that Enrique's flowers and attention have contributed a great deal to her happiness. I wonder if his sudden interest in her is just a ruse to find out how much Alan told her about him. She still hasn't heard from Alan.

I have to set up an appointment with Annette to get to her aunt Clara. Annette worries me. I have problems believing what she's told me.

It's six o'clock and I've just finished a very good shift. I pick up the phone at the reception desk, hunt for my phone book in my large bag and dial Annette's home number. It rings many times before I hear Annette's husky voice. I can tell she's been drinking from her first "hello."

"Annette? It's Gloria Berk."

"Who's Gloria Berk?"

"The disc jockey, from WVVV Radio? We met at Sweet Carolina's? Don't you remember?"

"Oh, yeah. The little runt with the red hair and perky boobs. I remember. What's up? Heard from the jerk yet?"

"No. But I'd like to ask you a favor."

"Shoot."

"Could you set up an appointment for me to meet with your Aunt Clara?"

"Whatever for?"

"I've been thinking about doing a program on rural America," I lie. "Go to different towns, discuss different ways of living, you know, to bring the many cultures of our country to my audience."

"Uh, uh," she says. "So what about my aunt?"

"Well, I thought she might be my first interview. Show how people in the South live."

"Will you pay her?"

"I can arrange it with my manager to give her a small honorarium..."

"What's that?"

"Money."

"Good. I'm sure she'd like that. When do you want to see her?"

"I need to be in South Carolina this weekend for a business meeting and I thought I'd combine it with a visit to your aunt."

"You can see her on Saturday after her Bible group meeting, around ten a.m. How much are you paying her?"

"I'm not sure yet. Maybe a hundred dollars."

"See if you can make it two hundred. She can use the money."

"I'll try. Tell me what she's good at, what her interests are, so I can ask her good questions."

"She's an accomplished herbalist. She knows everything there is to know about herbs and potions. Everybody's always asking her for her concoctions. You can get her going on that for hours—that and religion, the Bible."

"Terrific. Please set it up for me. Listen, Annette, would you like to come along? I'm leaving Thursday night."

"That's mighty kind of you, Gloria, but I can't go. I'm busy Friday night."

"At the clinic?"

"No," she says brusquely. "Not at the clinic."

"Oh, I didn't mean to..."

"That's O.K. I know you didn't. I made a promise to my aunt that I would atone for my sins by helping others. So every Friday night I go to Ruth's Kitchen to feed the homeless."

"You're quite a surprising woman, Annette. At least let me take you out to dinner when I get back."

"Why? Are you some kind of lesbo?"

"No, I'm not," I smile. "But then do you have to be one in order to invite a friend to dinner?"

"I guess not."

"Great. I'll call you as soon as I get back and fill you in on what your aunt said."

"I like steak."

"Good. I'll buy you the biggest, juiciest steak in D.C."

"You have a deal," she says. "Give my sweet aunt a big hug for me. Tell her I love her." She hangs up the phone without saying goodbye.

❧ ❧

IT'S TIME TO GO HOME, PREPARE FOR MY LAW CLASS. THE TRAFFIC congestion as always, is dreadful, but this evening there's a luminosity in the air. The sky is clean, tinged with red clouds and a sliver of a shy moon peeking from behind them. I'm listening to my station, to Manny's evening request show—mellow voice, poignant songs of longing and of love. I start singing out loud to the Natalie Cole's "Unforgettable." My windows are wide open and a sweet magnolia scent is tickling my nostrils.

I cut across traffic lanes and try to speed up my trip by taking back streets, but I always seem to end up in the snail-like pace of Wisconsin Avenue. I'm singing at the top of my lungs and pedestrians passing me smile and wave. I wave back. I wish I had the station T-shirts with me, and buttons and coffee mugs to pass around. It's ratings time again and we can always use all the support we can muster.

I notice a dark green car behind me that hasn't left my tail for the last ten minutes. Wherever I go it seems to be there. I can't distinguish who's sitting behind the wheel, but I see a pair of very large glasses and a man's fedora pulled low. I feel my stomach tighten up. One of Ray's guards? I'm sure he wouldn't be so obvious. I make a sharp left onto a side street as soon as there's an opening in the traffic. No more green car. I relax a bit and open up a package of cheese crackers, my late lunch. My mother would be horrified to see me eating this just before dinner, but it'll be at least another hour before I can prepare a decent meal.

It takes me longer than usual to get home. I park my car in its assigned spot below my balcony, and when I get out of the car I have the strange sensation that someone's watching me. I look around, but see no one. I pull my bag out of the car, close the door and start sprinting toward my apartment building. As soon as I step on the threshold the man with the fedora steps out of the darkened lobby. I utter a scream and jump back. He comes over to me. His thick glasses swallow up his face. His cheeks are drawn, like an old man's, and his lips are pale and thin. He pushes an envelope into my hand and disappears. I sprint up to my apartment, breathless, scared to death. I lock the door, lean on it, and look at the envelope trembling in my hand. My name is on it, in dark blue ink, in flawless penmanship. I rip it open in one furious tear and read the carefully scripted note.

> *Your tale is being heard, and yet it wasn't told*
> *Your fruit is falling and yet your leaves are green,*
> *Your youth is being spent and yet you are not old,*
> *You see the world and yet you are not seen;*
> *Your thread may be cut soon and yet it is not spun,*
> *And now you live, and soon your life is done.*

"I LIKE POETRY YOU KNOW RED?" LUIS TELLS ME AS WE'RE DRI-ving down Route 95 on our way to South Carolina. He looks happy, carefree, relaxed. His arm is warmly draped around my shoulders and I feel cozy inside his Jaguar. "I never told this to anyone," he goes on. "I guess it's not a macho thing to admit. And you know how macho I am, right?" He looks at me and squeezes my arm tenderly. "Other people in my family like poetry too, so it's not like I'm doing something bizarre. My mother once found a notebook of my poetry I was hiding in my sweater drawer and she read it and showed it to my father. Man. I thought I was going to die or I would have to run away from home. My mother was gushing all over the place and my father just looked at me with one of those mean looks he sometimes has and he asked me, 'So, are you gay?' Can you believe it? And this from a man who's always quoting some poet or another. It's good enough for them. Just not good enough for me."

Luis had picked me up at the law school, right after my class was over. He wasn't happy we would start our trip after nine at night, but I've missed too many law classes this semester. I didn't want to miss this one too.

He was waiting for me at the entrance of the school, standing by his flashy brand new maroon convertible, and eyeing every student who came out with me. He smiled broadly when he saw me. It made me feel like a teenager meeting her boyfriend after class. I was actually happy to see him, happy I didn't have to travel to South Carolina on my own, happy that he was there.

We've stopped at a fast food place for sandwiches, fries and a soda, and Luis is still munching on the fries. It's a comfortable, delightful trip.

"What were they about, your poems I mean?" I ask after a while.

"Stuff. Love and hatred and jealousy. Life and death. Things like that," he grabs another fry.

"Why would your father even think you were gay?"

"Who the hell knows. That's the way he is. I guess he feels that if you write poems you are sensitive, no matter what the poem is about. And if you're sensitive that means you can't be a real man. That you must be gay. In his eyes. No matter. He'll never understand me. But that's all right." He pops the last fry into his mouth and puts his arm around my shoulders again.

"Hmmm. You feel good," he says.

"Are you still writing poetry?"

"Sometimes."

"Anything about us?"

"Sometimes."

"Do you think I could see it?"

"No. Not yet. Maybe some day. Not yet. Where do you want to stop to sleep?"

"We can go a couple of hours more. Let's do as much as we can tonight so we don't have to drive too much tomorrow."

"Sounds good to me."

"What did your mother say about your poems?" I ask.

"She liked that I was writing them. She writes too, so she was proud."

"Your mother writes poems?"

"Yes, pretty good ones, too. My father wanted to have a collection of her work published, but she absolutely refused. She said they were just for her and for the family. That they were too private, much too personal."

"A talented woman," I say.

"Yes, she is. She's also a bit of a nut. All those potions she makes, and salves and ointments. She made us do all kinds of crazy things when we were kids—embarrassed us to death."

"Like what?"

"Crazy things. For example, if one of us kids was coming down with a cold, or a virus, or something, she'd make us wear a garlic around the neck."

"A garlic?" I laugh.

"Yea. A head of garlic. Sometimes a whole strand of garlic heads sewn together."

"Like a necklace?" I laugh again.

"Exactly. And it's not funny. She really made us do it. We were wearing necklaces of garlic to go to St. Albans School. Fabulous. We would've been the most popular kids in class."

"You didn't wear it?"

"Just until we stepped out of the house. My father would then hide them for us. It was strange. She had a million of those remedies. Bayberry tea gargle for a sore throat. God-awful tasting stuff. One time I skinned my knee really badly playing soccer in the street with my friends. It was bleeding a lot and didn't stop. She immediately ran to the kitchen and brought out some cayenne pepper to put on my scrape. Pepper. It stung like crazy. It humiliated me in front of my friends who were staring the whole time. But it did stop the bleeding right away." Luis is talking happily. He seems to take it all with a great deal of humor and affection.

"You know, Luis," I say, "the woman I'm meeting on Saturday, Annette's aunt, is an herbalist. Come with me to visit her. You can talk to her, interest her with your stories, get her involved. Maybe she'll open up to you and talk to us about Alan and the kid."

"Yes, boss." He takes my hand and kisses it.

"You know what would be great? What I would love?"

"What, Red? You ask for anything and I'll get it for you. Anything."

"A hot, delicious bath—not a shower. A bath with bubbles in it where I can immerse myself and soak for a good, long time."

"No problem, my lady. We won't stop at a motel that doesn't have a nice big bathtub for my girl."

He starts whistling some tune I don't recognize, hugs me tighter and I snuggle against the crook of his arm. The warm breeze is whipping my face. I close my eyes and try to understand Luis' wildly fluctuating moods. He's usually gentle with me, funny, even loving, until his frenzies transform him.

"You asleep, Red?" he whispers.

"No. Just thinking."

"Me too. Thinking about you. About us. About how calm and exciting it is for us to be alone together. Without my family beating on us. Do you feel how great this is?" He slides his fingers closer to my underarm and places them inside my sleeveless blouse. He starts playing with the seam of my bra and pulls at it coyly.

"Take it off," he says. "Let me touch you."

"Here?"

"Yes."

I open my eyes and look up at the starry sky. There's light traffic on the road at this time of night and the headlights from the oncoming traffic light up the bugs dancing above us. I sit up straight, put my hand on my back, unhook my bra and pull it out from under my shirt. My heart is beating fast, the adventure excites me. Luis' changing moods excite me. His tenderness moves me and his unpredictability electrifies me. Driving to a new place in the heart of the night arouses me. Even looking for Alan, whom I barely know, following a trail that seemingly has no beginning and an end I can't see, tantalizes me. It entices my senses, my imagination. Alan's family seems not to care too deeply about Alan's whereabouts. And Renata has lost her intensity now that Enrique is showering her with affection. But for me, this investigation has become much more than just finding out where Alan's hiding. It's trying to understand why someone who seems to have it all runs away from his wife, from his children, from his home and his lover, without leaving a trace. I've been wondering if I'd do it too, if I were pressured.

I lean on Luis' arm again and his fingers move softly, slowly, under my arm, inside my blouse, until they finally rest gently on my bare breast.

"Uhmm," Luis says. "There's nothing better. Nothing more delicious. Here's a good place for us to stop," he says in a husky voice.

I stay in the car while he goes into the well-lit, well-tended motel. We barely drove three hours.

"They have cabins by a small pond," he says, beaming as he jumps back in the car. I asked for one with a fireplace and a big tub." He smiles.

※ ※

I SUBMERGE MYSELF IN THE WARM WATER OF THE TUB. THE drops of the perfume I sprinkled on the surface make the whole white bathroom smell like a flower garden. Through the half open door I can hear the wood crackling in the fireplace and I can see Luis' strong arm poking the kindling. Some jazz sounds waft in from the radio in the bedroom. I close my eyes and let the water sweep over me. It soothes me to a light slumber. A gentle touch on my forehead yanks me awake.

"You're beautiful," Luis says in a warm, rasping voice. "I never really saw how beautiful you are." His dark eyes are moist and his lips are parted. I lightly press my fingers over his lips and he holds my wet hand and places the open palm on his cheek. "God," he says. "This feels so good, so right." He strips quickly. "Can I?" he asks me, as he starts climbing into the tub.

I move my legs to make room for him and he slides in beside me, holding me tight and spilling water as he submerges his body. He's so tall and the tub is so small, there's hardly room for the two of us. I start laughing uncontrollably until he presses his mouth to mine to quiet me down.

That night we make love sweetly, unhurriedly. There are no phone calls, no deadlines, no pressures. It's a night of kisses and whispers and delightful surprises. The songs of the cicadas lull us to sleep and we wake up in a cozy room with lace curtains that let the bright sun filter in with intricate and delightful shadows. I'm completely engulfed in Luis' arms, legs and body when I open my eyes.

"Oh my God," I sit up with a jolt. "It's almost ten, the alarm didn't go off. I'm sure I set it for seven."

"Come back to me." Luis pulls me back into his arms.

"We still have a good six hours drive to get to Aiken. We really have to hurry."

"No we don't. Let's stay in bed a little longer. This is great. Let's stay like this the whole day. The whole month."

I kiss his chin and rub the dark stubble. "Don't you want to get to the courthouse? To look for the kid's birth certificate?"

"We'll make it," he says yawning and stretching his arms. "Have no fear, sweet lady. Jesus, I'm starving."

He holds me by the waist as I try to climb out of the four-poster bed and he kisses my back. It sends a shudder up and down my spine.

‧ ‧

WHILE I FINISH DRYING MY HAIR, LUIS GOES TO THE OFFICE TO pay. As soon as I'm finished with my hair I start taking our bags to the car. Luis meets me half way. He's pale, frowning and huffing loudly.

"What?" I ask.

He throws a crumpled piece of yellow paper at my feet. "Look, look," he shouts.

I bend down, pick up the paper, smooth it out and read:

> *Running, running,*
> *you can't escape me.*
> *I'm watching*
> *the devil in you.*
> *Fornicators, evildoers,*
> *you'll pay for your sins.*

"Where did you find this?" I can barely speak.

"It was left at the office for us. They couldn't give me a description of who left it. Just a man, they said. They couldn't be more specific. The idiot at the desk last night, when the note was delivered was watching a movie on TV and didn't want to be disturbed. God. I hate this. I hate this. I hate this."

"Do you have any idea who's behind this? Could it be your father?"

"Why?" Luis asks me with a white rage. "Why would he do it? No, I don't know who's behind this. I only know that someone's following us, Red. And I don't like it. I don't even know why anyone would want to do this, but I'm so goddam angry."

He goes to the back of his car, carrying both bags in one arm, opens the trunk, throws them in and takes out a small revolver.

"My God, Luis. What on earth are you doing with that? Where did it come from? How long—"

"Quiet down, Red," he says with a dazzling fury. "Get in the car. Let's go. I don't know if they're still watching us. Don't make a scene."

"I don't want to get in the car when you have a gun with you."

"Do you want to stay here, then?"

"You can't mean that."

"Just try me. Get in the car. Now." He pushes me in and the windows shake when he slams the door.

"Whoever it is," he says as we start speeding down the highway, "is going to be very sorry he's messing with me. Who did you tell we were leaving?"

"Sue, she's my general manager. I also told my program director. He had to know I was leaving, so he could find a replacement for me."

"Who else?" he barks at me over the engine noise of his Jaguar. He's going over seventy.

"My parents."

"That's it?"

"Yes."

"Does anybody have anything against you? Anybody who could be following you?"

"I don't know."

We drive in silence for a long while. He suddenly jerks his car into the parking lot of a diner.

"Let's eat," he announces as he puts his gun under his belt and covers it with his Izod shirt. It still leaves a bulge, but you have to know it's there in order to notice it. He opens the door to my side, helps me out but doesn't look at me. His eyes have taken on a greenish hue and they're somber and threatening.

We order scrambled eggs with bacon, orange juice and coffee. It's a delicious breakfast. Fresh. Aromatic. He doesn't seem to know what he's eating. He's shoveling food into his mouth without pausing, without tasting, without even looking. He's scrutinizing every face in the small, cheerful, noisy diner. We're taking too long. There's still a long drive ahead. When we're finished, he throws the money on the table, pulls me to my feet and we walk out without having exchanged a word during the entire meal.

"Luis, we have work to do in Aiken. We can't let this incident derail us. We need to have a plan and stay focused."

We stop only once for gas and reach Aiken before five and ask for directions to the courthouse. We get there as the doors are closing. It won't be open tomorrow.

Did Luis do this on purpose? Did he turn off the alarm? Does he want to find the birth certificate or is he here just to keep an eye on me?

We drive around for a long time hunting for a place to stay the night. Luis keeps looking back in his rear-view mirror and is unhappy with every choice of hotel we make.

We finally settle for a small motel on the outskirts of town. We bring in soggy hamburgers and french fries, and eat in silence at the small table near the bed. Luis sits by the bed, dials a phone number, talks to a client about a pending case, and doesn't turn off the night light until well after midnight. We say goodnight and we each turn on our side, away from each other.

I make certain the alarm clock is set for eight, and that it's right next to me on the night stand.

❧ ❧

AUNT CLARA IS DELIGHTFUL. HER FULL, ROUND FACE IS ALL smiles when she opens the door for us. Her gray hair, cut simply in a pageboy, looks youthful and shiny. She ushers us into a small living room, her 'parlor,' as she calls it, and she offers us some tea and cookies. "My friend Beulah made them," she says giggling. "She knew I was expecting company and said it wouldn't be gracious of me to offer you one of my biscuits. They're hard, not much flavor, but that's how my mamma used to make them. Here, please take one of these. Beulah will be angry with me if she thinks I didn't offer you any."

Luis and I sit side by side on a brown corduroy couch with dainty lace doilies on the arms.

Aunt Clara sits across from us in a wood rocking chair that has a melodious sound when she rocks.

"How's my Annette? Is she happy up in Washington? You just saw her, didn't you?" Her brown eyes sparkle with a delightful warmth. "Lovely girl, my Annette. Lovely. And hard workin'. Don't know what I'd done if she hadn't been by my side when my Charlie died. She was there for me all the time." She dabs gently at her eyes with a handkerchief.

"She speaks with a lot of affection for you, too," I say, after taking a sip of a lukewarm, bland tea. I'd like to talk about Alan and Ricky. *Too soon. Patience.*

Aunt Clara smiles broadly and sips her tea noisily. Her hands are big and red. They look rough.

"And is this your young man? Good lookin' fellow, if I may say so myself. Very good lookin'."

Luis is actually blushing.

"Well..." I clear my throat a little. "We're good friends. He came with me to help me in the interview. He knows a great deal about herbs."

She cocks her head to one side, adjusts her pink sweater and gives Luis a knowing wink.

"One of us, hey boy?"

"Well..." Luis starts to say.

"I'll say," I interrupt. "He's known about herbs and potions since he was a child. Learned it all from his mother."

"That's the best way to learn it. With your mamma's milk. Everybody's talkin' now about herbs, like it's a new invention, isn't it true, boy? I hear of people just ravin' about the virtues of St. John's Wort. As though it's a new miracle. By golly, I've been usin' it since I was a little girl. My mamma gave it to me to calm down when I was actin' up. What does your mamma use, boy?"

Luis steals a glance at me, obviously embarrassed to talk about this, but I smile as reassuringly as I know how and nod to him three or four times.

"Same thing," he finally says in a very small voice. "She also uses Valerian to dispel stress."

"Yes, yes. Valerian's good. How does she use it? Powder or liquid?"

"Liquid. She adds it to her tea every day." Luis seems to be warming up to the subject.

"Excuse me," I interrupt. "Would you mind if I tape your conversation? I can use it in the program."

"You know, boy, how Valerian is also used?" Aunt Clara is talking animatedly to Luis without paying attention to my question. "If you hang it in your house you can guard against lightnin'." She points to a small brown pouch hanging near the entrance.

"Oh, that's interesting. I'll be sure to tell my mother." Luis has turned a bit from me and is now facing Aunt Clara completely.

"Excuse me," I interrupt again and whip out my small tape recorder. "May I?"

"Sure, child, sure." Aunt Clara takes small sips from her tea without taking her eyes off Luis. She's smiling a tiny, coquettish smile. "Where did your mother learn?"

"From her nanny. She was a Mestizo who believed in magic. She was the daughter of a famous witch doctor. She always used herbs and potions with my mother. And my mother continued the practice with us."

"It's powerful knowledge," Aunt Clara says gravely. "It's a power that few people have, but it's the energy behind birth, and life and love and death. Everythin' in the world has been created by that power, contains it, and has the answer to it. Your momma is a lucky woman to have that power."

"Well, sometimes we all feel she really tries to control the world."

They both laugh and we all have more tea.

"I, on the other hand," says Aunt Clara, "could never convince my Annette to follow my magic. Not when she was a young girl, not now."

"Did you try?" I ask. Annette seems such an unlikely candidate.

"Oh, yes. All the time. She's a stubborn girl, that one. Always has to have her own way. With her life, and her child, and her work. I gave her my secret potions. I wanted to share my magic with her. She knows how to use my potions, my herbs. I taught her that magic is love. But our magic should be performed out of love. Once anger or hatred enters the picture, we step into a world of danger, and misery, and pain. My poor Annette has been consumed by a powerful rage, by a hatred she can't shake. That's why magic never worked for her. She only wanted it as a weapon for revenge and it didn't work. It never will."

"She didn't follow your advice?" I ask.

"No."

"She seems happy with her life now," I say to keep her talking.

"I suppose she is—in her own way. It hasn't been easy. Raisin' that sweet boy without the help of the father."

"Do you know the father?"

"No. Never met him. She never brought him here."

"Why?"

"She told the boy the father was dead."

"And he wasn't?"

"No. The bum moved away. Had nothin' to do with her or the young one."

"Why?" Luis asks.

"Because she never told him she had his baby." Aunt Clara's face reflects the pain she has carried for years. "She thought that some harm would come to her if people found out about her son."

"What sort of harm," I ask. Luis is listening very carefully. His fingers are opening and closing in a rhythm all their own.

"She never made that clear, honey. Just that she was afraid. She told me not long ago that the father was involved with some mighty powerful people."

"Who is he?" Luis asks, almost in a whisper, pleading with her, touching her hand. "Please tell us."

She gets up without a word and opens a drawer in the small desk to the side of the couch where we're sitting. She hunts for something, making small noises with her lips. Finally she pulls out a yellowish paper. She unfolds it gently, smooths it out, and goes back to her rocker. She looks at it with great sadness and hands it to Luis.

"Here. Look for yourself."

Luis' hands tremble slightly.

"What is it?" I ask.

"The birth certificate."

"Who is it?" I ask. "Who's the father?"

"It says Alan White."

CHAPTER 16

I HAVEN'T HAD MUCH PREPARATION FOR THE SUNDAY evening show. Except for the short biography of Leonora Siqueiros that Ray gave me, I haven't been able to get much information on her. I look through my Mexican art books and can't find more than a passing mention of her name in a footnote about young emerging artists. I search the Internet for some background on her, some tidbit, anything, but I find nothing. However, I don't think that any amount of research would have prepared me for the Leonora Siqueiros I met.

I walk into the station this hot Sunday evening, half an hour before the show, fantasizing about the blast of cold air that will hit my face when I open the door. A young woman, probably no older than twenty-five, with long, black, shiny hair and a very thin body, almost frail, dressed entirely in black, is standing by the reception desk, apparently lost in thought. It's June in D.C. It's sweltering, and even though the station is well air-conditioned, the mugginess and the heat of the afternoon have filtered through every crack of the building. Even the silk flowers in the reception room seem to droop from the heat. But the young woman standing by the desk looks cool in her black turtleneck and tight black pants. She turns to me when I walk in and offers me a broad smile that seems to embody the vulnerability of a little girl and the allure of a woman of the world.

"Gloria Berk, right?" she says, offering her hand to me.

I nod and shake hands.

"By golly, Ray doesn't do you justice. He told me you were beautiful. I didn't imagine you this beautiful."

I'm flattered. "Beautiful" is not the word I'd use to describe me. Vivacious, yes, attractive, perhaps. 'Beautiful' is just stretching the truth to its very limits. But I smile back at her and feel flattered, nevertheless.

"Ms. Siqueiros?"

"Oh, please, please call me Lenny. Everybody does."

"Lenny? A boy's name?"

"Maybe. But I'm comfortable with it."

She looks comfortable with her name and with her long, shiny hair and her flawless olive skin.

"Lenny it is, then." I take her by the arm and start walking her to the conference room. "Tell me a little about yourself, about your work, so I can interview you intelligently."

"There's no need for that," Ray's voice booms in from the door of the station. "I've taken care of everything, Sugar. You just introduce her and sit back and enjoy the show."

"What... what... do...you... mean..." My rage prevents me from speaking coherently. I'm so angry with Ray I can hardly breathe. "What the hell are you talking about?" I finally manage to utter, still stiff with fury.

"Calm down, Sugar. Lenny here is a very fine artist, very fine. Unfortunately not too many people know about her, yet. I've arranged for my people to call throughout the show, asking Lenny questions about the things she wants to talk about. We'll make her look good. And we'll have so many calls, we'll make you look very good too."

"Listen to me, Ray," I say, taking a couple of steps forward and getting just inches from his large, protruding belly. His ever-present guards start to lunge toward me, but Ray keeps them in their place with a slight wave of the hand.

"Listen, Ray," I repeat, staring squarely into his face. "We'll do nothing of the kind. It's my show, it's my interview, and I'll conduct it the way I see fit. Do you understand? There are still twenty minutes before show time. I'll sit with Ms. Siqueiros and learn as much as I can about her. If I feel we can go on the air with a show that makes sense, then we'll broadcast live. If I feel either of us isn't ready, then I'll air an old, taped show. You get it?"

Ray smiles and pats my arm. I jerk back.

"If you want to stay here and listen to the interview, if we have one, you're welcome. There's a speaker in here, I'll turn it on for you," I say. "Meanwhile, I'm taking Ms. Siqueiros to the conference room to prepare. You stay right here. And please put that cigar away. There's no smoking anywhere in the building."

I strut back to where Leonora is standing, her mouth wide open, grab her by the arm and push open the large mahogany doors leading to the conference room. I turn back just before following Leonora in, and I see Ray putting his cigar in the breast pocket of his blazer. He grabs one of the magazines from the reception table and sits with a heavy thump on one of our antique chairs.

Leonora is an easy study and in twenty minutes she opens up for me a new world of revolutionary art and ideas. We go on live. The show is absolutely great. Her easy-going way, her intelligent answers, and her charm make her immensely appealing. She describes her paintings as a satire of society, somewhat in the style of the great Orozco. The interview part is over and I'm getting ready to open up the lines for the call-ins. I'm still worried about Ray's set-up.

During the commercial break Leonora leans towards me and whispers in my ear, "I'm having a terrific time. You're a great interviewer. Thank you. You're doing a very good job."

When the show is finally over there are still many callers who have stayed on the line without an opportunity to talk to Lenny. She takes the time to talk to each one personally. Finally, we agree on working together to set up an exhibit of her work at some Washington gallery.

She's flushed with excitement and shakes my hand effusively. "It'll be great doing things with you," she says. "I'm sure my art show will be a great success with your help."

"I know I'll enjoy it very much too," I say, as I stand up from my chair, ready to go. Lenny pulls me back down.

"I have a confession to make," she says.

My heart skips a beat. I take a deep breath and exhale loudly. "What?"

"I wasn't going to talk about my art during your show," she says, lowering her eyelids. The light of the studio casts shadows from her long eyelashes and she looks as if she has spiders on her cheeks. "Ray and I have been working together planning a way to empower our people, to give them confidence, to give them whatever they need to achieve their due. Anything," she says emphasizing the word. "In your show today, my plan was to call my Latino friends to arms. To show the whole world we're strong and united and powerful, and armed." My heart skips a beat. "But I changed my mind about it when you started asking me questions about my art. It excited me so much. I loved talking about my art."

"Did Ray know about what you were intending to do?" I ask curtly.

"Oh, no, no. Ray never knew anything about my plan. I wanted to surprise him. It was all my idea. I never told him. He just wanted for me to get some exposure here. He wanted to showcase me and my art. He's sweet," she says with a smile that sparkles. "He's done so much for our people. We owe him a great deal. He's lifted our souls, he's been great for our pride and our needs. And he's been an inspiration for me personally. I love the man. My meetings with him are extraordinary. I would never miss any of our sessions. Never. No matter where I am I'll fly back to D.C. to attend our weekly meetings."

"What meetings?"

"Oh, hasn't he told you? He formed a group of young people—we were mostly poor, aimless, some of us were runaways, some were druggies and we all considered ourselves revolutionaries. He collected us, like puppies, and we have been meeting with him every Friday night without fail. Come rain or come shine, there's Ray, with his two man-eaters by his side, teaching us, preaching to us, feeding us, you name it." She giggles. "And man, can he eat. He's great, I tell you. He taught us the basis to lead a real revolution, to understand the power of being united. He's fantastic. But tonight I had my own agenda. I wanted to show him I had learned my lessons well. I wanted to impress him. And then I lost my cool and I just couldn't do it. I was selfish, I think. I had to talk about my art." She smiles at me and sighs heavily.

"You did great," I say.

We both leave the studio smiling and Ray struggles to his feet from the narrow, straight-back chair.

"Great job, my dears. See, Sugar, you didn't need me after all. I'm deflated."

"You don't look deflated, Ray honey," Leonora says patting Ray's huge belly.

Ray takes a hold of her hand and kisses it softly while he winks at me. "Come, come," he hooks one of us on each arm. "Let's go celebrate. Let's go eat a great meal."

"I can't, Ray," Leonora says. "I have a plane to catch in a couple of hours."

"Right, right," Ray says without breaking stride. "I have a limo waiting for you in front." He turns to me. "Then it'll have to be just us, Sugar. Just you and me." He releases my arm and instead holds me tightly by the waist.

Leonora stands by the black limo, throws both her arms around Ray's neck and kisses him warmly and noisily on the lips.

"Bye, Ray darlin'. It was great, as always. I'll be back next Friday. Don't do anything naughty. At least not without me." He smiles, pats her on the behind, and she ducks into the limo with a seductive wiggle.

I'm sitting in the back seat of Ray's Mercedes without uttering a word. He slides in, puffing heavily, and as soon as he closes the door he lights up his cigar, enveloping us both in clouds of blue smoke.

"Jean Luc's O.K. with you, Sugar? You seemed to enjoy it last time we were there."

"It's fine."

"Why the long face? Your show was excellent. It'll draw rave reviews."

"Ray," I turn to him and face him squarely. Even though it's still light outside—it's not yet seven—it's dark inside Ray's car. When he puffs on his cigar the sparks illuminate his face. He's looking at me. Smiling. "You can't do this, Ray. You cannot take over my show, have people call in, dictate to me who I should interview." I'm getting angrier as I talk.

"But Sugar," he says mildly. "It was a great show. You did a good artist a favor, and on top of everything you're helping the downtrodden get a fair shake. Is that so bad?" He squeezes my arm lightly.

"That's not the point," I bark back at him. " I did this as a favor to you, Ray. Nothing more. I'm in charge of my show. I decide who gets invited and I ask the questions I think are appropriate. And I don't like the phone calls to be rigged."

"Sugar, Sugar," he shakes his head. "Nothing was rigged. Not a thing. I just asked my people to listen to your show. That's all. Nothing more, I swear." He puffs hard on his cigar and sparks fly between us. "And next time..."

"Next time," I interrupt, "if there's such a thing, it'll be the guest of my choice, the date I select, and with a lot of lead time so that I can prepare properly."

"Deal," he says, and hugs my shoulders.

We arrive at Jean Luc's and we're shown to the same table we sat at last time.

"Thank you, Marcel," Ray says, and sits heavily on the chair facing the entrance.

Marcel bows, massages his thin moustache and retreats into the darkened, almost empty restaurant. Ray's bodyguards take a seat a few feet away from us, dark glasses glinting with the light of the flickering candles.

"So how was your trip?" Ray asks as soon as he's ordered for both of us without looking at the menu. "Enjoyed the South?"

"It was O.K." I'm considering asking him bluntly about the anonymous note we got and the poem delivered to me by the man in the fedora.

"Ray," I say, after the waiter has poured the wine. "Are you having me followed?"

"Sugar," he sits back, smooths out his beard and smiles broadly. "What makes you ask me that?"

"Because I know you are, or somebody is, and because I resent it tremendously."

"I hope you believe this, Sugar. I'm not having you followed and I'm interested in finding out why you think somebody is."

"First of all," I point my finger close to his nose and the dark glasses of his men sitting facing me seem to glint more strongly, "you seem to know everywhere I go and everything I do. That's first of all. And I'd like to know how you found out I went away."

"Luis told me the two of you were going," he says simply.

I'm taken aback. "He told you? Why?"

"He's my son and he usually tells me where he's going. Besides, I had invited him last Friday to join me in my usual Friday meeting and he canceled out. He had to explain why he wasn't showing up."

"You meet every Friday night?"

"Never miss it. My people depend on it."

"The meetings you hold with Leonora and her friends?"

"Oh, I see she told you. She shouldn't be talking too much about it. We like to keep those meetings quiet, if you get my drift. Yes. Those meetings. With them. They're a group of smart, intellectual Latino

183

kids. A lot of them have been in deep trouble. We try to help them out as much as we can. They're good people, our next generation. But they want everything now. They can't wait for their turn. They all have great revolutionary ideas and I have to put the brakes on them once in a while. Teach them the ropes. They come from all over and we always meet on Friday nights. Then they can have some fun on the weekend." Ray digs into the onion soup that's so aromatic it smells almost like perfume.

We eat in silence for a while.

"The evening Luis was with you," he continues, "he was supposed to be talking to my people about immigration law, about helping our brothers and sisters who are here without the right papers. We need the numbers, Sugar. We don't want to have them sent back. You understand?"

"Yes."

"So, since my son was breaking his engagement with us, he needed to tell me why. I can't say I blame him," he says, reaching for my hand. "If I had a weekend with you I would be very tempted. Very tempted, indeed."

Our main dish arrives. Ray has ordered a rack of lamb that is so tender, I can cut it with my fork. It melts in my mouth. I forgot to eat lunch today and I devour every morsel on my plate.

Ray eats faster than me and he watches me eat with obvious pleasure.

"Hungry, weren't you? Doesn't that son of mine feed you at all?" He looks at my thin frame, fixing his gaze on my breasts, and smiles. "You look delectable anyway."

"Ray," I put my knife and fork down and look at him. He looks at me and tilts his head to one side. "I need to ask you something, but it's really crucial you tell me the truth, no matter what it is."

"I never lie, Sugar. It isn't worth the effort. Ask me whatever you want and I'll try my best to answer, if I can."

I take out the crumbled piece of yellow paper that was delivered to our motel. I smooth it out on the table and hand it to him. "Did you send this?"

Ray takes out his glasses, adjusts them deliberately, and picks up the paper. As soon as he starts reading his hand shakes slightly and the paper flutters as though a delicate breeze was blowing on it. Ray licks his lips and reads again.

"Did you send this, Ray?" I press him. My voice is louder.

"Sugar, this is a threatening note. I send you love notes, erotic poems, thoughts of sensuality and beauty. Why would I send you something like this? When did you get it?"

"Thursday," I say. "It was delivered to the motel where Luis and I were staying. We chose the place on the spur of the moment. We didn't reserve in advance, nobody knew we would be staying there. Not even us."

"Are you sure it was delivered to the right party? Maybe the people at the desk made a mistake."

"Luis told me it came in an envelope with our names printed on it."

"Did you see the envelope?"

"No."

Ray looks at the crumbled paper thoughtfully and asks, "May I keep it? I'd like to look more closely at the situation, do a little prodding."

"Ray, I really want to take it to the police."

Ray pales and the hand holding the piece of paper shakes visibly now.

"No. Not yet. Wait a few days. Give me a chance to look into it. I'll give it back in a couple of days, I promise."

"O.K., but you see from this that we were being followed. Somebody followed us to the motel in the middle of nowhere, in the middle of the night. And they left that piece of paper for us to find in the morning. Luis was extremely upset. Do you know he has a gun with him? He had it with him when we were traveling. It was very disconcerting."

"Of course I know he has a gun." Ray looks at me as though he were looking at a small child. "He has a license for it. He knows how to use it too. I taught all my children to use guns. You've got to know how to defend yourself. This is not a safe world. Did he use it at all?"

"No. But he was very nervous and made me feel extremely uncomfortable."

"You shouldn't have felt uncomfortable, Sugar." Ray's voice is even, soothing. "My son would protect you no matter what. That's how my boys were raised. But I see what you mean about being followed. Did Luis have any idea who it might have been? Did he see anything different, anybody that looked suspicious?"

"He didn't mention anything. His demeanor changed completely right after we got the note." I point at the paper still in Ray's hand.

"I can understand that. I'm going to find out for you, Sugar. I'm very surprised Luis never mentioned this little episode to me. You just leave it to me." He caresses my hand. "So," he says, after taking a sip of his wine, "it wasn't a great weekend after all, was it?"

"No."

"Relax, Sugar. I'll make sure we get to the bottom of whatever's going on here."

"Good."

"So," he says, while he munches on a piece of bread and butter, "I gather you found out our Alan's deep secret, huh?"

"You knew? I suspected you did." I don't mention it was Luis who put the suspicion in my mind.

"Yes."

"When?"

"As soon as that broad Annette what's-her-name showed her face around here. It didn't take too long to discover the dirty little secret."

"Does Linda know?"

"No."

"Does your wife know?"

There's a slight hesitation in Ray as he rolls his cigar between his fingers, sips his wine. Finally he speaks, almost meditatively.

"My wife, my wife, my dear wife." His voice has taken a mellow tone, a sweeter inflection. "She used to be a most amazing beauty. Glorious woman. I fell deeply in love with her the first time I saw her. So pure, so captivating, so innocent. She couldn't have been more than thirteen or fourteen at the time. I don't remember. I can only remember her beauty and my desire. I waited for her. I waited until we could get married. And she was so fragile, so delicate, I was truly worried I would crush her on our wedding night." I look away. "No, Sugar, don't turn away. I'm telling you the truth. There's no shame in that. She was the most beautiful thing I had ever seen. I was so awed by her, by her naked beauty, by her perfection, I was afraid to touch her. But she called me to bed, and to her side and we made love. God. I loved her." He pauses for a long time as if he's reliving those days. "Tell me, Sugar, do you know what real love is?"

"I'm not really sure."

"I'll tell you. When you can lie down in bed, close to a marvelous person, and her warmth swaddles you, and her perfume drives you crazy, and you fall asleep in her arms, and then you open your eyes and she's there, just lying there next to you—open, vulnerable—and the feeling of tenderness is so overwhelming you want to cry, and you thank God for having the person sleeping next to you, well, Sugar, that's real love. And nothing compares to it." He takes out a white handkerchief and dabs his eyes.

"So, if you love her..."

"How can I go to bed with other women?"

I nod.

"A few years after our kids were born, Miriam started resenting all the time I devoted to my people, my commitment to Guerra, to the movement. She said she felt abandoned by me. She especially hated the violence that's sometimes necessary. But some people need to be taught a lesson. So I used violence. And was attacked a couple of times. Miriam gave me a choice, either her and her religion full time or my cause. No middle ground. No room for negotiation. I couldn't give up the thousands of people who depend on me, on my support. And I told her that. She couldn't understand my passion for justice and she closed herself off from me. In every sense of the word. She never again wanted anything else to do with me."

"What did she do?"

"She devoted herself in the extreme to her spiritualism, and her religion, and to her herbalism. And to her children. I couldn't get her interested in our marriage any longer. Her children and her faith took all her time and her dedication. All of it. I had to look for my thrills somewhere else." He wipes his mouth with the crisp linen napkin. "She was not always the austere person you see now. But that's how life is." He sighs noisily. "She was my passion, Sugar, and in some way she still is. Yet, there's very little I can do." He pauses for a long time, lost in thought. "And to answer your question if she knows about Alan's child, the answer is no." He drains his wine glass. "And Sugar," he gets very close to my face, and I smell his odor of cigar and wine and expensive cologne, "I also know about the little blonde Alan was fooling around with."

I look at him in silence.

"The little blonde sex bomb who works with you."

"Renata," I whisper.

"Yes. Whatever her name is."

"She said they were very, very careful," I say.

Ray smiles. "She wasn't Alan's first," he says after a long pause. "And as long as my daughter doesn't get hurt, he can drop his pants any time he wants. As long as my daughter doesn't get hurt. But, as I think I told you before, he's the father of my grandchildren and I'll keep my mouth shut about his little peccadilloes. Hell, I do it. Why shouldn't he? As long as he's discreet and my daughter doesn't get hurt."

"I understand," I say. "Do you know that Enrique is now involved with her?"

Ray waits until the dessert of warm plum tart with fresh vanilla ice cream is served before he answers me.

"I know. And it's not the first time, either. He was seeing her before Alan. She's a hot little thing I've been told—full of fire and excitement and imagination. I, myself, wouldn't mind giving it a go."

"Ray," I say. I feel my face burning with anger and my throat closing. And for some strange reason I also feel jealous.

"No offense, Sugar. She doesn't have your depth, your intellect, your poetic soul. But I do hear she's a wonder in bed. I'd like to see for myself what men are raving about."

"Men? Plural?" I raise my eyebrows.

"Well, certainly more than one is what I hear. But I'm not judging her. I don't judge anyone. She can lead her life however she likes as long as she doesn't disrupt the rhythm of my life."

"Does Enrique love her?"

"I doubt it."

"Does Alan?"

"I doubt it too."

We eat our desserts in silence and I look into his moist, dark, luminous eyes gazing at me.

"Where's Alan?" I ask.

"I don't know."

When we get up to leave and the busboys come over to us, to Ray, they surround him and fawn over him. Marcel comes dashing at us as one of the busboys grasps Ray's hand and kisses it.

"It's O.K., Marcel. It's fine. These are my friends. They're all right."

He must have told Marcel this dozens of times—every time he comes in here.

189

Marcel moves back, a frown on his face. Ray prolongs the moments with his admirers and beams at them with delight.

I'm halfway up the stairs to the restaurant's doorway, flanked by Ray's men with their dark glasses, and I'm drinking in the sight of Ray's large figure in an almost deserted room, surrounded by several men touching him, kissing him, whispering in his ear. The maitre d', standing just a few feet from me, is a silent witness of this display of affection, and his grimace bespeaks his disdain.

Ray looks up, sees me standing there. He gestures grandly with his arm. "See Sugar, this is my life. This is what I gave up my love for. This is what Miriam resents."

❧ ❧

AS SOON AS I WALK INTO MY APARTMENT, I DIAL ANNETTE'S number. It rings for a long time before she picks up. It's only nine o'clock, but Annette sounds groggy, dazed. She must've been drinking for hours by now.

"Have a coffee with me," I say. "I have regards from your aunt and some potions she wanted you to have. Can we see each other tonight?"

"Only if we go have a drink. No coffee."

"I promised you a steak, remember," I say, hoping food might sober her up a bit.

"Yeah. And a drink."

"O.K." I say. "I'll pick you up in twenty minutes. Please wait for me outside your building. There's no place to park around there."

"You got it. Twenty minutes it is."

The traffic on a Sunday night is usually very light, so I'm surprised that just a couple of blocks from Annette's place the traffic has come to an almost complete halt. I'm honking my horn, drumming my fingers on the steering wheel, nothing helps, I'm inching my way towards her house.

Red and blue lights are blinking. *Great! A traffic accident. That's all I need.* An ambulance, siren blaring, horn honking, lights blinding, is crawling along in the median lane. Cars aren't moving to the side to make room for it. I shake my head and say out loud "lousy drivers." I don't know who I mean. Everyone.

I drive the car onto a side street and leave the car in a small grassy area with the hazard lights blinking. I'll go get Annette and walk her to my car. It'll save us time. As I approach the brown, peeling structure where she lives, I see the paramedics working on a limp body. The body of a woman with long, blond, unruly hair.

"My God!" I shout as I run towards it. "It's Annette. Let me through. Let me through."

"Back off, lady." A tall, burly policeman blocks my way. "Go away."

"I know that person, let me talk to her. Let me help, please."

"You're too late, lady. She's dead."

My head's spinning. "Dead?" I scream at him. "What do you mean dead? I was just talking to her a few minutes ago. What happened? Please let me be with her."

"No. Go away. She was hit by a car. She reeks of alcohol. She probably didn't see it coming. Please leave now, lady."

I sit on the sidewalk, bury my face in my hands, and start sobbing.

A small hand pats my shoulder and a very young voice whispers in my ear, "You alright, ma'am? Should I bring over the doctors?"

I look at the young boy, probably no older that ten or eleven. I can't focus. I can't catch my breath. "No, no. What happened? Did you see what happened?"

"The lady was your friend?"

"Yes." I'm sobbing. "Did you see what happened?"

"A car hit her."

"Who? Did you see who it was?"

"A white car. An expensive looking foreign car. A man was driving."
Dear God.

CHAPTER 17

MIRIAM VELASCO AND CARINA LOZANO ARE WAITING for me in the garden of the Velasco estate under a wonderful, old sycamore tree. Even though it's a hot, humid day there's a feeling of crispness here in this shady haven from the sizzling D.C. heat. A maid promptly brings out a frosty glass of lemonade for me and places it on the table between the two women, from which I gather it's the place reserved for me.

Carina stands up to greet me as soon as I step into the garden, her short white skirt showing off her pretty legs. She embraces me and kisses both my cheeks. "I'm glad you're here," she whispers in my ear. "You look good." I look into her eyes and a mantle of anguish seems to darken their luminosity.

"Thank you for joining us on such short notice, Ms. Berk," Mrs. Velasco says, extending her arm to greet me. She doesn't get up. "We certainly appreciate your coming here. Please take a seat." I do. "We need to finalize our plans for the fundraiser. Mrs. Lozano has been called out of town unexpectedly and I'd like her to be here for the final touches for our plans."

"Oh?" I say.

"She'll be back for the fundraiser, I'm sure." Mrs. Velasco looks at Carina.

"I hope there's nothing wrong," I say.

Carina merely shakes her head. "It's about…"

"No. Nothing's wrong," Mrs. Velasco interrupts. "It's some business matters she needs to attend to. Right, dear?" The heavy gold cross is heaving away from her body with every breath she takes.

"Right."

"So, if you don't mind, Ms. Berk, could you please inform us about the progress of your preparations." Mrs. Velasco adjusts her black leather belt, takes a sip of her drink, and spreads her hands on the table. My eyes are transfixed by her diamond ring. It looks bigger, brighter, in the daylight.

I turn to face Mrs. Velasco and tell her in numbing detail about the plan for the fundraiser for Children's Hospital. We're planning an all-day station marathon, giving away prizes, soliciting money, interspersed here and there with a song or two. Pledges will be taken on the air. It's going to kill our ratings and our billings for that day. The culmination of the day will be a glittering ball at the Four Seasons Hotel, sponsored and paid for by the Velascos. Mrs. Velasco is very pleased with the plan. She smiles and nods, interjecting "good, good" at intervals. I steal glances at Carina during my long exposition, but she's not listening to me. She looks lost in her thoughts, quietly nibbling on some kind of cheese cracker and sniffling once in a while.

"You're O.K. Carina?" I ask.

"Oh yes, dear girl. Allergies, you know?"

After an hour or so of Mrs. Velasco grilling me for more details, and after she has exhausted every bit of knowledge I have regarding the event, I stand up to leave. I make up an excuse to retreat from the tense, smothering atmosphere.

"Please call me at the station or at home if you have any more questions," I tell Mrs. Velasco.

She nods and barely touches my fingers when I shake her hand good-bye.

Carina stands up with me and slides her arm around my waist. "I'll walk you to your car."

"Please stay here, Carina," Mrs. Velasco demands. "I need your help with the seating arrangements.

"I'll be right back, Miriam. It'll only take a minute."

She's still holding me by the waist. I put my arm around her shoulders and the mismatched twins, the two redheads, walk out onto the street.

"Meet me in an hour at Café Milano in Georgetown," she says to me softly. "It's important. Do you know where it is?"

"Yes."

She leans toward me, takes my face with both her hands, bores her red-rimmed hazel eyes into mine and kisses me on the forehead. "Be careful, dear."

We linger for a second or two, her face close to mine, my arms around her waist, gathering strength from each other. Her breath is hot against my neck, her hands on my face, moist. "Be careful," she whispers again.

I open the door to my car and turn back to see Mrs. Velasco's mouth twitching as she watches us from the garden gate.

❦　❦

"WHAT'S THE PROBLEM?" I ASK CARINA EVEN BEFORE SHE SITS at the table at Café Milano. "Why are you leaving town so suddenly? What happened?"

She avoids my eyes and my questions and picks up the menu in front of her. "Carina, please. Talk to me. What's going on?"

Carina lowers the menu slowly, her hands trembling, her complexion tinged with a sickly yellowish cast.

195

"They're dangerous, dear. The whole lot of them." She's glancing at the door as we talk. She suddenly gets up. "Let's find another table—farther from the entrance. I hate the blasts of hot air every time the door opens behind me."

The restaurant is kept so cold it's actually a relief when a warm breeze sifts in through the glass door.

"Fine," I say.

We get seated in the farthest corner of the restaurant, behind the glittery bar, very close to the kitchen.

"Better here?" I ask.

"Yes."

We order cheese ravioli and a bottle of white wine, a dangerous combination for me just hours before my show. Carina doesn't care what we eat, she says, as long as we can have a few minutes alone.

I wait until she's ready to talk, and chew carelessly on a cheese bread-stick. I'm looking at her and amusing myself by sweeping the golden crumbs under my plate. I don't press her. We're both silent for a long while. The wine arrives and we both drink in silence.

"He's a brute," she finally blurts out. I stare at her. "Ray. He's a brute."

"Why? What did he do to you?"

"He confronted me yesterday. In my own house. Appeared there uninvited and made some lewd comments about my chest. Made a pass at me and tried to grab me. Told me he wanted to know if it would feel different for him knowing that I wasn't a complete woman. I told him, with as much delicacy as I could, after all I am a well-bred woman, that if he didn't leave me alone, if he tried any more funny stuff, I'd go to the kitchen, grab a knife, and take his manhood."

I smile. She doesn't.

"His mood changed instantaneously," Carina continues. "He became a fury and he hissed at me that my little game with his daughter, my game, he called it, was becoming a public scandal." She takes a napkin and gently wipes her lips. "He said people were talking about it, and all that talk will hurt his Linda. And that he'll do whatever's necessary to prevent his daughter from getting hurt. He gave me two alternatives: either I leave town as soon as possible, or else."

"Or else what?"

She shrugs. "Sounds like a threat. Maybe an accident coming my way?"

I stare in disbelief. "What do you mean 'an accident'? What kind of accident?"

"People in Ray's orbit sometimes find themselves caught up in accidents."

"Carina," I say loudly. "Please talk to me clearly. No riddles. No double-talk. What are you talking about?"

She's so pale I'm afraid she might faint. I offer her a glass of water and she grabs it with both hands and drinks it thirstily, slurping, spilling water on her white skirt.

"He might have me killed," she murmurs.

"I don't believe it. He may be militant, he may be somewhat violent, but I don't think he's a murderer. He couldn't be."

"Why? Because he reads poetry? Because he likes music? Because he collects art? Does that make him a saint?"

"How can you even think that he'd kill you?"

"Dear, not everything has to be spelled out," she tells me in a condescending tone. "You don't know the Velasco's history, Ray's violent streak. Why do you suppose Miriam will have nothing to do with him? She abhors violence. She told him so. Begged him to give up his ties to the underworld. Groveled to him. Prayed for him. He would have none of that. He preferred his hunting, his violence, his killings, to his adoring wife. That's why she gave up on the marriage. That's why she gave up on him." Carina is flushed as she talks. Her brow is covered with a fine veil of perspiration which she doesn't wipe away. "She's a religious woman, a devout church-goer, and he's a violent, masochistic tyrant."

She seems spent. She takes a bite of her ravioli and puts down the fork, looking at me. I don't say anything.

"Do you understand, dear? I'm sure you're having a hard time believing me. He appears to the world as a martyr—his wife won't have anything to do with him, he says. He's a self-sacrificing human being working for the good of his people, he says. It's all bullshit, my dear. All of it. He does it because he loves the power and the adulation that comes with the giving. He does it because power and violence and blood excite him." She looks at me and I just stare in silence. "I know," she continues. "I've witnessed his hunting sprees. His glee at killing. His orgasmic delight at the sight of blood."

I'm having a hard time eating, swallowing, breathing.

"He sends poems," Carina continues as though she were in a trance. Her intonation is monotonous, her breathing very shallow. "And flowers. Has he sent you his special ivory roses, whatever they're called?"

I don't answer.

"Oh, I see he already has. It's his style. His surprises. His late night erotic phone calls. He tried them all with me before my love affair with Linda started. When I had just arrived here fresh from my own separation. He wants to conquer every woman who crosses his path. It's the game they all play."

I look up at her. "Who?" I ask.

"The whole lot of them. He and his sons and probably Alan too."

"Luis too?"

"I don't know. I don't know about Luis. Maybe not. He's more like his mother—less violent, more religious, more sensitive. Luis is his mother's passion. She loves him, dotes on him. And I think he would do just about anything for her. He has her spirit. But still, he is his father's son. I don't know." She takes hold of my hand and I let her caress it.

"I'm sorry if this hurts you, baby. I don't know how much you care for Luis."

"I care." I look at her, at her swollen, red-rimmed eyes, at her pale skin, and I feel a tenderness taking over my spirit. "I'm afraid of him sometimes," I finally confess. "I don't know how to react. He's so volatile, so unpredictable."

"I'm sure that makes him more mysterious to you, more enigmatic."

"Yes," I say. "But I'm not sure I trust him."

"I understand."

"What about Enrique?" I ask her. "Is he as mercurial as his brother?"

"Enrique is a very complex man. He has his good side and his rough side. He has a soft spot that I don't quite understand. There's a poor family in Anacostia, from El Salvador, I think, or some other place in Latin America, I'm not sure where, and for some reason he's devoted to them. Collects things for them. Gives them money. Takes the kids out to the movies and to restaurants. Why, I have run into him when he was with that family, and he was a different person. Gone was the aloof, arrogant Enrique we all know and love. He was sweet with them, gentle, playful. I can't understand it. Nobody's been able to explain to me what makes him change so much when he's with them." *She's such a close family friend and yet she doesn't know anything about the man Enrique killed. She doesn't know about the man he ran over.*

Carina's color has started to improve, her manner is less cautious, she's more animated, friendlier. She starts eating her ravioli and with every bite she takes her usual vibrancy seems to grow in her. She's talking excitedly, happy to have an audience, delighted to be alive.

"You know," she says, tapping her fork on her plate, "the last time I saw Enrique was with that family, at the circus. It was a charity affair and I was doing a photo spread for the Washingtonian on the life of a clown. As a matter of fact I got an award for a picture of a clown," she says, pride shining in her eyes. "You know, my dear, I'd like you to have that picture so you don't forget me. Come to my place tonight and pick it up. We'll have something to drink." I nod and she continues with her story. "So, I'm at the circus and there's Enrique with his little friends. All of them—Enrique too—were munching on cotton candy and peanuts. The usually immaculate Enrique didn't seem to care that his silk shirt and his fancy pleated pants were soiled with butter and caramel. He was holding a kid with each hand and he looked delighted."

"I was invited to that charity at the circus," I say. "Wasn't it about three weeks ago?"

"Yes. On a Friday. You didn't go?"

"I wanted to, but couldn't. I had an appointment with an important client."

"Oh, you see clients? I thought you only did work on the air."

"Sometimes—very rarely—I'll go with one of our salespeople to do a sales call. I went with a friend that Friday. She got hurt that evening."

"Oh, the poor girl who got attacked with some sort of acid thrown on her face?" she asks to my utter amazement.

"How... how... Who told you?"

"Linda. She said that Enrique was very upset about it. He used to go with the girl. I was surprised to hear he was upset. I never thought he really liked her. I don't think he likes women too much."

"Oh, I thought he'd been happily married," I say.

"Only for as long as he could control his wife. When he discovered she was having an affair he hit her so hard, he almost killed her. Her parents wanted to press charges, wanted him arrested. Ray convinced them to drop the charges and apparently gave her a huge chunk of money for her troubles. Ray arranged for their marriage to be annulled eventually."

I take a sip of wine and start picking at my cold ravioli.

"Do you know he's seeing my friend again?"

"Yes. Miriam told me."

"Miriam knows?" I ask. *Why am I still surprised by anything in this family?*

"The whole family knows."

"He's showering her with flowers and gifts and attention," I say.

"It's part of the game."

"What game?" I'm exasperated.

"The game of let's get her to bed, let's get her to talk, let's get her to spill what Alan has told her."

"God almighty."

"Yes. We all know about Renata and Alan," she says with a smile.

"Does Linda?"

"Yes."

"Oh my God."

"Don't be surprised. Renata wasn't the first. Linda's used to it. She knows about her father's trysts and her brothers' women, so she wasn't dismayed about Alan's. I guess it's part of her upbringing, of how she expects the men in her life to behave."

"She wasn't upset that Alan loved Renata?"

"Is that what Renata thinks?" Carina's eyebrows rise with the question.

"Yes. She told me they were very much in love."

"Poor child. And to have that terrible accident happen on the eve of her trip."

I look at her questioningly.

"Yes. We knew that too."

"He wanted to take her away," I say. "Doesn't that mean he loves her?"

"But for how long, my dear? For how long? Tell me, have the police found out anything about the attack? How are they doing in their investigation?"

I shake my head.

"I see. You still think I'm one of them. You don't trust me yet."

"It's not that. I just don't know anything."

"I understand."

"Carina, do you know where Alan is?"

"No," she says with moist eyes. "I wish I knew." She sips her wine and looks around the room. "Alan's not a bad man, you know, even if Linda dislikes him. He's not bad. He loves his children wildly and he has always been interested in babies and families."

"Oh?"

"He's asked me on more than one occasion about some of my childless friends. He was deeply interested in them. I thought that showed caring and a soft heart."

"I guess it does," I say. *Especially if you're involved in selling babies.* "When are you leaving?" I ask.

"As soon as my bags are packed. No use staying around while every move I make is being monitored. I feel I'm being observed all the time. It's an unsettling feeling. And I can't see Linda so I really have nothing holding me here."

"What does Miriam say about all this?" I ask as the waiter brings us our cappuccinos.

"She hasn't said a word to me about any of it, which is very strange. Miriam's not the kind of person who holds back from telling you how she feels. She's been uncharacteristically quiet for the past few weeks. Perhaps Ray never told her the whole story, to spare her feelings for me. We're still friends."

"You will be back for the fundraiser, right?" I ask as we get up to leave.

Carina's pallor returns as we walk out onto the Georgetown street. A green car—small, non-descript, a little banged-up—seems to be waiting at the entrance of the restaurant. Carina looks at it, her eyes narrowing, her breathing shallow, and takes a hold of my arm.

"We'll just see if I make it, dear. We'll see if I can."

CHAPTER 18

I'M STANDING IN FRONT OF THE WATERGATE CONDOMINIums. Carina lives here. It's imposing and solemn. I've never been inside and I'm curious to see the place.

The doorman tips his hat and holds the heavy glass doors open for me, and I step into a softly lit, carpeted lobby.

"Good evening, Ms. Lozano," he says.

I turn and look at him.

"Oh pardon me, Miss," he says. "I got you confused with one of the tenants here. You look so much like her. So sorry."

"Don't worry about it. I'm coming to see her. Where's her apartment?"

The doorman walks me to the reception desk and returns to the front door.

"Mrs. Lozano isn't here," the man at the desk says without even ringing her apartment.

"I have an appointment to see her," I say, checking my watch. "It was for seven. I'm just a few minutes late. I'm sure she's expecting me."

"Mrs. Lozano isn't here," he repeats. "She left a few hours ago."

"Did she say when she's coming back? Should I wait for her here?"

I'm very surprised Carina would break our engagement. I'm certain it was for this evening.

"You can wait if you'd like, Miss. And I wish I could tell you when she's coming back. But I'm not sure she's coming back..."

"What do you mean?" I'm starting to grow concerned. "Did she leave alone? What did she say?"

"I'm not a liberty to disclose..."

"What? Please," I plead. "I've got to know."

"Who are you, Miss?" He eyes me suspiciously.

"I'm Gloria Berk." I take out my radio station I.D. "I'm a very good friend of Ms. Lozano. Please," I say. "This is very important. We had a very important meeting planned for this evening," I lie. "Did she leave alone?"

"No," he says after a long pause. "She didn't. There were two men with her."

"Who were they? Have you ever seen her with these men?"

"I don't know who they were." The clerk starts busying himself with some notes on the desk. He's lost interest in our conversation.

"Please tell me what they looked like."

"Nothing special. Two young men."

"Were they tall?"

"Yes. And stocky. Well dressed. I'm sorry miss," he says, turning away from me. "I'm very busy here. I wish I could help you."

"Where they wearing dark glasses?" I have a sinking feeling about the answer that's coming next.

He merely looks at me and raises his eyebrows. "Inside? Of course not."

"Did she say anything? Anything at all? Did she leave any message for me?"

"Not really. She just said goodbye and that she didn't know when she'd be back."

God. Oh God.

The telephone at his desk rings and he turns away from me to answer it.

"Can I get you a taxi, Miss?" the doorman asks me. "Do you need some help?"

"No, thank you. I have my car parked across the street in the Kennedy Center lot."

I'm walking slowly, almost stooped. As I turn to the right of the driveway, I see from the corner of my eye a green, banged-up car is slowly moving towards me. I walk faster toward New Hampshire Avenue and the green car is behind me.

When the hell are they going to leave me alone? This is just too much.

I speed up my pace, my shoes feeling heavy and clumsy and a few sizes too small. I reach the Kennedy Center and walk briskly to my car parked near the lit entrance. As I approach it, the green car gets closer to me. The lights of the parking lot illuminate its interior. As it slowly approaches I turn quickly to face it and see that the driver is the man with the fedora that handed me the threatening note near my apartment. By his side I think I see a long-range rifle. My heart takes a tumble. He stops in front of me, face fully lit. He cracks his window open, looks straight at me and mumbles, "Stay away from the Velascos, Miss, if you value your health." And he speeds away.

A piercing, soundless scream drowns in my chest.

※ ※

THE PHONE'S RINGING AS I OPEN THE DOOR TO MY APARTment. I can barely make it to the phone. I pick it up and throw myself onto the couch, legs propped up on the cocktail table.

"Where have you been Red, I've been calling you all evening."

"I was out."

"I know that. Where were you?"

"With friends, Luis. What's up?"

"Don't get mad. I want to make up to you for my bad behavior in South Carolina. I didn't conduct myself like a gentleman."

"I don't know what you mean. Being totally silent the entire trip back is bad behavior? I'd never guess it."

"Fine, fine. I deserve that. Let me make it up to you."

"No. I'm tired. I've got work to do and I've got to call my parents. Let's talk later in the week." I'm ready to hang up.

"Listen, Red. I have news for you that I think you're going to like. It's a surprise."

"I hate surprises. What is it?"

"I want us to go to Casa Marina this weekend..."

"No!" I interrupt. "No more. No more trips, no more guns. No more notes. You heard that Annette got killed, didn't you?"

"Yeah. I heard. I also heard it was ruled a hit and run. Sorry for the poor broad. But you've got to go with me to the Eastern Shore. I've got somebody who's going to meet us there. You've got to come. No funny stuff, I promise. I'll even leave my gun behind, if you want."

"Who? Who's going to meet us there?"

"I promised I wouldn't say. The person thinks it's dangerous, but is willing to meet with you as long as there's nobody else there. You've got to come. It's really very important."

"Is it Alan?"

"I promised I wouldn't say. Don't make me break my promise."

I kick off my shoes, sigh with relief, and go to the kitchen carrying the phone cradled in my shoulder. I don't answer Luis right away. I have to weigh this.

"Red, are you still there?"

"Yes, I'm here. Let me have a few days to think about this."

"You can't take too long deciding. I've got to go there beforehand, have the place ready, get us some groceries and drinks and tell the staff to leave us alone for the weekend. Are you game?"

I hesitate a few seconds while I pour myself a glass of wine. "O.K.," I say.

"Terrific, Red. I swear you won't be sorry. I'll pick you up right after work Friday evening. Don't have dinner. I have a great place I want to take you for dinner in St. Michael's. Best crabs in the world. You're going to love it."

"What about the mystery person? When do we meet?"

"First thing Saturday morning. Oh, and Red?"

"Yes?"

"Pack very, very light. You won't need too many clothes." He cackles and hangs up.

"WELL, GLORIA," SUE SAYS IN A GIRLISH SING-SONG ON HER way out the door on Friday afternoon, "heard anything new from the Velascos?"

"No. Not lately. It's been a quiet week on all fronts."

"Planning an exciting weekend?"

"Just a quiet weekend with Luis and preparing for my Sunday show."

"Good girl. Have you heard the news about Renata?"

"No. What news?"

"Apparently Enrique Velasco is getting really serious about their romance."

"Oh?" I try to show little emotion, but I don't think I succeed in hiding my anxious look. "How do you know?"

"I went to see Renata this afternoon to tell her her job is safe here at the station. She was talking to her mother about engagement rings."

"Wow. That's a fast courtship."

"I'll say. But Renata told me they knew each other from before and Enrique seems to have swept her off her feet."

"It would appear that way," I say sullenly. *And I believed she was pining away for Alan.*

"It'll be nice to have a wedding around here. Maybe it'll give Ron an idea or two." She winks at me. "Ta, ta, kid. I hope my evening with my guy is not so quiet." She walks out of the station in a gale of papers.

An hour later, as Manny takes over the six o'clock shift with love songs and dedications, I walk out the building to Luis' tight embrace. "Yumm," is his greeting.

He opens the trunk of his Jaguar and swings my small bag in. I steal a glance inside.

"No gun, Red," he says with a smile. "Didn't I promise? Let's get going. We have quite a bit of traffic to the Eastern Shore. Maybe we'll make St. Michael's by eight. We'll have ourselves a feast. You'll see."

I climb into the car and he promptly drapes a possessive arm around my shoulders.

"You're quiet, Red. Everything O.K.?" he asks after a while.

"Sure." How can I tell him that Peter called last night, that my heart was heavy with yearnings for his warm smile and reassuring presence. I miss Peter—the one man I wanted desperately. I've had others, although my experience is short: a few times with a student in college, whom I loved and lost. It was fast, in my dorm, when my roommate was away, and a few times with a fellow disc jockey who had just separated from his wife and who kept calling her name while making love to me. Terrific. But I hungered for Peter. It just wasn't the right time. We had some good times, Peter and I—our easy-going friendship spiced with romantic longings and playfulness. I felt safe around Peter, protected somehow.

"Anything the matter, Red? Why don't you say something?"

"I heard today that Enrique's getting serious about Renata."

"Looks that way."

"Pretty sudden, isn't it?"

"Oh, no. He's carried a torch for her ever since they met quite a while ago. Then she dropped him and now they're back together, but he always had designs on her. He didn't really date seriously after he started going out with her."

"Why did she drop him?"

"Some other guy, I think."

"What happened to the other guy?"

"Out of the picture now, I guess."

No mention of Alan. If Carina knows about Alan and Renata, I'm sure Luis knows too, but if he doesn't bring it up, neither will I.

"Hey, does that give you any ideas, baby doll?" He caresses my breast greedily and I remove his hand.

"Like what?" I ask irritably.

"Like getting hitched too? Making it a double?" He pinches my shoulder and places his entire hand over my breast. I remove it once more.

"Very cute, Luis. My first marriage proposal and it comes as a joke."

"Who's joking? I think we're great together—just love that cute little body of yours." Another squeeze.

"Maybe we should wait a bit. We hardly know each other."

"Is it a maybe?"

"It's a let's wait and see."

"As you wish. As long as I know you're not fooling around with anybody else I'll wait for you forever." He winks. I start playing with the radio.

"I'm serious about this, Red. I really like you a lot. I don't want to see you jeopardizing this relationship with any foolish goings on." His tone is becoming less affectionate. "I don't like losing—in anything—and I want you for me. Just me. So, whenever you're ready, just whistle, I'll come running. Just don't make me lose my temper. Don't you fool around. Don't make me mad."

I sit low in the bucket seat of his car, listening to Manny's dedications, feeling my throat constricting under Luis' veiled threats. And here I am, going to a secret rendez-vous with an unknown person, who might be Alan, but might not be him. And nobody else seems interested in finding out about him. Even Renata, so forlorn, so heartbroken barely a month ago, is now considering marrying somebody else.

209

But I've set a course of action—a quest. I'm not looking for Alan for Renata's sake anymore, not even for Annette and her son. I'm doing it because a human being seems to have vanished from the face of the earth and somebody ought to care.

"You get it, Red? Do we understand each other?"

Luis' voice comes filtering into my consciousness as though it were cutting through a thick fog. I just look up at him and sink deeper into my seat, humming softly under my breath. "Snap out of it, girl, whatever your funk is. We're going to have a terrific week-end. I have everything planned for us, to the last detail: sailing, dancing, good food, lots of kisses. There's nobody there. We'll have the whole house for ourselves to do as we wish. How does it sound?"

"Who's meeting with us?"

"What? What did you say?"

"Who's meeting with us?" I repeat slowly. "Tomorrow. Who are we seeing?"

He squeezes my knee. "Red, baby. You don't want me to spoil your surprise, now. Do you? Wait until tomorrow. Tonight it's just you and me. Alone. Reliving those amazing moments when we first met. I still can't get out of my mind what it felt like to see you riding that horse bareback, so tantalizing, so sexy, so exciting. I started wanting you right then. And later, my God, what a feeling when I walked into your room in total darkness and felt the touch of your naked body. I thought I was going to explode, and right under my parents' bedroom. God. It was so exciting I get hot just thinking about it. I want to feel all that all over again."

"Do they know we're going there this weekend?"

"Yes."

"No problem?"

"None that I know."

꙳　꙳

AT AROUND EIGHT-THIRTY WE PULL INTO AN ENORMOUS GRAVEL parking lot that appears to be completely full. We have a hard time finding a parking space. Finally, after a few minutes of riding around, we pull in between a large dusty RV and a sparkling brand new SUV. I climb out wearily and step into an overflowing pile of beer cans, cigarette butts and crumpled paper napkins.

"What is this place?" I ask. "It looks like a warehouse."

"It's just the best crab place in the world. No place better than this. People come here from everywhere just to taste the most delicious crabs. You're not too particular, are you, Red? You have to open them yourself and you eat them straight from the shell. No plates, no silverware, no linen tablecloth. Just fabulous people food. Real food. You'll see," he says as he holds my hand and pulls me through the narrow paths crowded with dozens of vehicles.

"Friday and Saturday nights it's a madhouse here. Noisy and crowded. We'll probably have to wait a while," he says as we approach a long line of people milling about by the entrance. He looks at me and hugs me hard. "The wait's worth it," he says. "You'll see."

He goes in and comes out with a large pitcher of cold beer and two glasses and sits by a stone wall. He runs his hand through my disheveled hair and pulls me down on his lap. After what seems like an hour and several glasses of beer, we're ushered into a cavernous space—cement floors, tables covered with thick white paper and the din of hundreds of people cracking huge crabs right on the table. We're served an enormous bucket teeming with crabs, two mallets, and another pitcher of ice-cold beer.

"Dig in, Red. This is heaven isn't it? My mother can't stand this place, you know?"

The noise is so deafening it's not worth even trying to hold a conversation. While I'm cracking and breaking claws, and sucking up the soft meat, I look around. Right in front of me I see a face from my past. A delicious, electrifying face from my college days—Patrick. Patrick Russell, my first love, my first romance, my first sexual encounter and my first heartbreak. The green eyes that I adored, the curly dark hair that I caressed during my sleepless nights.

I stare at his rugged chin and at the dark stubble that used to leave my skin red and chafed after our lovemaking. My palms get sweaty and I take a sip of beer. It's been over seven years since we last saw each other. I cried all night in his arms when we said goodbye and he left for a small radio station in Salisbury, Maryland to become their morning deejay. I heard he's since become the general manger. I try to blot out the noise around me to catch an echo of his caressing laugh.

Patrick seems to feel my persistent stare. He looks up, and holding a crab in one hand and a mallet in the other, looks at me in disbelief. I wipe my hands on the roll of paper laying unceremoniously on the table, the noise seems to die down, the huge room fades into nothingness and the only person in the place is Patrick, gazing at me. I lick my dry lips with the tip of my tongue and try smiling through my excitement. My old love.

He smiles back and then, in a sudden flash of recognition, he grins widely, throws his arms up in the air, leaps from his chair and rushes over. He pulls me up from my chair, holds me tight and kisses me long and tenderly on the lips. I kiss him back. I'm back in college, swept off my feet by the handsome university radio jockey and teaching assistant at the Communications Department. I'm dazed with emotion and shyness. Blind to the world around me.

Strong fingers digging at my arm pull me away from my reverie. Luis is standing next to me, looming, pale with rage, two dark lagoons of fury searing into my eyes. He raises his arm and Patrick steps back.

"She's with me," he barks above the noise of the place. He pushes Patrick away. "Leave her alone."

There's a quiet around us.

"Hey, buddy, I didn't mean any harm. I just wanted to say hello to an old friend."

"Well, then, go say hello to your mother. Leave her alone." Luis throws a hundred dollar bill on the table, grabs me by the arm, scratching my underarm with his class ring. "She's with me, you understand?" He yells.

We leave the restaurant amid the stares of the diners and I turn to look at Patrick, crestfallen, near the table where he kissed me.

As soon as we set foot outside I start yelling. "This is enough. You're a brute and an egomaniac. This is just ridiculous. You won't push me around, Luis. I won't allow it. Not any more. That was an old friend I hadn't seen in a long time and it was a nice surprise to see him here. You've got to stop behaving like a nut. I'm tired of your stupid jealousy and I'm not going to put up with it any longer. Let's get back to D.C. right now."

Luis doesn't utter a sound. Still holding me by the arm, seemingly oblivious to my tirade, he's dragging me towards his car, kicking beer cans as we walk through the rows of cars.

"Let go of me," I cry out. "Let go."

He doesn't answer. He keeps pulling me until we get to his car. He releases my arm, leans against his car, sickly pale, his forehead drenched in sweat. He places a shaky hand on my shoulder.

"Don't do this to me," he says in a hoarse whisper. "Don't. Let's go home. I need to lie down."

He looks like he's about to faint. "Do you want me to drive?" I ask.

"I'll be fine in a minute. Let me get my breath back. I'll be fine." He takes a few shallow gasps, wipes his moist face with an immaculate handkerchief, and slowly opens the door for me to get in.

"Are you all right?" I ask before getting in. I'm very worried about him, he looks so wan.

"I'm O.K. Get in. Let's go home."

⚜   ⚜

VILLA MARINA IS IMMERSED IN DARKNESS. IT LOOKS AND FEELS abandoned. The gravel, as we drive over it on the long road to the main house, sounds like an angry sea. The moonless, cloudless sky with all the flickering stars looks like a gem-studded mantle.

I open the car door after a silent trip and inhale the sweet smell of magnolias and honeysuckle.

The sounds of horses seem to come from far away.

"You'll stay in the same room you stayed in before," he says in a husky, gravely voice.

"Fine." I'm surprised he doesn't want me to sleep in his own room.

"Settle down and I'll come see if you need anything," he says when I walk into the small room. It smells musky and dank. As though the doors and windows have been shut for a long time, but the moisture of the bay has nevertheless filtered in and lodged in every pore, in every slit. It's an unpleasant aroma and after turning on the small night lamp by the bed, I go to open the window. The crank that operates it doesn't work. I notice a slim wooden stake attached to the frame that won't allow the window to open.

I wash up and unpack the few things I brought along. I open my handbag to retrieve a book I brought along and notice my cell phone is missing. *Goddam it. I lost it. Where could I have lost it? I know I had it with me at the station. God. It's the station's property. Sue will be furious with me. I may have dropped it in Luis' car. I'll look for it in the morning.*

There's a soft knock and Luis pushes the door open carrying a tray with glasses and a bottle of champagne. He's wearing a pair of denim shorts and is freshly showered, hair still wet, a strip of moisture on his upper lip. He strides into the small room, the muscles of his bare legs rippling with every step. He smells good and is smiling broadly. I'm still angry with him, but must admit to myself he brings up in me a raw desire. He's a very handsome sight.

"Here, Red," he says, placing the tray on the night table next to my bed. "Let's forgive and forget. Let's have a helluva good time and let the world around us go to hell. What do you say?" He hands me a full glass of champagne. "To us," he says and he clinks his glass to mine and gulps down the amber liquid. And then he pours a second one, and a third. When the bottle is empty he tosses it into the waste basket, gets undressed and jumps into the small bed. "Come to me, sweet baby, let me feel your body. Make me feel something. Make me feel alive." And he opens his arms to me.

I glide into bed next to him and slide my arms around him.

"Do you like me?" he asks in slurred words.

"Yes."

"How much? How much do you like me?"

"I like you a lot, Luis. You know that."

"Is it because of my father's money?"

"What?"

"Do you like me because my father's rich?"

"That's ridiculous."

"Then if you like me why don't you want to marry me?"

"Because I hardly know you. You hardly know me."

"I know enough about you to want to marry you, but you don't care enough for me. I know. Like all the rest you just see the glitter, the money, the wealth. Isn't is so, Red?"

"That's stupid. You know it's stupid. Stop talking like that."

He turns on his side in a violent move and faces me. His breath is hot and smells of alcohol.

"Don't you dare call me stupid, you goddam broad. Nobody calls me stupid. That's what my great father used to call me when I couldn't do one of his brutal deeds. 'Stupid,' he'd say. 'That's stupid.' No more. Nobody in the world will call me that again."

"Settle down, Luis. You know very well what I meant," I whisper in his ear. "Your father's wealth has nothing to do with the way I feel about you."

"How do you feel about me?" a gentler tone has returned to his voice. "Tell me. Whisper it to me in your lovely voice." He caresses my naked shoulder.

"I like your body. I like the way you smile, and your face, and your caresses."

"Do you like the way I make love to you?" He kisses my lips sweetly.

"I do."

"A lot?"

"Yes. A lot."

"Did that man we saw in the restaurant ever make love to you?"

I don't answer.

He shakes me by the shoulders.

"Answer me."

"Yes."

He opens his arms and lets me drop onto the bed. Then he turns around on his hands and knees, grabs me hard, kisses my mouth until I feel his teeth digging into my lips. I can feel a warm drizzle coming out of my mouth—I can't tell if it's saliva or blood—and I can't move. I can't talk. I can hardly breathe. He makes love to me wildly, desperately, violently. "Was he better than this?" he asks. "Was he better than this?" He jabs into me. He pushes against me. "Was he better than this?" Again and again. His hands are pressing against mine. His mouth is hard against mine. After some violent spurts he collapses next to me.

I'm hurting and angrier than I've ever been.

"Get out of here," I hiss at him. "Leave the room. Go. You are a rapist..."

"Was that guy better than me?" he laughs.

I get out of bed and grab my clothes.

"Where the hell do you think you're going?" he says as he lies in bed, arms above his head, legs crossed at the ankles. "Are you crazy? Where are you going?"

"Away from you."

He jumps out of bed and in one leap he's at the door, pushing it closed with one hand.

"You're nuts, Red. Maybe that's why I'm so hot for you. You excite every part of my body. Come, get into bed. Let's fuck again."

"Get out. Get out right now." I pick up the empty champagne bottle and throw it at him.

He ducks and smiles and the bottle shatters.

He looks at me, standing naked by the mirror, disheveled, hot with fury, and he rubs his hands.

"What a life we're going to have together, my sweet undomesticated cat. I love your temper and your sweet little body."

He opens the door slightly. "I'm going to my room. I need to get some sleep. Don't worry. You'll be fine here. Nobody will disturb you. I have your cell phone and I've secured your window. I'll lock the door from the outside so the big bad wolf can't harm you." He smirks. "Oh, and by the way, the mystery guest?"

I look up at him. "That was just one big lie to get you here. If you thought dear old Alan was going to show up you'll be very disappointed. That jerk ain't showing up here any time soon."

He goes out and sticks his head in one more time. "Ah, and Red, don't even think of escaping. There are guns all over the place here. And you know I can use them."

He closes the door behind him and I hear the loud click of the lock.

CHAPTER 19

IPRESS A WET TOWEL TO STOP THE BLEEDING IN MY MOUTH and walk around the room in a daze. It's hot in here. Suffocating. I'm drenched and in pain. I sit on the disheveled bed, but jump up quickly because it's moist and bloody and sticky. It turns my stomach. I quickly jump in the shower.

The door's locked. I insert a tooth brush, and then a pen to try to unlock it and start laughing out loud at my own clumsy attempts. I try the window again, pushing, shoving—it won't budge. I could break the glass, I guess, maybe by throwing my shoe against it, but I don't want to make any noise and alert Luis to my escape attempts.

I pace around a little longer. It's been an exhausting, long, draining day. I need a little sleep. I strip the moist linen off the bed, lay out a clean towel and lie down. Sleep takes over me in just seconds. Let me rest for just a few hours, that's all I need.

Bright light pouring into my room wakes me. Six a.m. The only sounds around me are the birds singing somewhere near and the crickets. I press my ear to the door and don't hear any footsteps nearby. I have to leave this place. Now. I try once more to open the door. It doesn't open. I'm locked in. A prisoner of Luis' whims.

Suddenly I see with a new eye the painting of the Madonna and Child over the bed. I climb on the bed, lift down the painting and place it on the bed. It's in a very heavy frame and the dust flies all over the room, into my nose, into my throat. I cough softly and try to muffle it with the bloody towel. There are two nails sticking out of the wall. I need to make a lancet to cut the glass. I've seen glass cutting since I was a child. My father used to create beautiful glass art designs which he would cut carefully. "Patience is all you need, dear," he'd say to me when I tried to help. "Patience and a little imagination."

I turn on the radio, softly, to mask any noise I might make, and with one of the nails I draw a circle on the window using the wooden stake as its center. I go over the circle again and again—gently, softly, carefully. I push the nail around and around the circle ten times, fifteen times. When it starts to make a screeching sound I spread a little body lotion on the glass to oil it a bit and patiently, slowly, I push the nail on the circle again and again until it's so dull I have to throw it away. I have only one nail left and again I push on the circle, deeper now, a little deeper. My palms are moist and the nail slips away from me so I have to wipe my hands again and again. I tiptoe over and press my ear to the door. Still no noise outside my room. No footsteps. No signs of life upstairs. It's close to seven. I'm afraid he could be waking anytime. I wrap a towel around the leg of the chair near the dresser, and with the back of the chair resting on my stomach, I push hard against the circle on the window. It's budging a little. I take a deep breath and push hard once more. *My God, it's moving.* One more strong push and the circle of glass in the window pops out and lodges against the wooden stake. No noise. I sigh as the sweetest breeze comes in and cools my sweaty face. Seven fifteen.

I wrap the dirty towel on my arm, stick it through the hole, and push hard against the stake. It doesn't move. I push again, harder, with my entire body bearing down against my hand. It's starting to dislodge. I can feel it moving. I take a deep breath, push one more time and the stake goes careening down, landing softly on the grass below the window. I'm bathed in perspiration. I put on my jeans, a T-shirt, sneakers, and grab my bag. Slowly, very quietly, I crank the window open and inhale the morning mist. I look right and left. Not a soul around. Far away, in the waters of the bay, some sailboats shining in the morning sunshine look like butterflies opening their wings to a new life. I jump out of the window, scraping my arms in the process, and land on the grassy knoll leading into the bay. Luis' window may also overlook the bay. I can't let him see me. I press my body against the wall of the house, leaving a red streak from my bloody arms, and I walk as quickly and quietly as I can, half-bent, toward the stables.

I run fast, hiding behind trees as I go. I keep looking back at the main house, but I can't see anything moving there. Seven-thirty. At the stables, the horses seem to feel my presence and they start to stir. I hear them neighing. I push the door to open it, but it doesn't give. The doors are locked. The mechanism looks old and rusted. I skulk around to an open window and climb in. I rip my T-shirt on a nail by the window with a piece of cloth hanging from it. I start to wipe my face and arms with the cloth, but drop it immediately. It has a terrible smell and it's stained with dark spots. I wipe my face on my torn T-shirt.

The horses are fidgety. Slowly, slowly I approach the mare I rode last time I was here and I pet her. "Sh, sh, sh, here, Beauty," I say to her. "That's a girl. We're going for a little ride." There's a pitchfork leaning against the wall, near the horses' hay. I wedge the tines into the double door's mechanism, raise the handle hard and the door gives. I push it with my shoulder and it gives way. I mount the mare and gallop, bareback, out of the barn. I take the gravel path out of Villa Marina and have started toward the main road when the muffled sounds of a powerful engine reach my ears. I turn around and see Luis' Jaguar in a gale of dust.

The horse and I leave the gravel path and cut across corn fields. There's no trace of Luis, but I don't know where I am. I keep galloping until the first traces of civilization appear: a house, a tractor, a road. I finally see a main road and take it to town. Easton. People stare at me. I must be some sight: a wild-eyed, wild-haired woman in a torn T-shirt, a swollen mouth and bloody arms, galloping into town on a horse without a saddle or bridle.

I ask someone standing at a bus stop where the police station is and he tells me. I ride on before he can make a comment.

When I reach the police station Luis' Jaguar is parked right in front. I freeze. And then I see him coming out of the station flanked by two burly policemen. The three of them are smiling and Luis has an arm around each one of them.

"That's her," he says, pointing at me. "The horse thief. I'm sure she'll have some crazy story. See? That's Beauty with her. You recognize her?"

The two policemen approach me and Luis stays behind, looking at me and smiling smugly.

"Step down, Miss," one of the policemen says. "Have any identification?"

"Please, please," I say. "He had me holed up in his place. He locked me up. He raped me. You've got to believe me. My things are still there. I was a prisoner."

The two policemen look at me as though I'm crazy. "Just step down, Miss," one of them says. "Show us some I.D."

I comply. Luis is still standing back.

"Mr. Velasco has lodged a complaint against you," the policeman says. "We'll have to investigate."

"Please, you have to believe me. Call my manager. Here, I'll give you her phone number."

Luis approaches slowly. He doesn't look at me. "She stole my horse," he says softly.

"Is this horse yours, Miss?" The tall policeman asks.

"No, but..."

"Miss, I'm afraid we'll have to hold you."

"Please, please. Take me to Mr. Velasco's house. You can see my things there. You can see I cut a hole in the window to escape. Call his father. He knew I was coming here for the weekend."

The four of us walk into the police station and they allow me to use the bathroom to clean myself up a bit.

"Make your phone call, Miss," the policeman says, handing me the phone as soon as I come out. I call Ray. "Please come here and explain," I whisper. "I'm in trouble."

"I'll be there," he says.

They bring me coffee and a doughnut, which I gobble down hungrily, and we all settle down to wait for Ray to come to the station. I'm half-crouching in one corner of the small police station, shivering even though it's a warm and sunny June day. "Wanted" posters are pasted on every spare wall space and I read them and sip cup after cup of coffee while I wait the two hours it takes Ray to arrive from D.C.

Luis, sitting comfortably in the chief's swivel chair, is chatting amiably with the police officers the whole time, laughing loudly and exchanging stories I don't want to hear.

I'm surprised to see Miriam Velasco come in the door of the station with Ray. After a short, quiet conversation, Ray pats the chief on the back, offers him a cigar, comes over to me and gently lifts me by the arms. I can hardly walk. He puts his arm around my waist and I lean against his chest and slowly we make our way to his car. Luis and his mother stay behind. I don't see them come out.

Ray opens the door for me and helps me into his car while his two guards look on without moving.

"Get in, Sugar," he says tenderly. "Do it carefully. You're hurt."

He gets in on the other side, takes my hand in both of his and kisses my fingers. "I'm truly sorry, Sugar. Truly sorry. I shouldn't have let it go this far."

"What, Ray?" I whisper, eyes closed.

"Nothing, Sugar. You wouldn't understand."

As soon as we get to Villa Marina he leads me to what must be his bedroom and sits me in an easy chair. He runs the water in the tub and when the tub is filled he leads me into the bathroom and softly closes the door behind him.

I don't know how long I soak in the tub. When I finally come out, swathed in a huge towel, I find my own fresh clothes laid out on the bed. I dress and walk downstairs, following the sound of muffled voices to the main room—angry voices. I knock and Ray promptly opens the door, takes me by the arm, and sits me down on a gold-colored, plush couch. He gives me some alcoholic beverage in a tall glass. "Here, drink it," he orders. "You're so pale you're scaring me." And I do.

"So," Ray says to Luis. "Gloria stole your horse, you say."

"Yes."

I open my mouth to complain but Ray, sitting close to me, shakes his head slightly. I keep quiet.

"What happened here?" Ray asks.

"He already told you," Miriam says in an angry voice. She's sitting directly across from me in a high-backed chair playing with her gold cross, eyeing me with a mixture of hatred and pity that I find disconcerting. I try not looking at her.

"She just went wild when I said we shouldn't make love," Luis says, looking at his mother. She smiles at him. "And then she tried to attack me and ran away."

"That's why she's bleeding?" Ray asks.

"She must've hurt herself somehow."

Ray gets up, starts pacing, and finally approaches Luis. Luis seems to sink into his chair.

"Do you think I'm an idiot? Who do you think you're talking to? When are you going to learn to behave like a man? How many more times do you plan on playing this stupid game?" He shakes his head in disgust. "To get pleasure out of scaring women, out of hurting them. My own son. I think you're worse than stupid. I think you're a coward."

Luis is immobile. He seems to be asleep with his eyes open.

"And now what?" Ray continues. "Are you going to hide behind your mother's skirts, like always?"

Miriam makes a move to get up.

"Sit down, Miriam." Ray's voice is softer. "Please sit down. He's like this because of you, because of your pampering and your overprotecting him. He's not a man. I don't know what he is."

Miriam sits back, eyes riveted on me. She purses her lips and her hand moves slowly down to her skirt to brush off some invisible lint. Ray turns his attention to Luis once again.

"You listen to me now, Luis. No more of this. Ever. No more games. No more scaring people. No more hurting others. No more lies. I've had enough of you and your stupidity and your goddam childish behavior. You want to prove yourself? You want me to respect you? Then be a man. Behave like a man. Do something in your life I can be proud of."

"Father..." Luis says.

"Please go. I can't stand to look at you."

"No!!!" Miriam gets up and walks over to her son. "No. He's a good boy. He's a good boy. I tried to warn you," she says, pointing a long finger at me. "Whore."

"Shut up, Miriam," Ray says. "Please shut up." He turns to me, eyes moist. "Gloria, I never thought it would get so bad. We thought the medicine he's taking had it under control."

"What?" I ask in a panic.

"His terrible rages. His anger. His tantrums. He could never control them as a child. That's why I had my eyes on you. To protect you..."

"Ask him about Alan," I say.

"He doesn't know anything," Miriam says. "He had nothing to do with it. Leave him alone."

Ray walks over to Miriam. He's very pale, shaking as he walks. He takes her hand and sits her close to him.

"What happened, my dear, please tell me."

Miriam doesn't talk, she doesn't move. Ray holds her close to him, petting her, caressing her, murmuring to her.

"What happened, my love, my dearest. What happened?"

She finally turns to him, eyes burning, hands shaking. "My life was going to pieces, Raymundo. I could no longer control it. I had to do something."

"What Angel? What did you do?"

"First I lost you. I couldn't get you back. No matter how much I tried. No matter how much I begged and groveled. Then I saw my lovely boy here getting sicker and sicker. I asked God to help him, but even God couldn't make him better. Then he was so taken by this woman," she looks at me. "I tried to scare you away. I sent you notes. I put a pouch of Celandine to make you run away, but I couldn't win. He wanted you so much."

"Do you know what happened to Alan?" Ray asks very softly.

She doesn't seem to hear him, and in a trance-like state she continues with her monologue that sounds almost like a prayer.

"I saw Linda, my sweet Linda's life disintegrating. Do you know Alan was going to leave her? She told me he left her a note."

"There was no note," Ray says.

"What do you mean? She told me."

"There was no note. Linda made it up because she wanted us to feel sorry for her when she found out that Alan was taking off with the little blonde. Linda wanted us to leave her alone. To let her lead her disgusting affair with Carina. Alan didn't leave her a note."

"God Almighty. May God forgive me. I thought he was leaving my Linda for good." Miriam says softly. "That is why that Friday night... Oh, God. May God forgive our sins."

Luis gets up and slowly walks out of the room. Ray and Miriam don't seem to notice.

"What, Angel? What?"

"I damaged the poor girl's face."

226

"Renata's?" Ray asks.

"Yes. I hated her for taking Alan away from my Linda, for hurting my only daughter the way I've been hurt by you, Raymundo. I was not going to allow the pain that marked my own life to devastate my daughter's life. May God forgive me. I threw a potion made with Drano on her face. The day Linda told me Alan was going to desert her, I followed Renata and you, Ms. Berk. I waited until you left, and then I rang the bell and she opened it and I just threw my potion on her face." She lets out a laugh that sends shivers down my spine. "It was really so easy."

Ray is very pale, holding onto his wife. "Do you know what happened to Alan, dear?"

"Yes."

"Where is he, dear?" Ray is talking very softly.

"Let me die, Raymundo. Let me die."

"Where's Alan?"

"I lured him here on the eve he was to run away with that whore. I called him up at work and told him that his little Mary, his darling, had fallen off a horse and was asking for him. I guess the love for his daughter was stronger that his desire for that harlot because he came here. My Luis was waiting for him. He used one of your hunting guns, Raymundo. The one you taught him to use to kill little animals. He did it for me. For me. To show me he loved me."

Ray holds her tighter. "Oh, my God. My dear, dear wife."

"Let me die, Raymundo. I don't want to live any more. Just a sip of my potion. That'll do it."

"Where's Alan body?"

She turns to me, sears me with her burning eyes. "Do you remember, Ms. Berk, the day of the party here? When you bewitched my son with your tantalizing tango? The night you were dancing in the garden under the stars? With your dissolute charms?" She turns to Ray, "Your little friend here was dancing over Alan's grave."

At that moment, out of nowhere, there's a gun fired in a deafening sound. An explosion. Like windows shattering very close to us.

Miriam covers her face. "Luis," she sobs.

"My God," Ray jumps up and runs out. "Stay here, Miriam. Stay." He shouts. We hear his steps running up the stairs.

I look at Miriam. She's very pale. Almost static. Like a statue done in alabaster. Her eyes fixed on a spot on the floor. The only thing moving is her cross that gently heaves on her chest.

Ray comes in a few moments later, sits next to his wife, cradles her in his arms and they both cry.

THE BLUE FLEECE COVERLET THE STEWARDESS HANDED ME IS hugging my body. The plane to Europe is half empty. I'm flying to Greece to spend my vacation with Peter.

I just read in *The Washington Post* that Mrs. Velasco died yesterday. Of natural causes, it said. I know what the real causes were. And so does Ray.